FAMOUS CHINESE SHORT STORIES

Retold by
LIN YUTANG

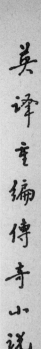

Washington Square Press, Inc.
New York

Famous Chinese Short Stories

1961

L

Published by
Washington Square Press, Inc.: Executive Offices, 630 Fifth Avenue;
University Press Division, 32 Washington Place, New York, N.Y.

WASHINGTON SQUARE PRESS editions are distributed in the U.S. by
Affiliated Publishers, Inc., 630 Fifth Avenue, New York 20, N.Y.

CONTENTS

CONTENTS

SATIRE

TALES OF FANCY AND HUMOR

CONTENTS IN CHINESE

CONTENTS IN CHINESE

FAMOUS CHINESE
SHORT STORIES

INTRODUCTION

THE short stories in this volume are some of the most famous Chinese tales ever told. They comprise some of the best — though not all of the best are here. The selection and retelling of these stories for Western readers impose a necessary limitation. Many famous stories have been omitted, either on account of theme, matter, or basic assumptions of a different society or period, which make the retelling an impossible or unprofitable undertaking. I have selected those which I believe have a most nearly universal appeal, and which answer more to the purpose of a modern short story.

The purpose of a short story is, I believe, that the reader shall come away with the satisfactory feeling that a particular insight into human character has been gained, or that his knowledge of life has been deepened, or that pity, love, or sympathy for a human being has been awakened. Nothing in the reader's basic assumptions should stand in the way, requiring elaborate explanation, in order that this desired effect may be achieved. I have chosen stories which present no such difficulties and which make the achievement of this effect easy or possible, although I recognize that some of these stories will appeal to the reader because of the strangeness and exotic charm of a remote atmosphere and background.

The instinct to listen to a good story is as old as humanity itself. Tales have been told in China since history began. The Tsochuan (probably 3rd century B.C.) and certain chapters of Shiki (2nd century B.C.) abound in vivid descriptions of human character and immediate scenes of human conflicts. There were also numerous collections of brief, superficial records of strange, supernatural events in the first centuries of the Christian era. But the beginning of the written short story as an art form can be definitely placed in the Tang dynasty (especially the 8th and 9th centuries). These were the so-called *ch'uan-ch'i*. Usually brief, running under a thousand words and written in the limited classical medium, these art tales have a strange vitality and power to excite the imagination. They are still the best of their kind, unrivaled by later imitations; in cases where the stories were retold in the expanded vernacular versions of a later period, they were hardly improved by the elaboration. The Tang period was not only the golden period of poetry; it was also the classical period of the literary tale. Men's imaginations were bolder, as in Elizabethan England; their fancy was a little freer and livelier, and their hearts were a little lighter, when the pedestrian realism of later generations did not prevent the winged flight of their fancies. By this time, Buddhist tales had already penetrated deep into Chinese society, Taoism was officially revered, and nothing seemed strange or impossible. Theirs was a world of magic, chivalry, war, and romance. As Sung was the rationalistic period, so Tang was, in a broad sense, the romantic, imaginative period of Chinese literature. There was, properly speaking, no drama yet, and other mediums, like serious fiction, were not yet available; but what these writers did with the classical tales of wonder and mystery was unsurpassed by later dynasties. I find that half of the stories selected come from this period.

The Tang *ch'uan-ch'i* in time gave place to the Sung *hua-pen*, or story-teller's copies in the vernacular. This was an entirely new development, so that these two forms continued to represent the two main classes of Chinese short stories. The great collection of classic tales, the *T'aip'ing Kuangchi,* published in A.D. 981, at the beginning of the Sung dynasty, may be said to be a final compendium of tales told in the literary style for a thousand years, nearly up to A.D. 1000. In a way, it symbolized the closing of a period. All the best Tang tales are preserved in that collection and some are found nowhere else. But naturally and silently, without literary fanfare, a new form of spoken literature had grown up in the teahouses as a form of popular entertainment. We know definitely that at the Sung capital there were different types of professional story-tellers, some specializing in historical romances, some in religious tales, and some in the exploits of a popular hero. Su Tungpo in the eleventh century told us in his *Journals* that some parents, annoyed by their children in the house, would send them away to listen to the professional story-tellers. We also know that Emperor Jentsung (1023-1063) used to ask his courtiers to tell him one story a day. Two collections of these story-teller's copies, called *haupen* or *hisaoshuo*, have recently come to light, and are of extreme interest because they contain some of the earliest, yet the best, stories in the vernacular. The authors of these story-teller's copies are unknown, but internal evidence shows that they belong to the Sung period (11th and 12th centuries). The collection known as *Chingpen T'ungshu Shiaoshou* is the sources of the *Jade Goddess* and *Jealousy*. It contains eight stories, all of them excellent, including two ghost stories, a story of crime, and a highly pornographic story usually omitted from current editions. The other collection, *Ch'ingp'ingshan T'ang* (present earliest known edition published between 1541-1551), is the source of *The Stranger's Note*, the best mystery story I have come across in Chinese literature, and very neatly told. The collection also contains some horrifying stories of ghosts. In one of these, a woman ghost used to have young men brought to her for pleasure, and when a new young man was brought, the ghost always commanded, "The new one has arrived, take the old one away," and the latter's heart was plucked out to be eaten. Many of the stories in these two collections were later expanded and incorporated in the Ming collections of short stories.

Readers acquainted with Chinese literature may be surprised that I have included nothing from the many collections of short stories in the Ming period, like *Chinku Ch'ikuan*. There were at least five or six such well-known anthologies, *Chinku Ch'ikun* being the best known, and being itself a selection from earlier anthologies like *Chingshih T'ungyen*. Unfortunately, these stories are told in narrative style and fall between the imaginative, exciting Tang tales, and the truly modern short story; their themes are conventional and their narratives pedestrian and mediocre. To be sure, many interesting things happen, but few of them reveal insight into character or have deep meaning. The earlier Tang and Sung stories may be shorter, but they often leave us with a sense of wonder at life and human behavior.

I have tried to have the various classes of short stories fairly represented in this volume. Of the group of adventure and crime stories, I have placed *Curly-Beard* first, because it is regarded as one of the best of the Tang tales; the dialogue is good, the characterization and incidents are vivid, and nothing is contrived.

Love and the supernatural seem to dominate the rest of the stories. There are few stories, crime, adventure, and the supernatural included, which do not have a love element in them, which merely shows that, East or West, the surest way to hold the reader's interest and make his pulse beat a little faster is to tell of love between man and woman. There are many love stories not included here because, especially in the Ming collections, the first thing the lovers do when given a chance is hop into bed, which is somewhat ridiculous. *Passion*, the best known love story included here, has this feature, but at least there is an element of emotional intensity — a quiet and dignified highly born girl seeking sex experience. Because this story was written by a first-class poet, and because its dramatization known as *Western Chamber* was written in the most beautiful and poetic language the Chinese medium was capable of, it has become the classic tale of love. The popularity of this story is indicated by the fact that there are eight different plays based on it. *Madame D.*, the story of a married woman's adultery, was relieved by many other features, and justified by an unhappy marriage. The best story of pure young love is, I believe, *Chienniang;* besides, it illustrates a perfect blending of the two elements of love and the supernatural. One does not question that these things happened. They simply did. The reader who questions them is beyond redemption.

Ghosts in Chinese literature do either of two things: they horrify or they charm you. More often they do the latter, for, as I have said elsewhere, these charming, seductive female ghosts are the products of wish fulfillment of the poor Chinese scholar, married or single, who, shut up in his studio, liked to conjure up a dream beauty as his companion. Nothing can be more delightful to a man, when he is sitting alone at night, than to see a beautiful, smiling apparition appear in the soft lamplight and use her wiles to seduce him; then, later, she nurses him in sickness and bears him beautiful children. *Jealousy,* a story of two jealous women ghosts, is intended to fulfill the first function of ghost stories, and I hope it will give the reader proper goose pimples. *Jojo* is typical of the other kind of amusing, playful, and doggedly loyal girl friends who are really ghosts. P'u Sung-ling (1630-1715), author of *Jojo,* is the only writer in the Ch'ing Dynasty included in this volume. His *Bookworm,* a satire upon politicians, tells how an embroidered picture of a girl on a bookmark steps out of the pages of a volume of history; she makes love to the man and teaches him not to hope to be a success in politics by just being a good scholar. Of the hundreds of writers of tales of the supernatural, P'u Sung-ling alone achieves subtle characterization and gives convincing, supporting incidents. He is most famous for his stories of jealous women and henpecked husbands, and he has a special liking for fox-spirits (i.e., women who ruin men by their lust and beauty). But I have already included three of the best by P'u, including the juvenile, *The Cricket Boy*.

The Tang tales of fancy and humor seem to fall into a separate category and are best represented by the four stories of Li Fu-yen. He is not as well known as Li Kung-tso, author of *The Drunkard's Dream*, but I confess to a partiality for him. All his tales are characterized by a light whimsical fancy typical of Tang tales. He lived in the first half of the ninth century, the period when the greatest and best *ch'uan-ch'i* tales were produced. For in going over these famous Tang stories, I find that four fifths of them fall within the range of the first half of the ninth century. A great number of these tellers of tales were Li Fu-yen's contemporaries, like Tuan Ch'eng-shih (*Cinderella*), Li Kung-tso (*The Drunkard's Dream*), Tsiang Fang, Hsueh Yungju, Ch'en Hung, Po Hsing-chien (brother of Po Chu-yi the poet), and Yuan Chen, author of *Passion*, to name only a few. As the eighth century was the century of Tang poetry, so the ninth was the century of Tang tales. This form of writing had become so popular that Niu Sengju, a premier, was the author of one of the most popular volumes, with tales of supernatural beings three inches high engaged in battle, and other adventures. Li Fu-yen wrote his supernatural stories as a continuation of Niu's tales. I think his tales are superior to Niu's in material and manner of telling. They return us happily to a world of wonder and magic in which all things are possible, with a touch of the humor of the *Arabian Nights*. The Cinderella story, produced also in this period, is the earliest written version of this story in the world. It has the wicked step-mother and sister, the lost slipper and all, but it antedates the earliest European written version of Des Perriers in 1558 by seven centuries.

I make no apology for the fact that in rendering these stories into English, I have not confined my duties to those of a translator. I have sometimes found translation impossible.

The differences in language, in customs and practices that could be taken for granted and those which have to be explained, in the reader's natural sympathies for this or that character, and above all in the pace and technique of modern story-telling — all these make it necessary that the stories be retold in a new version. In the stories by P'u Sung-ling and Li Fu-yen, I have made the fewest changes. If I have omitted parts of stories and added others for story effect, I have not taken more liberties than Chinese story-tellers have always taken with earlier versions. In what I have added I have always striven for historic authenticity. Readers interested in the source materials are referred to the preliminary notes at the beginning of each story.

The Jade Goddess and *Chastity* were published in the *Woman's Home Companion* and the Cinderella story was first published in *The Wisdom of China and India* (Random House).

Adventure and Mystery

I. CURLY-BEARD

This is a favorite Tang story, distinguished by sharp characterization and dialogue. It was most probably written by Tu Kwang-t'ing (A.D. 850-933), a highly distinguished Taoist himself and an author of many works. It forms No. 193 of the T'aip'ing Kwangchi, but slightly varying texts exist, some of which ascribe it to one Chang Yueh. Legendary tales had grown up around the figure Li Tsing, who is also the hero in "A Lodging for the Night." There were two dramatizations of the story. I have supplied some details in the part at the Taiyuan inn.

I⁣T WAS a world of chivalry, adventure, and romance, of plucky battles and faraway conquests, of strange doings of strange men which filled the founding of the great Tang dynasty. Somehow the men of that great period had more stature; their imagination was keener, their hearts were bigger, and their activities more peculiar. Naturally, since the Sui Empire was crumbling, the country was as full of soldiers of fortune as a forest is full of woodchucks. In those days, men gambled their fortunes on high stakes; they matched cunning with cunning and wit against wit. They had their pet beliefs and superstitions, their virulent hatreds and intense loyalties, and once in a while, there was a man of steel with a heart of gold.

It was nine o'clock in the evening. Li Tsing, a young man in his thirties, had finished his supper and was lying in bed, bored, puzzled, and angry at something. He was tall and muscular, with a head of tousled hair set on a handsome neck and shoulders. Lazily he jerked his biceps, for he had a peculiar ability to make these muscles leap up without flexing his arms. He was ambitious, with plenty of energy, and nothing in particular to do.

He had had an interview with General Yang Su that morning, in which he had presented a plan to save the empire. He was convinced that the fat, old general was not going to read it and regretted having taken the trouble to see him at all. The general, who was in charge of the Western Capital while the Emperor was sporting with women at Nanking, had sat, bland and self-satisfied, on his couch. His face was a mass of pork, with blubbery lips, heavy pouches under his eyes, fat hanging down under his chin and lumpy, distended nostrils, from which sniffs and grunts issued regularly. Twenty pretty young women were lined up on both sides of him, holding cups and saucers, sweetmeats, spittoons, and dusters. The dusters, which were made of hair from horsetails, over a foot long, and fixed with a jade or red-painted wooden handle, were more decorative than useful. The silky, white horsetails swung gracefully, though idly. There could not be a more convincing picture of a misfit in high office, or a neater contrast between the luxurious setting and the debased sensuality which was no longer capable of enjoying it.

A tanned, soldierly Li Tsing had stood silent and tall, looking removed from the scene, as if with a veil of thoughts over his eyes. The empire was going to fall like an overripe, rotten apple, he thought, and pretty soon, too. The whole country was in revolt. And here was this mass of pork surrounded by a screen of female flesh. It was believed, and of course it was true, that the bodies of the young women helped to keep the room warm.

Yang Su had looked at the visitor's card and said in a tone of bored fatigue. "Who are you?"

"A nobody. I thought in times like these you might be looking for a man with an idea and a plan for action — and you might be more courteous. You could have asked me to sit down."

"Sit down, I forgot. I am sorry," said the general. Yang Su always received his visitors without rising from his seat, but no one had ever spoken of it to his face.

Somewhere there was the sound of a short breath, like a gasp. A duster almost dropped to the ground, and a tall, slender girl in pink hastily retrieved it. Li Tsing looked up and saw two beautiful black eyes, excited and wondering, looking at him. Leisurely he sat down.

"What do you want?"

"I want nothing. Don't you want something, Your Excellency?"

"I?" The general spluttered at this impertinence.

"I mean, are you not looking for something. Perhaps a plan to save the empire, and a man with decision . . . " He let his words die on his lips.

"A plan?"

"I see that you are not. I am afraid I am wasting your time, General."

But he drew the plan from his pocket when the general asked for it. He saw him place it squarely on the low stool on his right, in an effort at politeness, and then he asked, "Is that all?"

"Yes," replied Li, and he rose and left.

While he talked, the girl in pink continued to look at him, and their eyes had met. As he turned to walk out of the room, she dropped her duster again. It had been the only pleasant feature of that interview, and he now chuckled in his bed as he thought of the way she had stared at him.

He heard a light tap at his bedroom door. Who could have come to visit him at this hour? It could not be that

the general had read his memorandum. He rose and found
a stranger at the door, in a purple cloak and hat, holding
a bag at the end of a walking stick across one shoulder.

"Who are you?"

"I am the duster girl at General Yang's house," she
whispered. "May I come in?"

Li hastily threw on a robe and asked her in, excited by
her mysterious visit and by her disguise. The girl, between
eighteen and nineteen, laid aside her cloak and hat, revealing
a lissome figure in an embroidered jacket and a red skirt of
cloud design. He looked at the beautiful troubled vision.
With her white face bent, she made a curtsy and explained.

"You must forgive me. I saw you at the audience with
the general this morning. I found out your address from
your visiting card and came to see you."

"So you did!"

The girl's eyes followed him as he tied the belt of his
robe and peered out of the window.

"Please listen, Mr. Li. I have run away."

"Run away! As simple as that. You know the entire city
police will be after you."

"Do not worry," said the girl with a sweet and enticing
smile. "I have a young friend who wants to take over my
position and that carcass of a general will not even miss me.
The inside of that household is like the empire itself. No
one is loyal to the master — in fact, they hate him and want
only to get the most out of him."

Li asked her to sit down in his best chair. The girl's eyes
were still fixed on him. "Mr. Li, I have read your memorandum."

"You have! What do you think of it?"

"I think you are casting pearls before that swine."

Li was amused. "Did he read it?"

"No. What do you think?"

Li saw the remarkable intelligence in the girl's eyes and
smiled at her. "So you are thinking of running away."

"Let me explain," said the girl, only now seating herself slowly in the chair. "Everybody knows that the days of the empire are numbered, that the deluge is coming. Everybody except that walking carcass. We girls know, too, and we are looking out for ourselves." She paused for a second and then added, "Many have run away. A year from now, or perhaps more, and there will be no General Yang. When I saw you this morning I thought I would like to make your acquaintance."

Li studied the girl. He was moved not so much by her beauty as by her plan to escape and by the intelligence of her foresight. He knew too well what would happen to a girl in her position when war came to the capital, and the general fled or was captured. She would be taken by the soldiers and raped or sold as a slave.

She was tall and slender, with eyes set wide apart and slightly longer than usual; her somewhat prominent cheekbones complemented her longish face.

"What can a girl do? I am serious. Please believe me."

The suggestion of sadness in her voice, the serious look in her eyes, her whole deportment and manner of speech fascinated him.

"What is your name?" asked Li Tsing.

"Chang."

"And what seniority?"

"Number one in my family." The girl looked at him steadily. "Mr. Li, I have seen hundreds of people who came to see the general, but never one like you." It was obvious that she intended to run away for good, and had chosen to come to him. He admitted to himself that he was not unwilling to have her.

"It is going to be hard, Miss Chang, sharing a soldier's life, one month here, another month there, marching and campaigning, in uncertainty and danger."

"I know all that from reading your memorandum."

"You saw me only this morning. Just what makes you think I am the right man for you to join?"

"I saw you make the general apologize for his bad manners. No one else had dared. You spoke without fear. I said to myself, there is the man. If you say yes, I will go back and make some final arrangements."

When the girl came back in an hour, Li could hardly believe it. He was as delighted and flattered as he was worried over the consequences, for he was poor. Every few minutes he peeped out the window to see if anybody was coming after her.

Curiously, the girl appeared very calm. Her eyes dwelt on him fondly and followed him everywhere.

"You have no relatives?" asked Li Tsing.

"No. Otherwise I would not be in that household — I am happy," she said suddenly. This was the only indication of the excitement that was lurking all the time in the light of her eyes.

"I have no job, you know."

"But you are ambitious. You will do big things."

"How do you know?"

"The memorandum."

"Oh, yes, the memorandum," he answered with a cynical smile. It was not that he thought lightly of his own composition. He was a well-read and gifted scholar, and his plan of action was clear, bold, and incisively stated. "No nonsense, do you mean to say that you fell in love with that piece of paper?"

"Yes, I did — or rather, with the man who wrote it. It is a pity that the general passed it by." She did not tell him until much later that what had fascinated her was the beautiful carriage of his head on a strong, well-shaped neck and broad proud shoulders, his clear eyes, and his whole manner of being every inch a man and soldier.

After a few days, Li heard a rumor that the girl was being sought for by the guards of the general. Although the search was perfunctory as the girl had told him it would be, Li dressed her in a man's disguise and set out with her on horseback.

"Where are we going?" she asked.

"We are going to see a friend at Taiyuan."

In those chaotic days traveling was far from safe, but Li had no fear so far as physical self-protection was concerned. He could handle a dozen men at a time, short of a dastardly ambush. He was one of that ilk of gallant, ambitious, daring warriors who was feeling the ground of the tottering Sui Empire, making friends, and studying the political and geographical situation, in order to be ready to rise in revolt when the opportunity called. There were many others like him, men traveling in disguise and working secretly, looking for brave, trusty and loyal comrades.

"Do you believe in fate?" he asked the girl as they rode along.

"What do you mean?"

"In destiny. There is a young man, the second son of the commander of Taiyuan. My friend Liu Wentsing knows him very well and is plotting a rebellion without his father's knowledge. Liu has enormous faith in the young man. He thinks he is the True Dragon."

The girl gasped. "The True Dragon!"

"Yes," said Li and his eyes darkened. "He will probably mount the Dragon Throne one day. He has an extraordinary face. Do you believe in physiognomy?"

"Of course I do. That was how I chose you. How extraordinary is he?"

"I cannot tell you. Of course he is handsome, well-built, and all that. But I cannot describe him. You feel his presence when he enters the room. Something comes out of him, as from a born leader of men. I wish you could see him, then you would know what I mean."

"What is his name?"

"Li Shihmin. People address him as 'Erlang' because he is the second son of the commander."

Li Shihmin was, of course, the man who was to found the great Tang Empire, to become the most beloved emperor in the last thousand years, brave and wise and kind, his reign marking a golden period in history. It would be only natural to suppose that such a man's beauty of character should find expression in his physiognomy. He must have been extraordinary to do the things he did, and his face would have shown it.

At a small inn where Li and the girl were stopping at Lingshih the bed was already laid out. In one corner of the room stood a small earthen stove with a good fire going, over which a stew was simmering. The girl, having removed her disguise, was combing her extraordinarily long hair, above the bed so that it would not touch the ground. Li was grooming the horse just outside.

A man of middle weight, with a red, curly beard and whiskers arrived at the inn on a scrawny donkey. Without ceremony and without regard for the girl's presence, he threw down his leather bag for a pillow, reclined on it, and sprawled on the ground, looking at her with his powerful eyes. The impertinence of the stranger angered Li, but he went on brushing his horse, keeping an eye on the stranger.

The girl also stole glances at the stranger. His face was a copper brown, and he was dressed in a fur jacket and trousers. A scabbard hung obtrusively at his waist. He did not look like one who could be trifled with. She turned sideways and, holding her hair with her left hand, she signaled to Li with the right that he should not be angry and should leave the man alone.

As soon as she had done up her hair, she went over to

the stranger and asked his name courteously, to be friendly. Slowly the man rose and said that his name was Chang.

"And what seniority?"

"Number three in my family."

"My name is Chang, too," she said sweetly. "I am your clan-sister, then."

"What is your seniority?" asked the man.

"I am the eldest in my family," answered the girl.

"In that case, I shall call you 'Imei' (number-one-younger-sister). I am glad to meet a clan-sister like you."

Li was inside the door. "Tsing," said the girl, "come and meet my third brother."

The stranger was friendly, but his words came abruptly in clear crisp tones. He had the air of a widely traveled man who knew where he stood. His eyes searched Li and the woman, and he seemed to have drawn his own conclusions about them. Li studied the man's manner and dress and decided that he was a soldier of fortune like himself. He had wanted to meet men like him, men of the open road with short manners and speech, with a disdain for the conventional life of safe, cautious, and meek citizens, men who would rise to action when the opportunity arose and act like men of steel, loyal to their friends and deadly to their enemies.

"What is cooking in that pot?" asked Curly-Beard.

"Mutton. It is almost done," replied the girl.

"I am famished."

Li went out and came back with some wheat cakes to share the dinner with the stranger. Curly-Beard took out a sharp knife to cut the mutton and chop up the gristle for his donkey. He ate without regard to manners and finished amazingly fast.

"You two are an interesting couple," he remarked, addressing the girl. "Poor and romantic, huh? How did you happen to pick him? I can tell all about you. You are not married and you have run away from something. Am I right? No, do not be frightened, Imei." There was a certain warmth in his voice as he addressed the girl.

Li's eyes did not even flicker, but he wondered how this man knew. Could he read faces? Perhaps the girl's long fingernails may have told the secret that she had lived in a rich mansion.

"I am afraid you are right," replied Li with a laugh. Their eyes met, Li trying to fathom the stranger's purpose, and then adding with a smile, "She has chosen me, as you say. Do not underestimate women. She knows that the deluge is coming."

"The deluge?" Curly-Beard's eyes had an extraordinary sparkle.

"Figuratively, of course."

Curly-Beard's eyes swept to the girl with a glow of admiration.

"Where have you come from?" he asked.

"From the capital," said Li calmly, looking steadily at him.

"Is there some wine?"

"There is a wine shop next door."

Curly-Beard rose and went out.

"Why did you tell him?" asked the girl.

"Do not worry. The sons of the forest have a stricter code of honor than the officials. I know a fellow spirit when I see him."

"I do not like the way he cut up the mutton when you were away, and fed his donkey with the leftovers without asking me. As if it were his meat."

"That is the best part of him. If he were courteous and a little unctuous, I should be worried. I have an idea that a man like him can have small consideration for a few morsels of mutton. He evidently likes you."

"I can see that."

Curly-Beard returned with the wine. His face glowed and he began to talk. The veins on his temples stood out. His voice was split and low, but his sentences were slow, clear, and deliberate. He thought very little of all those generals who had raised banners of rebellion. None of them would amount to anything. As he listened, Li was sure that Curly-Beard was planning something big himself.

"What do you think of Yang Su?" asked Li, to sound him out.

Curly-Beard struck his sharp knife into the table and laughed. The sharp blade pierced the wood, flashing a scintillating white light and singing as it vibrated before it gradually came to a stop.

"Why talk about him?"

"I was asking your opinion." Li told him of his interview with the general and how the girl had made her escape.

"Where are you going now?"

"To Taiyuan, where I can keep my identity unknown for some time."

"Do not think you can do it. Have you heard of an extraordinary person in Taiyuan?"

Li told him of Li Shihmin, the reputed True Dragon.

"What do you think of him?"

"Very extraordinary."

Curly-Beard's face grew very serious. "Can I see him?" he asked after a while.

"My friend Liu Wentsing knows him very well. I shall ask him to introduce you. Why do you want to see him?"

"I can judge faces pretty well."

Li had no idea that he was promising a fatal interview. They arranged to meet on the Fenyang Bridge at dawn the day after their arrival at Taiyuan. Curly-Beard offered to pay for the room, and even insisted, saying he was doing it for his Imei. He trotted off on his thin donkey and disappeared.

"I am sure he wants to see the True Dragon for some good reason of his own," said Li, as they turned back into the inn. "What a strange man!"

Li Tsing and Curly-Beard met at the appointed time, two dark figures at the head of the Feysang Bridge in the early mist-covered dawn. Li took his friend by the arm and after a light breakfast, walked with him to Liu Wentsing's house. The two men were silent with a feeling of something deeper than friendship — a common purpose. Li was the taller, a stout, soldierly figure. Curly-Beard walked with an easy swinging gait, like a veteran with plenty of power in his knees, who thought nothing of a jaunt of a hundred miles.

"Do you believe in reading faces?" asked Li Tsing, thinking of the True Dragon.

"A man's physiognomy is the record and the expression of his character. The eyes, the lips, the nose, the chin, the ears, the color and tint of his face and complexion — everything tells a story as plain as a book if you know how to read it. Whether a man is strong or weak, sly or honest, determined and cruel, or sensuous and crafty — it is all there. It is the most complicated book because human character is the most complex thing on earth, and all combinations are possible."

"So a man's destiny is determined at his birth?"

"Almost. He cannot escape it any more than he can escape his own character. No two faces are alike. As a man thinks, his face records, accurately, infallibly. As a man lives, so things will happen to him, and it is not so much what happens to him as how he is going to take it."

As they approached Liu's house, Li noticed the faint suggestion of excitement in Curly-Beard's quickened breath.

Arriving at the house, Li Tsing went in first and said, "There is a friend of mine who would like to meet Li Erlang. He is a good judge of faces. He is outside."

"Show him in, by all means," was the reply, and Li hastily went out to the door to welcome Curly-Beard. Liu had already been planning an uprising with Li Erlang, or Li Shihmin as his proper name was, and when he heard of one who could read a man's destiny in his face, he was delighted. Curly-Beard came in and they were invited to stay for lunch while Liu Wentsing sent a note to Li Shihmin to come over.

Soon Curly-Beard saw a young man walk into the room, with an unbuttoned fur jacket over his shoulders, his head thrown back, a towering figure, gay and hearty and confident. Handsome was not the word for him. As he entered the room he seemed to radiate. His eyes, without moving, seemed to take in all that was happening in the room. Below his sharp, pointed nose, which had a remarkably straight, prominent bridge, red, stiff whiskers curled upward as if you could hang a bow on them. Li saw Curly-Beard scrutinize the tall figure with the eyes of an eagle.

"I wish my friend the Taoist were here to see him," he whispered to Li after lunch.

You may not believe it, but when they left there was an expression on Curly-Beard's face as if someone had struck him a death blow. He walked with his head bent, his face beclouded, uncertain, troubled. His breathing was quick and audible.

"What do you think of Li Shihmin?" asked Li Tsing. When he received no answer, he repeated his question. "What do you think of him?"

Slowly, Curly-Beard mumbled, almost to himself, "I am eighty or ninety per cent certain of it. He may be the True Dragon. But I would like to have my Taoist friend see for himself. Where are you stopping?"

Li told him he was stopping at an inn.

"It is all right for a few days. Come with me."

Curly-Beard took him to a silk shop. After a short while, he came out and handed Li a paper package containing some bits of broken silver, about thirty or forty ounces, saying, "Take this and provide a good shelter for Imei."

Li was amazed.

"Never mind. Take it." Such was the way of those adventurous heroes.

"Did you rob the shop?"

Curly-Beard laughed. "No, the owner is a friend of mine. Do you want some more? I can leave word with him. Come and get what you want. I have an idea you are not so well off, and I should hate to see my sister put to any inconveniences. I don't think you should stay here too long. Come to Loyang and stay with me. Come in a month." He raised his head and counted on his fingers. "On the third of February, I shall be back. Come to a wine shop east of the stables at the East Gate. When you see this donkey and a black mule tied outside, you will know that I and my Taoist friend are upstairs. Walk right up."

They reached the inn where Li was stopping, but Curly-Beard was not prepared to say good-by and followed Li inside. He treated the girl like his own true sister and Li like his brother. He ordered a big dinner for them that night and did not seem to want to leave. They sat talking deep into the night.

"Please never mind me, Sister. You retire first." But he stayed in the room. He did not seem to be at all sleepy. Mrs. Li got into the bed, because she could not keep her eyes open. She was embarrassed, but amused. Curly-Beard had a superhuman vitality. In the early hours of the morning, Li dozed off while he was still talking.

In the morning, Li was waked up by the strange guest. "Where did you sleep?"

"Right here, on the floor."

"Why, did you think I needed a bodyguard?"

Curly-Beard appeared as fresh as ever. "I am starting for Mount Wutai. I have certain things to attend to. I will be back at Loyang on the third of February. Do not forget, and of course I want Sister to come too."

It was perhaps the way of those heroes who roamed the country, who traveled fast and made friends fast, wearing their hearts on their sleeves, generous to a fault. When a man insists on treating you like his brother and your wife like his own true sister, you cannot help liking him.

Li and his wife arrived at Loyang according to their agreement with Curly-Beard. They found the wine shop as described, and when they saw the two animals tied outside, they went upstairs.

"I knew you would come," said Curly-Beard, rising to welcome them. He introduced them to the Taoist, student of magic, astrology, physiognomy, everything which had to do with *ch'ishu*, "forces and numbers," everything which determines our lives through these invisible influences. The Taoist was a soft-spoken man, and did not utter many words. If he was looking at Li Tsing and his wife, they were not particularly aware of it, and he was cordial in his quiet way.

"So you prefer the sword to the pen," he said suddenly to Li Tsing.

"Yes. Such times call for action, not for books."

Li was amazed at the accuracy of the Taoist's remarks. He was a well-read man, and he said that when he was sixteen or seventeen, the question of deciding whether to be a scholar or a soldier had been a struggle for him.

Curly-Beard showed them to a room. "Here you can stay if you like. It will be safe. Do not worry. I know what you are thinking about. The shop is mine. Help yourself to the cash downstairs and buy something nice for my sister."

So they stayed at the wine shop, and Curly-Beard often came and sat with them to talk far into the night, discussing military strategy. Li Tsing had much to learn from him. It was the tactics which he later put to practice and used to such advantage. It was not a matter of physical bravery, as many imagined. It was a matter of knowing your enemy, of seeking out his vital spots, where one good blow would count for a hundred. When you strike a snake, you strike

at his head. You do not fight an enemy, you fight around him.
And so it went. Such discussions always lasted beyond midnight. The astrologist was often occupied watching the sky
in the direction of Taiyuan, looking for star conjunctions and
aura and nebulous phenomena which Li and Curly-Beard
did not understand.

After a few weeks, the Taoist said that he would like to
see Li Shihmin.

"You will introduce my friend to Li Shihmin," said Curly-
Beard to Li. "I should like him to tell me whether he is
the True Dragon. This is going to be crucial. Everything
will be decided then."

"What will you do if he is the True Dragon? Fight
him or join forces with him?"

"I do not fight Destiny."

"With him, then."

"Do not be silly." Curly-Beard cut off the discussion with
a laugh. Quoting a proverb, he said he would rather be the
head of a chicken than the tail of a cow.

They set out to Taiyuan. The Taoist was introduced to
Liu as a great astrologist who could foretell the future. Liu
was playing chess with some of his friends and asked the
Taoist to sit down and have a game with him, while he sent
a note to Li Shihmin to come over and watch the chess.
Curly-Beard and Li Tsing stood around to watch.

Li Shihmin came in and silently took a seat beside the
chess table. He did not utter a word, which was the correct
form for all watchers of the game. Curly-Beard nudged Li
Tsing in silence. The world was full of brave soldiers and
saber-rattling heroes, but a True Dragon was of a different
order. The Taoist, apparently absorbed in chess, was watching
the Dragon's breath, feeling his radiations, testing them,
evaluating them. Li Shihmin sat perfectly erect, shoulders
straight his hands placed squarely on his open knees. Now
and then his black eyebrows danced a little as he watched the
game, and in the back of his eyes there was a light, as if he

saw all, understood all. Five minutes later, the Taoist pushed the chessboard away from him and said to Liu Wentsing:

"The game is lost, definitely. There is no way of saving it. You made a splendid move with that pawn, splendid indeed. I give up."

So far as the watchers could see, the game was not as irretrievably lost as the Taoist indicated. But he apparently had decided to save himself a useless fight. He rose from his seat and sighed.

The game being ended, the three friends thanked their host and left.

When they were outside, the Taoist turned to Curly-Beard and said, "Your game is lost. The Man of Destiny is inside. There is no use trying. But you may seek some other land to conquer."

For the first time, Li saw Curly-Beard's back slump and his whole frame relax. Something had happened to Curly-Beard, inside.

"The situation has changed, and I am afraid I have changed my plans. You wait for me at Loyang. I shall be back in a fortnight," said Curly-Beard and went away alone.

Li did not like to ask questions. He returned to Loyang with the Taoist.

When Curly-Beard returned, he said to Mrs. Li, "I want you to come and meet my wife, Sister. And I have something important to lay before you and Mr. Li."

Li Tsing had never known where Curly-Beard lived. He was continually amazed by the man. He was led to an entrance consisting of a small one-paneled door. But on entering the first courtyard, they saw a hall magnificently furnished. Dozens of servants and maids stood about. They were ushered into the eastern room where the guests were to make their toilet. The dressing table, the ancient mirrors, the bronze basins, the crystal lamps, the tables, cabinets, and screens were all of the finest quality and some of them were obviously priceless.

Curly-Beard soon appeared with his wife and introduced her to them. She was a woman about twenty-eight or thirty, of remarkable beauty. Li and his wife were overwhelmed by the open, stout hospitality, which made them feel like very distinguished guests.

At dinner there were girl musicians playing strange music with a lovely melody, the like of which Li had never heard. When dinner was almost over, servants came in carrying ten hardwood trays, all covered with pieces of silk, and laid them on low stools against the eastern wall. When all was prepared, Curly-Beard said to Li, "I want to show you something."

The silk covers were lifted, and Li saw that the trays held documents, deeds, records, and bunches of very large keys.

"There are about one hundred thousand dollars in these," he said, "including some jewels and other valuables. I am making a present of them to you. What do you say? I had made plans and collected them, looking to the time when I should organize an army and buy troops, weapons, and ammunition. I hoped to do great things. Now I have no use for them. That young Li of Taiyuan. I am convinced, is the True Dragon. You take these and help him to accomplish what he is destined to do. He is your man, and do not forget the strategies I have taught you. In five or ten years, Li Shihmin will be able to conquer all China. Serve him loyally, and power and fortune will be your reward. I have my own affairs to attend to. A dozen years from now, when you hear that across the borders of China, some one has conquered a foreign land and established a new kingdom, you will know that it is your old friend. You and Sister can then face the southeast and drink a cup to my health."

Then he turned and said to all the servants and members of the household, "Hereafter Mr. Li will be your master, and owner of all that I possess, and my Sister will be your mistress."

Having given the proper instructions, he went and, dressed in traveling clothes, set off on horseback with his wife, followed only by one manservant. They never saw him again.

In the ensuing years, Li was busy winning battles in the long campaigns which united China under the great Tang Empire, Li Shihmin became the great emperor ruling the country in peace, and Li Tsing was his most trusted friend and commander-in-chief of the Tang armies.

One day Li read in an army report that someone whose name was not mentioned, had landed a force of thirty or fifty thousand men at Fuyu, across the southern border of China, and had conquered it and made himself king. Li was sure it was his old friend who had helped him and his wife during his young days. It was almost incredible that the man had chosen oblivion and had banished himself from China rather than be subordinate to anybody. He had made up his mind to be king somewhere, and now he was a king.

When Li went home that night he told his wife about the report.

"Good old Curly-Beard!" she said, greatly moved.

"Yes, good old Curly-Beard. He has got what he wanted."

Remembering their friend's last words to them, they lighted two red candles after supper and went into the courtyard. There standing face to the southeast, they drank a toast to their old friend.

"Can't you do something for him — perhaps tell the emperor to decorate him?" His wife's voice sounded strangely guttural.

"Leave him alone. Rewards and honors from the emperor will only worry him. He must be sovereign and lord, second to none, wherever he is. A wonderful man," remarked Li Tsing, and then added with a sigh, "A great man!"

2. THE WHITE MONKEY

~~~~~~

The story forms No. 444 of T'aip'ing Kwangchi, author unknown. It bears the curious title, "Supplement to Chiang Tsung's Story of the White Monkey," Chiang Tsung (519-594) being the person who saved the White Monkey's son by hiding him. The story goes that it was written to make fun of Ouyang Hsun (557-594), one of the greatest calligraphists in China, who was as ugly as a monkey. Ouyang Hsun was supposed to be the White Monkey's son. As such, this story was probably written in the early part of the seventh century.

I have changed the story to make the Chinese general's humiliation in losing his wife to the White Monkey the main theme. Sources for additional material on the customs of the aborigines are taken from one Tang and two Sung records: Tuan Kung-lu's Peihulu, Fan Ch'eng-ta's Kweihai Yuheng, and Chu Fu's Ch'iman Ts'unghsia.

A similar story about a Chinese general losing his wife in the Kwangtung mountains is found in the Ch'ingp'ingshan T'ang collection ("Major Chen Loses His Wife in the Mei Mountains").

EVERYBODY has heard, of course, how General Ouyang was caught in battle, beheaded, and his family exterminated in the year A.D. 569, when he threw in his lot with the rebels. Opinions differ. Some think the general deserved it because his family had for generations enjoyed the favor and trust of the emperor; they only regret the fact that the illustrious record of so great a general and his father should have ended in disgrace and disaster. Others, like Chiang Tsung, sympathize with him, and believe he was trapped and forced into rebellion because the emperor had grown suspicious of his power in the south.

But all this is beside the point. When he was in his thirties, something happened to change the man's character. His sensibilities had been wounded. The young Pacification General of the Southern Provinces became an embittered, raspy, unhappy man. His friend Chiang Tsung, who was able to save his son and bring him up in hiding, told something about it in his story of "The White Monkey," but according to the general's aide, one Mr. Lei of Kwangtung who was an old member of the general's staff, he did not tell the whole story. The general could not outlive his disgrace. This is the story told by Mr. Lei, now a man of sixty. He saw it all.

I had been in the service of the general since he inherited his rank and position when his father died. As an old member of his father's staff, I enjoyed his confidence. The general had a young wife. She was pretty and came of a high family. One day she was kidnapped. We all knew — everybody took it for granted — that the White Monkey had done it again. I did not like to see the general's face as he sat alone at breakfast.

We were stopping at Changlo at the time. The general had been warned not to take his young and pretty wife along on the campaign in the region of the southern aborigines. For about a hundred miles around his region, the White Monkey had been in the habit of capturing Chinese women, who disappeared completely without a trace. Guards had been posted around the house day and night, and, as an extra precaution, a number of maids had slept in her room and some menservants in the anteroom. In the small hours of the morning, when one of the maids woke up and heard a noise, the general's wife was gone. No one knew how the kidnapper had entered, for the doors were locked. I was awakened by the scream of the lady's maid, who dashed about, her dress unbuttoned, yelling that her mistress was gone.

We started the chase. The house, which was a military station on a well-known mountain route, stood a hundred feet up a precipitous cliff on a ledge, overlooking a deep chasm. On the other side of the chasm rose a moss-covered cliff, which faced the door only fifty feet away at the level. A heavy mist made it impossible to see beyond twenty feet in that early dawn. Chasing after the kidnapper along those mist-covered cliffs was extremely dangerous. A slip of the foot or missing of a turn in the road would mean a straight plunge into the chasm below and instantaneous death. After half an hour of futile chase, we gave up.

The general was wild when he returned with us and questioned the maid for details. He gripped the maid's shoulder and shook her. "What did you see?" he demanded.

The maid was crying. "I didn't see anything. When I heard a noise and woke up, the lady was gone."

For the first time I saw the general lose his temper. He slapped the girl on the head. We had never seen him so beside himself. He had been a just man, and we older members of the staff had great admiration for him when we saw how he led the campaign at Shih-hsing.

"Has anyone of you ever seen the White Monkey?" he asked.

None of us had. But I told him that the White Monkey had been seen by many people in widely separated towns for a hundred miles around. He had been observed by fuel gatherers from a distance as a white figure climbing vine-covered steep mountainsides and disappearing into the cloud-capped peaks.

"Do you think he is one of the aborigines? And this is for revenge?" the general asked me. In his recent campaigns, he had bottled up the different aboriginal tribes in their mountain settlements called "caves."

"I don't know. The townspeople say that from time to time, he came to town on perfectly legitimate business, carrying a deer, a few beaver skins or boar tusks, and perhaps one or two dried glands of musk, trading them in exchange for kitchen knives, choppers, carpenter's tools, and salt. He spoke Chinese fluently and made honest bargains, but let no man cheat him of his barter, or the next day or week that man would be found dead with an arrow in his back."

"What is his appearance?"

Lieutenant Wang who was born in this region said he was unlike the *Miaos,* the *Yaos,* or the *Holaos,* for those tribesmen were generally dark and small of stature, with wrinkled faces even in their youth. People who had seen him said that the White Monkey stood five feet ten, with thick-set, round shoulders, powerful arms, and apparently no neck. The most disturbing feature was the whiteness of his eyebrows, his eyelashes, and the hair which grew all over his chest and arms and legs. When he ran, his soles always touched the ground, which gave him a peculiar, ape-like, swinging gait. Whether this was developed from his habit of climbing rocky mountain roads we do not know; but this gait, along with his wide-split, big toes and the silky white hair on his comparatively thin legs, gave him a gruesome, grotesque appearance.

"He wanted only girls and very young women," Wang added.

The general sat with his chin on his chest, breathing audibly. "Have they ever found the women he kidnapped, or their bodies?"

"No, that is the mystery," said Lieutenant Wang. "If he had raped them and left them to die, some of them would have made their way back, or their bodies would have been found."

"Has he kidnapped children, too?"

"No. The mothers only cry 'White Monkey' to frighten the children. We heard that he captures only girls between eighteen and twenty-two." Lieutenant Wang hesitated a moment. "And, General, he seldom takes wives with children. I can't explain it, but here in this neighborhood, a curious tradition has grown up that mothers are safe from him, and some mothers say that he is fond of children."

The general felt humiliated and helpless. We could not be sure whether the White Monkey had done this deed as revenge or as a joke on the Chinese general. Apart from losing the wife he loved, he felt that his honor and the name of the Chinese Army were at stake.

The general was confronted with a unique enemy. The problem of hunting down such a lone kidnapper, who by all reports had superhuman energy, cunning, and endurance, was hardly the same as that of mapping an ordinary campaign. Soldiers were sent ten and twenty miles around, up the crags and down the chasms, to hunt for traces of his wife and to look for any clue which might lead to her recovery.

About two weeks later, one of our men reported finding a woman's red, embroidered shoe on a tree branch, some thirty miles from the place. It was a certainty that Mrs. Ouyang could not have marched on the way and that the kidnapper had carried her. The shoe was presented, limp and discolored, drenched by rain. It was identified by the maid and by the general himself. The probability was that she was alive and being held captive, but where to find the White Monkey?

We felt so sorry for the general. He sat alone all afternoon, and an aide said he pushed the food away from him after he sat down to supper. No one dared to speak to him that day.

The next morning the general called me early, before breakfast. "Lei," he said, "we are setting out today to search for my wife. I have decided to delay the campaign. Pick out two dozen men to come along. Bring all necessary provisions. We may be camping out for a month — who knows? I want Lieutenant Wang to come along, of course."

I did as I was told. I picked two dozen young men, some of them the best archers in the land, and all handy with their spears and knives. We did not have to bring many provisions. Fruit was plentiful, bitter oranges grew wild in the mountains, and our men knew how to dig wild taroes and bake them in the ashes of an open fire. Thus armed and provided, we had nothing to fear. The general himself was a superb swordsman, and he could split an orange with an arrow a hundred feet away.

In fact, we rather enjoyed the trip, traveling in those high altitudes. The landscape was magnificent. We passed mountains and virgin forests and cataracts, and wooded country full of giant vines, spruce, and "tear-stained" bamboo which grew to a hundred feet. There was also good game to be had. We had nothing to fear from man or beast on the way. The tribesmen whom we met knew who we were. These tribesmen were, as a matter of fact, the most hospitable people in the world when they were allowed to live in peace with the Chinese. It is true, they think nothing of spearing a man in the back if it is a matter of revenge, but they make their living by hunting and rice cultivation and want no quarrel with people who are fair in their dealings with them. But it was hopeless to get any information about the White Monkey from them. All of them "did not know." The general suspected that the White Monkey not only lived in most amicable relations with these tribes, but was a kind of hero to them.

We had been going in a southwesterly direction toward a region where the general had not been before. Here the landscape opened on a dry, broad river bed. As if by arbitrary division, the luxuriant jungles stopped and a vast stretch of denuded rocky hills lay before us, relieved only by spots of tough, dwarfed underbrush. Great boulders testified that this had once been a fertile valley with a big mountain stream running through it. Then nature seemed to have changed her mind and directed the course of the river elsewhere. On the western horizon rose a formidable rock formation of columns, the like of which man's eyes had rarely seen. It is correct to speak of them as columns, for these hills of limestone had been so eroded by rain, wind, and moisture for millions of years that they had now assumed the shape of perpendicular towers or pillars, making a weird, jigsaw outline on the horizon. All traces of human habitation had disappeared. The sun setting behind those rocky columns cast long, strange shadows of alternate black and white across the broad open valley. It would be difficult to find water in such a barren place. Besides, we had come over a hundred miles from our station. The desert seemed to indicate the proper end of our journey, quite fruitless as far as our objective was concerned.

But the general was attracted by the curious topography of the place. Across the river bed the land sloped upward, and two or three miles away, vegetation began to appear again and thicken. A little to the southwest, the jigsaw outline of the hills stopped and was replaced by a long, majestic solid wall of impenetrable mountains. Their rocky peaks caught the glory of the sun's rays and shimmered in a golden glow like a mysterious city on a hill. A company of egrets flying high in the sky toward a mountain indicated that their roosting place lay there.

The general had also the idea of tracking the dry river to its source. He was still hopeful and commanded us to strike for the mountain. The day was long and if we marched steadily without stop, we should be able to find a camping place soon after sundown. After an hour's journey along the untrodden bank, filled with fine water-worn pebbles, we reached the grassy foothills.

"Look!" cried Lo, who was a bright young lad of twenty, one of the general's aides.

We saw a pile of charred stones grouped together, with ashes around them. Some one had no doubt made a camp fire and cooked here. Some dried-up orange and banana peels lay about. For two days we had not met a human being, and the sight of the campfire ashes gave us once more a reassuring sense of contact with the human world. Young Lo went around examining the ground and suddenly again cried, "Look!" We all rushed around to see. Lo showed us a piece of black ribbon such as ladies used to tie their hair while dressing.

"It must belong to Mrs. Ouyang," said Young Lo.

We would be glad to believe him, but there was no reason to suppose that a woman's ribbon should necessarily belong to the general's wife. The general, of course, could not tell whether it did or not. He merely stared at the piece of ribbon and sighed. But all of us are wishful thinkers when a search is futile and the prospect hopeless. The atmosphere became tense. We would all enjoy finding our prey and seeing some action. We knew we were going to meet a dangerous enemy, but the hurly-burly of combat was better than this monotonous march.

We encamped for the night under the starry sky. Hiking on a hot June day on a sun-scorched river bed was tiring even for veterans, and we fell soundly asleep.

The next morning we resumed our journey. It was all climbing. We must have gone up three thousand feet in two hours. Only a small stream ran and trickled at the bottom of the ravine and disappeared again on the ground. The white giant boulders below reflected the intense heat, and a column of vapor was coming up. The wooded slope was rich in pheasants, and we often saw glimpses of their brilliant plumage trailing through the branches. Vines the size of palms stretched everywhere, providing convenient support. The air became rarefied. Once more we were on high altitudes.

When we got to the top, we saw an astonishing sight. A dam had been built at the nape of the range out of great boulders and hewn stones. When, how, and by whom this had been built it was difficult to imagine, for the stones were so great that, without proper tools, they could have been moved only by a race of superhuman giants. It was clear that this had been built by the people living on the other side to divert the stream, for a swift and deep current ran past to the left and fell into a deep pool below. An old tablet stood at an angle, half buried in the ground, bearing the strange script of the *Mans*. A soldier who came from the *Mans* told us that it said, "Great High Heaven Protected Place." Apart from the deserted and fallen tablet, we were as far from any signs of human abode as we had been.

After some scouting, it was established that the swift mountain stream falling into the deep chasm made an unbridgeable barrier between where we stood and the other side. It skirted the mountain for miles, and no bridge — wood or rope — was in sight. The opposite banks consisted of cliffs so steep that a bridge would serve no purpose anyway. It seemed that the inhabitants of the mountain had built the dam to turn the current more for military defense than for agricultural purposes, making the mountain into an invulnerable fortress.

Still there should be some access from the north. We turned right, up the stream. For a short distance, the brambles were so thick and heavy that we lost track of the current. As we came out, we saw towering five hundred feet from us a wall of solid granite shaped like the natural rampart of a city on a hill. Along a fissure between the rocks, stone steps were visible at intervals, ending again, however, in the rocks' shadows. Without question, we had found the entrance, but the approach was so difficult that we looked at one another for a moment.

"Well," said General Ouyang, "this looks crazy. It is impossible to know what lies on the other side. It takes more than brawn to gain access to that natural castle. We are the equal of any, so far as spears and arrows are concerned, but we'll be fighting in a blind country without a way out. People who live out there don't like intruding strangers, you may be sure. Still, I would like to explore. If the White Monkey is in there, there will be some brisk action. If not, the tribe may be friendly. What do you say?"

We were all in favor of investigating the entrance.

When we reached the top, we found it was a deathtrap. There was a level space some thirty feet across, vulnerable to spears and arrows from above. Our only cover would be a few feet under a big rock. A narrow passage zigzagged for ten feet between two rocks and led to a heavy door made of some hard wood, securely fastened from the other side. Only one person could pass through the passage at a time. No fortress had been better built or conceived.

We knocked at the door in vain. Upon close listening we heard the voices and laughter of women and children far away. We banged at the door and hallooed. After some twenty minutes, a head appeared over the rocks to ask who we were. Lieutenant Wang, who spoke their dialect, said that we were a party of hunters seeking passage to the south. The head disappeared, and soon there was a great noise of evident excitement inside. When we looked up again, a dozen arrows were pointed down at us. The general assured them of our peaceful intentions and begged them to open the door.

It was a hopeless situation. When the door opened, Wang stood first in the passage. He glanced around. Twenty arrows in two rows were poised and pointed at the entrance, the first row of men kneeling and the second row standing. Wang found himself presenting a perfect target. Nearer at hand, five or six men with their short knives drawn stood on both sides of the gate. Each unwelcome intruder's head could be chopped down conveniently the moment it protruded out of the cave entrance. In such a situation, discretion was the better part of valor. Wang advanced with a smile and the men with knives closed in. Wang tried to talk. They were taking away his knife from the scabbard. At that instant, the second and third man rushed out of the entrance. Knives clanged and arrows flew. Three or four persons already lay on the ground.

Suddenly the scuffle was stopped by a voice. We looked up and saw the White Monkey standing close by on top of a rock, some fifteen feet high.

General Ouyang came forward and the White Monkey stepped down to meet him.

"This is all a mistake," said General Ouyang. "We are on our way to the south and would like to ask permission for passage." He introduced himself.

"I am greatly honored," answered the White Monkey. Any other chieftain would have shown the greatest respect for the general's authority, but the White Monkey acted as if he was merely a proud host to a passing traveler. His hair was done up in a coil and like all the other tribesmen, he was barefooted. In spite of his frightening white eyebrows, he had a certain calm and dignity. "As you are my guests, I would ask you to command your men to lay down their arms. You see, I am unarmed," he said, and made a broad, loud laugh.

"We are friends," said the White Monkey. "You have never seen my country. You will enjoy it."

The general ordered us to disarm. Seeing this, the White Monkey was greatly pleased and became extremely cordial. The wounded were helped to their feet.

It is difficult to describe the sensation I felt when I surveyed the country. A broad plateau, surrounded by tall peaks on all sides, shaded by orange trees and dwarf palms and dotted with rice paddies, looked like an enchanted kingdom. The air was balmy and pleasant, in marked contrast to the heat outside. There was something in the light of the sunny valley and the fresh colors of the flowers and fruits and leaves which gave an exhilarating feeling, as if we had been suddenly transported to another world. Here and there stood shacks of logwood, covered with dry leaves, their floors raised a few feet from the ground. Women and half-naked children were playing about and laughing in the sun. Parakeets in snow-white and an unbelievable vermilion flitted from tree to tree. It was almost impossible to think of evil in such an enchanted land.

"What a pretty country you have!" remarked the general politely and sincerely. "It makes me envious."

"And well guarded, no?" the White Monkey replied with a quick laugh.

The White Monkey lived in a cabin built of heavy logs. The floor was covered with rough planks. There was hardly any furniture outside of a few planks, serving as benches, and a big board of teakwood, supported by sections of trunks, which served as the only table in the house. A big, curious and happy crowd had come to watch the visitors, and among them we could see some Chinese women. It was noon, and we were served rice and a dish of sharp, odoriferous flavor, which seemed to be a stew consisting of vegetables, spices, and pigs' entrails thrown together.

The White Monkey had several wives, called *meiniang*. The women were not secluded as in Chinese society. The general did not mention his missing wife, but I could see he was tense while he talked and joked with his host at lunch. The White Monkey proposed to take the general to see the country after lunch.

Perhaps the White Monkey wanted to show his guests or captives (we did not know which) how helpless any attempt at escape would be. This strange creature walked in fast, jaunty steps in spite of his two-hundred-odd pounds. His top-heavy shape and relatively thin legs seemed especially adapted to jungle marching and climbing. He seemed to be in harmony with the place. Somehow the colors and the light of the valley made his white eyebrows on his coppery complexion less formidable than I had imagined. The deep lines around his mouth and cheeks, his sinewy arms, and his enormous back and shoulders all spoke of great muscular strength and prowess. He was proud and happy, and looked as if he did not owe anybody anything — certainly not as if he had kidnapped his guest's wife.

The chieftain and the general walked ahead, followed by Wang, myself, and a few others. The general saw a Chinese woman of about thirty standing with a child at her door and remarked to his host, "She is Chinese, I believe."

"Yes, there are a number of them. You like pretty women, don't you?" asked the White Monkey quite casually.

The woman looked at us silently, and we passed on. "Their children are prettier, too," said the chieftain somewhat inconsequentially, pursuing his own thoughts. "You see, nothing makes my men happier than to have pretty women for their wives. I want my people to be happy. We have everything in this country — fish, game, poultry, rice. We have no use for money, and I don't collect taxes from my people. If they catch a big fish, they eat the big fish, and if they catch a small fish, they eat the small fish. If you care to stop tomorrow, I shall show you where we fish. We lack only salt and women — and knives, of course."

"What do you mean you lack women? I see plenty of them here." I could see the general was carefully steering the conversation.

"Not enough. We have over three hundred men and only a little over two hundred women. You see, this rich plateau can feed at least a thousand more. I want to see this whole kingdom," he said with a sweep of his hand, "filled with people, beautiful people, strong people. We have not enough women."

"How is that?" asked the general in surprise.

"There are about three hundred women, if you count the old ones. I don't. Only women between eighteen and forty-five produce children. Chinese women produce many children. There is one I brought here ten years ago who has borne seven boys in succession, and all pretty, too. I don't know why it is, but our women generally produce only two or three. I prefer women of your race."

"What did you do? Kidnap them?" The conversation was drawing close.

"No. I just brought them here. If other people could, they would take ours, too. But let them try." The White Monkey stopped with a laugh and then he added, "Your people are funny. Pardon me for saying so. I cannot imagine how you have marriages arranged between parents of the boy and the girl. I wouldn't take a bride into my house unless I could carry her across my threshold."

"And you think it is better your way?"

The White Monkey looked at him curiously. "We have more fun and excitement this way. You've seen a girl. You like her. You ask your parents to arrange for her to come quietly into your house. The bridegroom does nothing about it. Where is the excitement?"

The general felt depressed. He thought it useless to argue with the White Monkey over the "excitement" of kidnapping girls for wives.

"Did you bring the Chinese women here by force? My government does not approve, you know."

The White Monkey laughed, implying that it was none of his business whether the Chinese government approved or not.

We had reached the top of a knoll, where we obtained a full view of the entire plateau. A difference in the shade of the vegetation on the opposite banks enabled us to trace the course of the river, which encircled it on the south and east, until it stopped at a cliff where the rocky mountain on the west and north began. If it was the White Monkey's intention to impress us with the strength of his position and the hopelessness of invading his country, he was quite successful.

That night, the chieftain gave us a grand dinner of guinea hen and pheasant, ending with turtle. The chieftain made an occasion of it. He put on a tan tunic, and over it, a vest of elephant skin, painted red. A few smaller pieces were strapped around his arms. The whole was shaped like an armor, which in fact it was, impenetrable to weapons. A dozen tribesmen with spears stood along the wall. The White Monkey's women came and went, serving food at the table.

We had not dared to ask the people of the village about the general's wife, for fear our mission might be discovered. But the White Monkey must have known what we were there for, though he remained the most cordial of hosts. All through the dinner, the general's mind was preoccupied. The White Monkey had as much as admitted that he had kidnapped her.

Suddenly we heard a woman's scream inside. The general recognized his wife's voice and stood up. She had seen a chance to break away while the other women were occupied and had torn her way into the room. When she saw her husband, she fell upon his shoulders and wept piteously. The White Monkey looked on, while the general tried to calm her.

"This lady is my wife," said General Ouyang, waiting for the worst to happen.

"Oh, no!" exclaimed the White Monkey in feigned surprise. "That makes it difficult, doesn't it?"

"Chieftain, I come here as a friend and shall depart as a friend. You must allow me to take my wife back with me."

"I don't give back what I take. She is mine until you take her from me. I don't give back. It is bad luck."

The White Monkey's face was suddenly fearful to look at. His hand was upon his scabbard.

"Guards!" he shouted and the tribesmen took out their knives.

"Remember I am your guest," said the general firmly, looking at his opponent. He know the tribesmen had a strict code of hospitality.

The White Monkey let his hand drop to his side. He came up to the general and said, "I am sorry that this has happened. But I rule in my territory as you do in yours. I wouldn't advise you to try to kidnap her from here. However, you are a good archer, aren't you?"

"Tolerable," answered the general proudly.

"Well, then, we will decide the matter honorably tomorrow, according to our custom." He approached the woman and said, "Until then, she is mine."

The wife trembled in fear and did not know what was going to happen. "It is perhaps not as bad as it looks," the general said to her. "I am sure I will be able to arrange to take you home. You go back."

The wife suffered the other women to take her inside. The atmosphere was tense and conversation awkward. But the White Monkey looked as if he had nothing on his conscience, and acted as if he was the most honorable of men. We knew, of course, of the aboriginal custom of *tuoch'in*, or kidnapping brides.

"I brought these women here for myself," he explained. "If after a year a woman does not bear me a child, I give her to one of my men. You know our customs, General."

He explained. Among these tribes, a girl chooses a man at the annual courtship dance, goes with him to the mountain, and lives with him afterward. If, after a year, a baby is born, she goes with him to see her parents. Then she is considered married. If not, the match is broken, and next year she selects another man at the New Year dance. This goes on until she has conceived, or becomes a mother.

"I do the same when a woman does not have a child by me," added the White Monkey. "I give her up. Somebody else ought to have a chance."

The general gasped a little. "What if some women can't have children?"

"It very rarely happens, if you change them around. If they can't they are disgraced. On the other hand, it would be criminal to separate mothers from their children. The children are the real reason for marriage, and the husband is the excuse. As you can see," he concluded, "they all become mothers and they are all happy here."

Next day, a lovers' contest was announced, to be preceded by a courtship dance which the White Monkey had ordered for the special occasion. Men, women, and children put on their best clothes. In the morning, the youth and girls, happy about the dance, left their work and strolled about in their holiday dress. A courtship dance usually lasted into the night when lovers, having chosen their partners, would go off into the forest. The young girls, usually gay, strolled past in groups, looking about and smiling at the young men, trying to make up their minds whom they would like to choose as lovers for the night.

The dance did not begin until about four o'clock. The White Monkey now appeared with his wives and children, and Mrs. Ouyang, looking bewildered, was among them. He was dressed in his war attire, proud of his elephant-skin vest. The deep lines on his weathered face showed clearly in the sun. On his waist hung a scabbard from which projected the smooth, well-worn handles of two knives, wound around with fine silver threads. He looked as happy and proud as a king.

The dance began informally and in not too good order. The drummers playing on snakeskin drums sat around a flag-pole fifty feet high in the center of the ground, while two men played long horns. The instruments were over five feet long, shaped like trumpets, and they made long, low notes which could be heard half a mile away. While the older men stomped their spears on the ground, the girls joined hands and danced in a circle around the pole, their finely embroidered, red marriage bands, flapping and flaunting at their sides.

Every girl had a marriage band, on which she had worked with the greatest care and skill. Their mothers looked on, while the young men stood around them and shouted and clapped. When a girl saw a man she liked, she would flap her band in his direction when passing him. If the man liked her, he took up her band and joined her. This went on, with a great deal of flirting, joking, laughing, and singing. Soon more and more pairs were formed, the men dancing on the outside and holding on to the long red bands of their respective partners.

Mrs. Ouyang looked on, fascinated. The general was getting impatient, but the White Monkey was enjoying the show and laughing and drinking with total unconcern. At the worst, he would be losing only one of his wives.

"Well," he said to his guest, "I know you are a great general, and I would not want to seem unfair to you. We will follow our ancient custom, and may the best man win."

He borrowed the marriage band of one of his wives and explained the contest, which was the method used when two men claimed the same girl. The band was four or five inches wide and on it was embroidered a snake. It was to be hoisted up to the top of the pole, and whoever shot his arrow closest to the snake's eye was to have the girl.

The embroidered band was hoisted up and it flapped lazily in the wind. All the men, women, and children stood around and watched with great excitement. Rarely was such a lovers' contest held.

"What is your choice? Shall we say a hundred paces away?" the White Monkey asked.

General Ouyang hesitated for a second, but he accepted. It was a small target moving irregularly, and hitting it was as much a matter of luck as of skill. His best bow and arrows were brought to him. The crowd stood off, the drums sounded, and the atmosphere was tense with excitement. Mrs. Ouyang understood now that her fredom depended upon her husband's marksmanship. He had three shots.

The general was an expert shot. He had shot flying birds at a greater distance, but a bird on the wing usually flies in a straight line. He aimed his shot at the snake's head nearest the pole — twing! He just missed it by the tricky wriggling of the pennant and his arrow disappeared into the distance.

"You didn't watch the wind," remarked the White Monkey, who was evidently in one of his best moods.

With the second shot, the general had better luck, for the arrow pierced the band close to the snake's neck.

"Bravo!" shouted the White Monkey. "You have another shot."

The last shot missed completely.

The White Monkey now stepped forward. He twanged his powerful bow as if it were a toy, glad of the opportunity to match his skill with the Chinese general. He stood motionless. At any moment his arrow would leave the string. He tilted his head, and for a moment he seemed to live in his eye on the target. In a split second, when he sensed a flagging motion of the pennant, he sent his arrow right across the snake's head.

A great shout went up from his people. The drummer beat the drum as if he would like to smash it. The band was pulled down and examined. The arrows had been marked and there was no possible dispute. General Ouyang swallowed hard, and his wife wept. It had been a fair contest and he had to accept the decision.

"I am very sorry," said the White Monkey. "But you did very well."

Mrs. Ouyang broke down and cried. It was a very sad and hard parting. The general bit his lip and tried not to show what he felt.

The weapons had been left outside the cave entrance for us to pick up on our return. The White Monkey accompanied us to the entrance and presented the general with an ancient copper drum.

"No hard feelings, General. Next year, if you care to come and visit me, you'll be welcome. If by that time my wife does not bear me a child, I will give her back to you."

The following year, a strange thing happened. The general went back to see his wife, and found that she had given birth to a boy. To his surprise, she was dressed like an aboriginal woman, and was happily dangling the baby in her arms, proudly exhibiting it to him. The general was losing his patience.

"I believe I can still persuade the chieftain to let you go back with me," he said to her.

But the wife was firm. "No," she said, "you go away without me. I cannot leave my boy here. I am his mother."

"Do you mean to say you prefer to stay? You do not love the chieftain, do you?"

"I don't know. He is the father of my child. You go away alone. I am happy here."

The general literally staggered when he heard his wife's words. It took him a little time to realize that the White Monkey's ways were not as stupid as he had thought. The White Monkey had triumphed over him inexorably, and he knew why.

This last humiliation was too great a blow to him. Thereafter, he was a broken man.

3. THE STRANGER'S NOTE

From the Ch'ingp'ingshan T'ang *collection, No. 2.*
Ch'ingp'ingshan T'ang *was the name of the publishing
house. These* huapen *or story-tellers' copies apparently
could be sold separately, for there was no general title
for the book, and both literary and vernacular stories are
found in it. As usual no author's name is given. The original of this story bears three alternate titles, "The Monk
Who Sent the Note," "Auntie Hu," and "A Misdelivered
Note," and the subtitle "Kungan ch'uan-ch'i," which
means that it was a crime and mystery story. It was,
therefore, a popular teahouse story, going under several
names. The same story is also found in another collection,*
Kuchin Shiaoshuo. *The next best crime story I have come
across is "Tsui Ning Wrongly Executed" in the other
Sung story-tellers' copies, the* Chingpen T'ungshu
Hsiaoshuo.

*The original shows the "stranger" as a thorough cheat
and villain disguised as a monk. Besides omitting and
supplying some details, I have switched the reader's
sympathy to the stranger and made the wife stick to him
instead of going back to her first husband, which was
more satisfactory to a Chinese audience. (The wife in
the original was a suffering, submissive woman, doing
nothing on her own initiative.) Otherwise, this version
follows the main outline of the original.*

IT WAS toward the noon hour. The day was hot and few passengers were on the street. Wang Erh's teahouse was situated two streets back of the covered passages and bazaars in the center of the East City, where the best restaurants were. The morning crowd, which had come to his teahouse for a cup of tea and exchange of gossip and news, had dispersed, and Wang Erh was washing his teapots and stacking them, some two dozen, on a shelf. This done, he took his pipe and prepared to enjoy a rest, when he saw a tall, well-dressed man walk into his shop. The visitor's bushy eyebrows and deep black eyes gave him a striking appearance.

Wang Erh had never seen this man before, but that did not surprise him. All sorts of people came to his shop; that was what made running a teahouse interesting. Businessmen and their families, scholars, salesmen, gamblers, cheats, and passing strangers all came to rest and refresh themselves. The tall stranger selected an inside table, and he gave the impression of being a little secretive, even a little nervous. Wang Erh saw that he was preoccupied, and thought it would be better to leave him alone.

Soon a boy peddler passed by in the street, calling aloud, "Fried partridge *hutu!* Hey-yo, delicious fried partridge!"

The gentleman called him in. The boy, whose head was shaven like a monk's, laid his tray on the table and began to pierce some *hutu* together on a stick, sprinkling some salt on it.

"Please, sir, here's your partridge."

"Leave it there. What's your name?"

"Seng-erh, that is my name, because I look like a little monk," said the boy with an innocent smile.

"Would you like to earn some extra money, little monk?"

"Certainly." The boy's eyes brightened.

"I want to ask you to do something for me."

The tall gentleman pointed to a house, number four from the corner, down an alley which opened on the street at a point just facing the teahouse. "Do you know who lives in that house?" he asked.

"That is the house of Mr. Huangfu, an officer of the palace, in charge of official uniforms."

"Oh, is he? Do you know how many persons are living in the house?"

"Just three. The palace officer, his young wife, and a little foster daughter."

"Good. Do you know the lady?"

"She seldom comes out of her house. But she often buys partridge from me and I know her. Why do you ask?"

The stranger saw that Wang Erh was not looking, so he took out a case and poured some fifty coins on the boy's tray, at which the boy's eyes brightened. "That's for you," he said.

He then showed the boy a package, which contained a pair of gold cable bracelets, two short hair brooches, and a note. "Give these three things to that lady. But remember, if you see the husband, do not give them to him. Is that clear?"

"I am to give these things to the lady. I am not to give them to the palace officer."

"Right. After you give the lady the note, wait for an answer. If she does not come with you, tell me what she says."

The boy went to the house, but when he lifted the screen and peeped in, he saw the palace officer sitting in the front room looking directly at the door. Huangfu was a short man in his forties, with broad shoulders and a wide, flat, rather rectangular face. He had been on duty at the palace for the last three months and had come home only two days ago.

"What are you doing here?" shouted the officer and ran after the boy, who had immediately started to run away. Huangfu grabbed him by the shoulder and shook him violently. "What do you mean by peeping in at my door and running away like that?"

"A gentleman asked me to deliver a package to your wife. He told me not to give it to you."

"What is in it?"

"I will not tell you. The gentleman told me not to give it to you."

The officer gave the boy's head such a loud whack that the boy winced and reeled.

"Hand them to me!" he shouted in his throaty, officer's voice.

The boy could only do as he was told, still protesting, "They are not for you. They are for her."

Huangfu broke open the package and saw the bracelets, the pair of hair brooches, and the note which read as follows:

Dear Mrs. Huangfu: You may think this presumptuous of me, but since I saw you at the restaurant, I have not been able to put you out of my mind. I would love to call on you, but that ass of your husband has returned. May I beg to see you alone? Come with the messenger of this note, or tell me how I can meet you. I am sending these little things as tokens of my great esteem.

Your admirer, (unsigned)

The officer ground his teeth. Raising his eyebrows, he asked coldly, "Who gave you this message?"

Seng-erh pointed to Wang Erh's shop just outside the alley, and said, "A gentleman with bushy eyebrows, great big eyes, a snub nose, and a wide mouth gave them to me."

Huangfu grabbed the boy by the arm and dragged him to the shop. The stranger was gone. In spite of Wang Erh's protests, the officer took the boy back to his house and locked him in. The boy was now thoroughly frightened.

Huangfu was shaking with anger. He called his wife out with a commanding voice. The young wife was a delicate and rather pretty woman of twenty-four, with a small, intelligent face. She saw that her husband was white and panting, and she could not understand what had happened.

"Look at these!" said her husband, grimly staring at her.

Mrs. Huangfu seated herself leisurely in a chair. She took out the articles and stared at them.

"Read the note!"

She read it and slowly shook her head. "Is this letter for me? It must be a mistake. Who sent it?"

"How do I know who sent it? You know! Whom did you have dinner with during the three months when I was on duty?"

"You know me well," replied the young wife gently. "I would not do such a thing. We have been married for seven years. Have I ever done anything a wife should not do?"

"Then where does the note come from?"

"How can I know?"

Unable to explain the letter and clear herself, the wife began weeping. "What kind of a strange disaster has fallen out of a clear, blue sky!" she wailed. Without warning her husband struck her on the face. Mrs. Huangfu cried aloud and ran into the house.

The palace officer called for the thirteen-year-old maid, Ying-erh, his foster daughter. Her short sleeves revealed her plump arms, red from washing. She stood stiffly erect, awaiting an order, trembling a little as she always did before her master. Fearfully she watched his movements. He took down from the wall a piece of bamboo and threw it on the floor. Then he took a rope and tied the maid's hands, swinging the other end of the rope across a beam in the roof. He hauled the girl up and, holding the bamboo in his hand, he asked, "Tell me, whom did the mistress dine with when I was away?"

"There was no one," replied the girl in a terror-stricken voice.

Huangfu began to beat the maid with the bamboo, and his wife, inside, trembled hearing her screams. The flogging and questioning went on for some time. Unable to stand it any longer the maid at last said, "When you were away, Mother slept with a certain person every night."

"That's better," said the master. He let her down and untied her.

"Now tell me, who was the fellow who slept with your mother every night in my absence?"

The girl wiped her eyes and said with hatred in her voice, "I will tell you. She slept every night with me."

"I will get to the bottom of this!" he swore, and went out, locking the door behind him.

The wife and foster daughter looked at one another. Mrs. Huangfu saw the bruises on the young girl's arms and back, and rushed to wash her wounds, crying, "The beast!"

The wife shuddered at the sight of the blood which had reddened the basin of water. As she poured it down the gutter, she muttered again, "The brutal beast."

The girl stood looking at her kind foster mother and said, "If it were not for you, I would have gone back to our village. And you should, too, Mother."

"Hush, you mustn't say that."

Mrs. Huangfu looked dazed, unable to understand what had happened. At last, she turned to the boy, who was cowering in a corner of the room, and asked, "What was the stranger like?"

The boy repeated the description and told her the story. The wife and her foster daughter sat silent, completely puzzled.

Half an hour later, the husband returned with four officers of the law. Dragging the partridge boy forward, he said to the men, "Take down his name." The men did as they were told, having respect for Huangfu's position as a palace officer.

"Don't go away yet. There are more persons inside." He called out to his wife and maid and demanded that all three be arrested.

"How dare we arrest the lady?"

"You have to. A murder is involved."

Frightened by his words, the men took down the names and escorted the prisoners out of the house. A crowd of neighbors had gathered outside. As Mrs. Huangfu stepped out of the door screen, she instinctively shrank back, and said to her husband, "*Koko*, I never thought I would see this day. You should have used your head and taken time to find out who sent the letter. It's such a disgrace!"

The officers had already pushed her outside the door. The neighbors made way for her to pass.

"If you were afraid of disgrace, you shouldn't have done it," answered her husband.

The wife said to him, "Why don't you ask our close neighbors if a man ever stepped inside our door during your absence? The idea of accusing me!"

"I will!" replied her husband angrily.

The neighbors, not knowing what the wife was accused of were altogether bewildered. They sympathized with the wife and shook their heads in answer to the husband's question.

Huangfu went with the accused to proffer charges before the magistrate, Chien of Kaifeng. Chien had a round, plump face and seemed to be a man of infinite patience, incapable of being excited by anything. The husband submitted the letter and the gifts and made the formal charge. The magistrate ordered the prisoners to be held in detention pending investigation.

Two jail officers, Shan Ting and Shan Chienhsing, were in charge of questioning the prisoners. They began with the wife.

Mrs. Huangfu stated that she was born in a village near the city, that she had lost her mother early, and her father at the age of seventeen, and that she had no close relatives. She had married her husband the following year, and they had been happily married for seven years. No relatives or visitors had come to her house during her husband's absence, and she never dined with anybody at home or in a restaurant, except her husband. She had no idea who could have sent the note.

"Why is it that you never see your relatives? Don't they come and see you?"

"My husband does not like it. Once my cousin, Chang Erh, came to see us to beg my husband for a job. He didn't get the job because it wasn't easy to get. My husband asked me to stop seeing my relatives after that, and I did."

"You do everything your husband tells you to?"

"Yes, I do."

"Do you often go out to the theatre, where you might be seen by people?"

"No."

"Why not?"

"He does not take me."

"And you don't go out alone?"

"No."

"Do you go to restaurants for dinner?"

"Very rarely. I am happy at home. Oh yes, several days ago, the night when he came back from the palace, he did not like my food and took me to a restaurant near by."

"And you two dined alone?"

"Yes."

The woman's neighbors were called in. In general they corroborated the wife's story. They had never seen any visitor at her house, nor had they seen her go out except with her husband. She was a woman who kept very close to the house. The neighbors had a rather good opinion of her and called her *Siaoniangtse,* "Young Mistress," because she was so small, although there was no "old mistress" in the house. A neighboring woman said the husband was short-tempered and mistreated the wife, who was always meek and submissive and never complained. The neighbor said Mrs. Huangfu looked like "a bird feeding from one's hand."

On the third day, Shan Chienhsing was standing in front of the magistrate's office, thinking about the mystery, when he saw the husband pass by. Huangfu came up to him and gave him a greeting.

"How is the case proceeding?" he asked. "Three days have passed. Perhaps you have received a present from the sender of the note and purposely delayed action."

"Nonsense! The case is not so easily concluded. Your wife insists on her innocence and we have learned nothing to prove otherwise. You did not send the note yourself by any chance?"

"Don't talk to me like that. We are happily married." Huangfu was angry.

"What do you propose to do?" asked Shan.

"If the court cannot clear the case, I will demand a divorce."

Shan went into his office and prepared the documents. That afternoon he presented his report to the magistrate. Magistrate Chien ordered the couple and the witnesses to trial the next day.

The magistrate first questioned the little boy. Then he turned to the thirteen-year-old maid as the most important witness. He banged the court gavel, an iron paperweight, by way of frightening her and spoke in a harsh, severe voice:

"You know everything that has been going on in the house, don't you?"

"I do."

"Did you see any visitor or visitors when your master was away?"

The maid answered impatiently, "If there were any visitor, would I not have seen him?"

The magistrate gave another loud bang with his gavel and shouted, "You little liar! You dare to lie in my presence! I will send you to jail for this."

The maid was frightened, but she said firmly, "Your Honor, I have not lied to you. My mistress stayed in the house all the time. You cannot wrong a good woman." She broke down, whimpering and sobbing.

The magistrate was impressed by the maid's testimony.

"Now then," he addressed the husband, "a charge of theft must be proven with the stolen goods in the thief's possession, and a charge of adultery must be proved by producing a co-respondent. I cannot condemn your wife without more evidence than a note from an anonymous stranger. You may have some enemy who planted this note." He looked at the woman and continued, "Certainly some one is trying to cause trouble. Don't you think you ought to take her home and try to find out who sent the note?"

The husband was adamant. "Under the circumstances, Your Honor, I am not willing to take her home."

"You may be making a mistake," warned the magistrate.

"I shall be satisfied if you will grant me a divorce," said Huangfu. He could not help looking at his wife out of the corner of his eye.

After more questioning, the magistrate said to the woman, "Your husband insists on a divorce. I hate to break up marriages. What do you think?"

"My conscience is clear. But if he wants a divorce, I shall not protest."

The divorce was granted according to the husband's wish. The boy and the maid were released and ordered to be taken back to their parents.

The wife completely broke down when the court was adjourned. Divorce was a great disgrace to the woman, and she had not expected it because her guilt had not been established.

"I did not know you could be so cruel after seven years of marriage. You know I have no place to go now," said the wife to her husband. "I will rather die than have my name dishonored."

"That is none of my business," replied Huangfu and abruptly turned his back.

Only Ying-erh, the girl, stood by her.

"Ying-erh," said the wife. "Thank you for what you did.

It is of no help now. You can go home to your parents. I have nowhere to go and I cannot keep you. Go home like a good girl."

They parted in tears.

The woman, now left all alone, could not completely realize what had happened. Aimlessly, she made her way through the streets and crowds without seeing anything. The day was darkening, and she wandered to the Tienhan Bridge on the Pien River where she stood looking out at the locks and congested water traffic. The masts of the boats stood close together rocking and swaying in the evening wind, giving her a heady sensation, as if she were rocking with them. She watched the golden disc of the sun disappear behind a distant hill, and realized she had come to the end of her road. She would never see the sun again.

Just as she was about to jump into the river, some one pulled her back. She turned around and saw an old woman, well over fifty, dressed in black. Her hair was thin and grayish-white.

"Daughter, what do you take your own life for?"

Mrs. Huangfu stared at her.

"Do you know me? I don't suppose you do," said the old woman.

"No," replied the young woman.

"I am your poor auntie. Since your marriage to the palace officer, I have not dared to come and bother you. It was so long ago when I saw you as a child. The other day I heard from the neighbors that you were involved in a lawsuit with your husband, and I came every day to ask for news. I hear that the magistrate has decreed a divorce. But why jump into the river?"

"My husband does not want me and I have no place to go. Why should I live?"

"Come, come, you can stay with your old auntie," said

the old woman. Her voice was strong for her age. "Such a young woman trying to end her own life! What nonsense!"

Mrs. Huangfu was not at all sure whether this old woman really was her aunt, but she allowed the woman to take her along, without a will of her own.

They went first to a wine shop where the old woman ordered her a drink. When the young woman came to the aunt's house she found it was situated in a quiet, out-of-the-way alley. It was fairly decent looking, furnished with green curtains and armchairs and tables.

"Auntie, are you living all alone? How do you support yourself?"

The old woman whose name was Hu, answered with a laugh. "Oh, I make a living somehow. I used to call you 'Missie.' I forget your name."

"My name is Chunmei," answered Mrs. Huangfu, and she did not push her question further.

The old woman, Hu, was very kind to her, and for the first days she made her guest rest. Chunmei lay in bed thinking of the sudden and strange turn of her life.

Several days later, the old woman said to her, "You must be strong. I am not really your auntie, but I wanted to save a young girl's life when I saw you about to take the jump. You are young and pretty. You have your life before you." Her old eyes narrowed into slits. "Do you still love your husband who has so brutally disowned you and left you to die?"

Chunmei looked up from her pillow and answered, "I don't know."

"I don't blame you," said the old woman. "But wake up, my daughter. You are still young and you shouldn't suffer yourself to be pushed around by people. Forget your husband, and get over your misery. Young people sometimes have foolish sentiments, I know. I have crossed more bridges than you have crossed streets. Life is like that. Up and down, up and down it goes, round and round in a circle. I lost my husband at twenty-eight. How old are you?" Chunmei gave her age. "Well, I was a few years older than you are now, but here I am. Look at me." Even though her face was lined, and the skin of her neck was a little loose, she seemed in perfect health. "You take a good rest and in a little time you will get over it. Life is like going on a road. You fall down. What then? Do you sit down and cry and refuse to get up? No, you pick yourself up and go on again. From what you told me, he is a rascal. Why, he has not deserted you. He has thrown you out. So what are you lying here moping about?"

Chunmei listened to her words and felt better. "What can I do? I can't be living with you forever."

"Don't worry. Take a good rest and get strong again. Then when you are well, find a good man and remarry. Pretty eyes and a pretty face like yours never need to go hungry."

"Thank you, Auntie. I already feel better."

Mrs. Huangfu could not help feeling grateful to the old woman for saving her life and helping her recover her spirits during this bitter period of her life.

They had dinner together every night. Old woman Hu always liked a little rice wine with her dinner; wine was the "water of life," according to her. "There's nothing like a little wine for recovering your faith in life," she said. "At my age, it makes me feel good and young once more." Chunmei admired the spirit of this hearty woman.

After dinner, they heard a man's voice calling outside, "Hu *potse*, Hu *potse!*" The old woman went hastily to open the door.

"Why do you close the door so early?" asked the man. It had been raining that day, and she had locked the door rather early.

The old woman asked him to sit down, but the man said he had to go away immediately, and remained standing.

Chunmei saw from the back room that he was tall and had thick eyebrows and big eyes. Her attention was arrested and she looked at him carefully from behind the screen. His mouth could be called broad, and his nose was not pointed, more or less answering the boy's description. Her heart pounded, but she made no sign of her suspicion.

"What is this?" asked the tall man in a tone of impatience. "It is already a month since you sold the three hundred dollars' worth of things. I want the money."

"They were sold, as I told you," replied Auntie Hu. "They are in my client's place, but what can I do if he has not paid up? As soon as he pays, I shall turn over the money to you."

"But this is long enough — longer than usual. Bring the money as soon as you receive it."

The gentleman left and Auntie Hu came inside looking quite upset.

"Who was the visitor?" asked Chunmei.

"I will tell you, Chunmei. The gentleman's name is Hung. He says he was the magistrate of Tsaichow and is now retired. I don't believe him. I know he lies, but he is a great fellow. He often asks me to sell some of his jewels. He says he is an agent for jewelers. Maybe he is, maybe he isn't. But he has good jewels, and the other day he asked me to sell some for him. They were sold but my client hasn't paid. I don't blame him for being impatient."

"Do you know him well?"

"Yes, in a business way — perhaps more. I never saw a fellow quite like him. I can't make him out. He is liberal with his money. When he sees I am in need of money, he gives me some without my asking for it. The next time he comes, I will introduce him to you."

Chunmei's interest was greatly aroused, but she tried not to show it.

Hung came again and again, and Chunmei was introduced to him as a relative of Auntie Hu. She was torn between the desire to find out if he was the stranger who had changed her life, and her liking for his undeniable charm. She could not quite get rid of the suspicion that he might be the very man they had been looking for, and she tried to make his face fit the partridge boy's description of the mysterious stranger. The point which bothered her most was whether his nose could be called snub.

At one of their meetings, she sat staring at him, lost in thought.

"What are you staring at me for?" remarked Hung in his jocular way. "Every physiognomist tells me I have a lucky face and lucky ear lobes." He pulled his heavy lobes, and said, "See? I always brought luck to people."

Hung was alternately amusing, helpful, and attentive. He was flashily dressed and inordinately vain. Because he had traveled a great deal, he could tell entertaining stories, and his swagger was part of his charm. But he was also interested in others. He asked Chunmei to tell her story and listened with sympathy. He took her part, interrupting only to express his disgust with the ex-husband's outrageous cruelty. His sympathy for her seemed sincere, even if he might be courting her.

After their second meeting he had asked Chunmei to sew on a button for him. Chunmei was fascinated. She saw that he really had business transactions to come and see the old woman about, but now he provided excuses for many more visits. He always brought a bottle with him, and sweetmeats and new delicacies which he had promised the women he would announce that he was coming for supper, complain of hunger, and then have the insolence to teach Chunmei how to prepare a dish of ham and candied ginger in his own way. When a man had the courage to command, it gave a woman pleasure to obey.

"What do you think of that rascal?" Auntie Hu asked Chunmei when he left.

"I think he is an interesting person."

"He asked me the other day to do something for him which I have not yet been able to do."

"What was it?"

"He is living alone. The other day he asked me to find a woman and make a match for him. Why don't you let me make the arrangements and suggest the match to him? I can see that he likes you and will be delighted at the suggestion."

"I see," said Chunmei thoughtfully.

"You see what? He is a charming man. What is holding you back? If you still haven't got over that ass of an ex-husband of yours, you are the greatest fool I know. Isn't he a fine fellow? He has money and will be able to take care of you, and you will be off my hands."

"I must tell you, Auntie," said Chunmei. "I like him, but there is something I should like to clear up."

"What is it?"

"I have an idea he might be the unknown person who sent the note, and broke up our marriage."

Auntie Hu broke into such laughter that Chunmei felt embarrassed.

"He answers the description, more or less, you know."

"What nonsense? How many tall men are there in the world, and how many have heavy eyebrows and big eyes? Is that his fault? Suppose he *was* that stranger, what then? You have been punished for eating a cake which you didn't eat. You've paid the price, and the cake is here. It's yours. If I were you, I would marry the stranger, just to show him off to that brute who was your husband."

Chunmei did not know what to think. If Hung was not the stranger, she would be doing herself a lot of good, and if he was, she would be doing her ex-husband no harm. She began to feel the sweetness of revenge.

The next time Hung came, she was gayer than usual. She had decided to test him.

He had brought his own bottle, and said, "Come on, drink to my luck in meeting such a fair lady as you."

"No, I will drink to your lucky ear lobes," the young woman replied. The drink helped her a lot. She could not contain her curiosity any longer, and in the next breath, she surprised herself by remarking, "The stranger was said to look like you."

"Really? I am honored. Think of a man who had the courage to do such a thing! If I had seen you before, I would have wanted to do the same thing, even if you were married to a duke. Once I did have an affair with a duke's mistress. You don't believe me? I don't suppose you would. However, here's to my lucky ear lobes!" He poured himself another cup and finished it at one gulp.

"See how he lies," remarked Auntie Hu pleasantly.

"Be sensible," said Hung, putting down his cup. "You have never seen the man. How do you know whether he is tall or short? But your husband was a brute to leave a pretty woman like you."

"Yes, he gave me no chance," she said. "It is all over now. What do I care? I am just curious to know who sent the note." In spite of herself, her eyes were a little red.

"Forget about the brute," said Hung. "Come on, drink. Such a pretty face is not made for tears. He did not want you, and you are still thinking of him. Oh, what a world, what a world!"

Chunmei was completely confused. The old woman encouraged her to drink and forget. Almost in revenge, she kept on drinking. Later in the evening, she became very gay. For the first time she realized she was free. She had never quite felt it before. It gave her a wonderful feeling of elation. She kept repeating in a silly way, "Yes, I have no husband . . . Yes, I have no husband."

"Yes, forget," said Hung.

"Yes, forget," said Chunmei. "Say you are not the stranger, are you?"

"Don't talk nonsense. What would you do if I were?"

"I would love you for setting me free from that brute husband of mine. Would it not be funny if my husband saw me drinking with the stranger here tonight?"

"Your former husband, I beg your pardon," corrected Hung. "You know what it would prove? It would prove that you had known the stranger and dined with him before. Thousands of women have done things behind their husbands' backs and are not divorced. You are divorced without having been unfaithful. What a world!"

"You are a devil," said Chunmei, and she began to laugh, and her laughter was gay as it had never been when she was Mrs. Huangfu.

"Am I?" asked Hung, and he put his arms around her.

She smiled up at him and said dreamily, "Hello, stranger," and offered him her lips.

Somehow she felt a sense of victory.

After their marriage Hung took her to live in a house far out in the western suburb. She had not thought it possible that she could be so happy. They talked and laughed and Chunmei seemed to be consciously trying to make up for what she had missed before. He often took her to small restaurants and she went with him gladly. He seemed well-to-do and was liberal with his money. He loved to press money into her palms and never asked her for an account, as Huangfu had. Then, too, he had friends whom he often invited home for dinner. It was as different as possible from her life with her former husband.

Hung had never openly admitted that he was the stranger. He always had a way of turning aside the question, or he would admit it with such a swagger that it seemed impossible to take him seriously. But one afternoon, after a little drink and some cold partridge, which they had bought from a street hawker, he was feeling very happy, and for once he made a slip of the tongue. "You know I sometimes think of that poor partridge boy — " he checked himself immediately and added lamely — "from what you told me about him." And Chunmei knew.

That night in bed after she had put out the light, Chunmei asked him, "Tell me why did you send that note?"

There was a long silence.

"He bullied you, didn't he?" he said at last.

"You knew? You had seen me?"

"Of course I knew. You don't know what a ridiculous couple you two made, like a swan married to a toad."

"Where did you see me?"

"I saw you the first time trailing your feet behind him on Kungchien Street. I stopped to ask you for road directions. He pulled you away roughly with a stern, censorious look I could not forget. That was last spring. You wouldn't remember. I thought of you as a bird in a cage. I was struck by you from the moment I saw you. I will let that bird free, I said to myself. I took a lot of trouble to find out. You had enemies, you know."

"I?" Chunmei gasped.

"You know that relative of yours, Chang Erh, who stayed in your house for some time to beg your husband for a job?"

"*You* know Chang Erh?"

"Yes. Do you know why your clan people never came to see you? Because of your husband's treatment of Chang Erh. He came home and told everybody in the village about it. I was in love with you and it was driving me crazy. I pictured you as a fairy enchained by a monster."

"But how could you do such a thing? I never had dinner with you. And I was happy."

"Yes, as happy as a bird in a cage. Remember two days before I sent you that fatal letter, when your husband had just come home, you dined at the Taiho restaurant in the passage with him? I was there, sitting at the next table. Yes, you were very happy. It didn't take me two minutes to

see that you were afraid of him. I detested the fellow. I
noticed that he never once consulted you about your food.
He ordered what *he* liked, and you ate humbly, sweetly, sub-
missively. I was boiling with rage. I tried to arrange to see
you, but that partridge boy bungled it. I was madly in love
with you and followed the trial every day through Auntie
Hu. I had hoped he would divorce you, but I did not expect
it to turn out exactly as I wished."

Next morning, she saw Hung writing a letter. She waited
until he had finished and then quickly snatched it from
him and said laughingly, "Do you know what this letter means
in my hands, if I hand it over to the court?"

Hung felt a slight shock and immediately recovered himself. "You won't," he said.

"Why won't I?"

"I know you mean the handwriting, but don't forget
that you are living with the adulterer now. At the most,
you will merely be convicted of adultery, and the judge
cannot convict a person twice."

"You devil!"

She bent and kissed him, a long hot kiss.

"You are biting me," Hung protested jokingly.

"That is how much I love you!"

New Year came around. Chunmei used to go with her
former husband to Siangkuoshih on that day to pray for a
lucky year. She suggested to Hung their doing it, and they
went to the temple together.

Huangfu, too, remembered their visit at the Siangkuoshih
on every New Year's Day. He had been feeling desolate and
unhappy since the settlement at court. The mystery of the
stranger had never been solved, and he had gone back
to the palace again. Now that he was separated from his
wife, he remembered more and more her good qualities, and
the more he thought about her, the more he believed in her

innocence. Everything pointed to it: her own behavior during the arrest and trial, and the testimony of the maid and the neighbors. His remorse was bitter. He forced himself to put on a good gown, took a box of incense, and went to the temple.

As usual, there was a big crowd at the temple on new Year's Day. As Huangfu came out, he saw his former wife going in with a tall man. They did not see him, so he waited outside for them to come out, chatting idly with a seller of clay dolls. When he saw them come down the temple steps, he hid himself in the crowd, trembling with anger and jealousy.

He followed them till they got outside the gate, and then he called to her from behind. Chunmei turned around and recognized him with a start. He was shabby and thin, and there was a new sad look on his face.

"Oh, you!" she cried with evident annoyance and contempt. Her tone and carriage were so different from his submissive wife that for a moment he thought she must be somebody else.

"Chunmei, what are you doing here? Come home, I need you." He glanced at Hung briefly.

"Who are you?" demanded Hung. "I should ask you to stop bothering this lady." Turning to Chunmei, he asked, "What is this man to you?"

"He is my former husband," she replied.

"Come home, Chunmei. I have forgiven you. I am lonely. I was wrong about you." Huangfu's tone was almost plaintive.

"He is not your husband any more, is he?" Hung asked the woman, accenting his words slowly and fixing his eyes on her.

Chunmei looked at Hung and answered, "No."

"May I speak to you for a moment?" Huangfu asked her again. Chunmei looked at Hung, and he nodded and stood aside.

"What do you want?" asked Chunmei. Her voice was suddenly angry.

"Who is this man you are with?"

"Is it any business of yours what I do now?" Her voice was bitter.

"For old times' sake," he begged. "Come home. I want you."

Chunmei went a step closer. Her eyes shone and she raised her voice. "Let's make this clear," she said. "You did not want me. I told you I was innocent. You would not believe me, and did not care whether I lived or died. You said it was none of your business. Luckily I did not die, and what I do is none of your business now."

Huangfu's face changed. He laid his hands on her tightly, and she struggled to get free, shouting, "Let me alone! Let me alone!"

The former husband was so surprised that his grip relaxed. She broke away and went to Hung.

"Leave her alone, you bully!" shouted Hung.

He took her hand, and they walked off without another word. Huangfu stood alone, stupefied. As they walked down the street, they heard him calling to her from behind them:

"But I have forgiven you, Chunmei! I have forgiven you!"

Love

4. THE JADE GODDESS

wwwwwwwwwwwwwwwwwwwwwwwwwwwwwwwwwwwwwwwwwwwwwwwwwwwwwwwwwwwwwwwww

Based on a story bearing the same title in the Chingpen
T'ungshu Shiaoshuo. *The original story ends quite
differently. The jade carver's wife was discovered by an
officer and buried alive in a garden, but she appeared
as a ghost to effect her revenge. I have followed the first
part of the story only, and developed the story according to the simple theme of whether a great artist should
destroy his art to cover his identity, or let his art betray
him. The story probably belongs to the twelfth century.*

THE VOYAGE up the Yangtze Gorges had been exciting and
hazardous, but I had finally arrived at the home of the
retired governor in a suburban town near Chengtu. The
governor was a famous art collector, and it had been said of
him that in his days of power, he had used his political position to obtain valuable objects of art. When he wanted a
bronze or a painting he had to have it, either by paying
for it or by other means. It could not be true that he had
practically ruined a family which refused to sell him a piece
of Shang bronze, for that was the rumor, but it is known
that his love of curios amounted to an obsession, As a result,
he had in his collection some of the most priceless treasures.

The governor received me in his parlor on the ground
floor of the Western Tower, which was reached by a succession of three courtyards. For a collector of art, the parlor
was almost bare of art objects, but was furnished with the

usual redwood furniture, covered with red cushions and leopard skins. The *décor* had that elegance of simplicity, suggestive of a fine, cultivated taste. As I talked with him, I constantly looked at the exquisite silhouette of a *sang-de-boeuf* vase, and a few sprigs of plum blossoms standing against the landscape window looking out upon his garden.

I was surprised that the governor was one of the mildest of men in his appearance. Perhaps old age had softened him, but looking at him, it was difficult to believe the rumors of his cruelty. He treated me as if I was an old friend who had dropped in for a morning chat. I began to wonder whether my friend who had arranged for the visit had told him of my purpose in visiting him, or whether the governor was too old to remember.

I envied this man, for the whole impression he gave me was that he was glad to be alive in this beautiful retreat which he had built for himself.

Politely I mentioned his famous collection.

"Oh," he said with a mild laugh, "today they belong to me, the next hundred years they will belong to somebody else. You see a family never owns an art treasure for more than a hundred years. Those things have a destiny of their own. They see us and laugh at us." His voice had acquired a certain animation as he talked. Now he put a pipe to his lips.

"Do you believe that?"

"Of course," he mumbled without taking his pipe from his mouth.

"What do you mean?" I asked timidly.

"Anything that is really old acquires a personality and a life of its own."

"You mean it becomes a spirit?"

"What is a spirit?" countered the old man. "It is what informs life, gives birth to life. Take an object of art. The artist pours into it his imagination and his life's blood, in just as real a sense as a mother pours her life's blood into the embryo. Why do you wonder that it should have a life of its own, when the soul of the artist enters into it — and in giving birth to it sometimes dies himself, as, for instance, happened with my Jade Goddess of Mercy."

I had intended only to see some of the manuscripts. I had not heard of the Jade Goddess, for very few people had. But my aimless question brought forth one of the strangest tales I have ever heard.

I was not quite sure what he meant when he referred to his Jade Goddess and the exceptional circumstances of its creation, and during our examination of the manuscripts, I constantly tried to lead the conversation back to that topic.

Pointing to an old manuscript, I said, "Of course, it is true that something of the personality of the artist is left behind and lives after him in his work."

"Yes, anything good and beautiful always lives. It becomes, as it were, an offspring of the artist," the governor replied with conviction.

"But especially when an artist dies in the creation of it," I added. "Like your Jade Goddess."

"That is a particular case. He didn't exactly die on account of it. But he might as well have been dead — might just as well have been dead after that," he added after a pause. "You see the whole circumstances of the life of this artist seem to suggest that he was born to create this piece of work and to be crucified for it. He could not have created it otherwise."

"It must be an extraordinary piece of work. May I see it?"

After more tactful promptings, the governor agreed to show it to me.

While some of his best things were on the first floor of the tower, the Jade Goddess was kept on the top floor.

"Who is the artist?"

"A fellow by the name of Chang Po, practically unknown to the world. I learned about his life from the old prioress of the Cockcrow Convent. I had to donate a large piece of farm property to the nunnery — to that sly, old prioress — before she would part with it. That was after the nun who owned it had died. It certainly is better taken care of here than it would be at the Convent."

The statuette, which was made of an extraordinary white lustre with patches of green, stood inside a glass case in the center of the top floor, protected by a latticework of wrought iron so heavy that no one could move it.

"Walk around her a bit," said the governor, "and she will still see you."

I was intrigued by the way he referred to the statuette as if she were truly alive, and, indeed, I had a weird feeling as I circled the jade figure that her eyes followed me.

It was a tragic statue. The expression of the goddess showed her caught in flight at some dramatic moment, with her right arm raised high up, her head turned backward, and her left arm stretching slightly forward. The expression was that of a woman being physically torn apart from somebody she loved. It might have been described as a statuette of the Goddess of Mercy going up to heaven, with her hand outstretched to bless mankind, but nobody who had seen the expression on her face could accept that interpretation. It was incredible how the artist had conveyed, in a figure no higher than eighteen inches, such a living, unforgettable experience. Even the folds of her dress were unconventional. It was an individual and completely personal creation.

"How did the nun come to own it?" I asked.

"Look well at the statue's whole posture, the posture of flight, and the expression of love and terror and agony in her eyes." He paused. "Let's go down," he said suddenly. "I will tell you the whole story."

The nun, whose name was Meilan, had confessed the tale before she died. The prioress may not have told the correct story in all its details and she may even have

embellished the story a little to make it more attractive. But
the governor had checked some important points and veri-
fied them for himself. According to the prioress, the nun was
very much confined to herself, but a well-cultivated person.
Not until she was on her deathbed did she tell anyone about
herself.

It must have been over a hundred years ago. Meilan was
then a young happy girl living in a large garden home in
Kaifeng. As the only daughter of a high official, Commissioner Chang, she was very much pampered. Her father
was a severe judge but upon his daughter he bestowed all
his affection. As always happens, a number of clan relatives
had come to live in the mansion, the better educated ones
being given jobs in the government and the illiterate ones
working as servants in the large household.

One day a distant nephew arrived. His name was Chang
Po and he was an intelligent lad of sixteen, vivacious and full
of spirit. He was somewhat tall for his age and his hands
with beautiful tapering fingers were remarkable for a country
lad. He made such a good impression on the family that the
mother decided he could be given the job of caring for visitors
though he did not know how to read or write.

He was a year older than Meilan and as they were still
children they often met and talked and laughed together,
for Chang Po could tell Meilan stories of the country and
she loved to listen to him.

But after a few weeks the family's first enthusiasm for
the boy was somewhat dampened. He was both unusual and
difficult. In the first place he was not a good servant; he was
often forgetful of his duties and would not, or could not,
take a scolding from his elders if he made a mistake. And so
the girl's mother asked him to tend the gardens. The boy
was finally happy doing this work.

Chang Po was one of those original people born to create,
not to learn what the world had to teach him. He was
perfectly happy alone with his flowers and trees and he

walked about and whistled as if he were lord of the creation. Left alone, he could do amazing things. He had taught
himself to paint without a master. In his spare time he made
wonderful lanterns and molded the most lifelike clay animals.

At the age of eighteen Chang Po was seemingly good for
nothing. What exactly attracted Meilan to him, she herself
could not say. He was just different and had grown tall and
handsome. He got away with everything and made himself
loved by the family with the exception of the father. A
natural intimacy grew up between the cousins, although it
was clearly understood that as they were of the same clan
name marriage between them was out of the question.

One day Chang Po suddenly announced to the mistress
of the house that he was leaving to learn a trade. He had
found a jade-worker's shop and had offered himself as an
apprentice. The mother thought it just as well, since he was
too often with Meilan. But Chang continued to live on at the
house, returning every night, and he had even more to say
to his cousin than before.

"Meilan," the mother said one day, "you are both grown
up now and although Brother Po is your cousin, you ought
not to see each other too often."

Her mother's words made Meilan think. She had never
quite realized that she was in love with the boy Chang.

That night she met Chang Po in the garden. Sitting on a
stone bench in the moonlight, she casually mentioned what
her mother had said.

"Brother Po," she said, blushing, "Mother says I mustn't
see you so much."

"Yes, we are grown up now."

The girl hung her head. "What does that mean?" She
spoke half to herself.

Chang Po stole a hand around her waist. "It means that
something in you makes you more charming every day to me,
something which makes me crave to see you. Something

which makes me feel happy when you are near and lonely and sad when I am away."

The girl sighed and asked, "Are you happy now?"

"Yes and everything changes. Meilan, we belong to each other," he said softly.

"You know very well I cannot marry you and that my parents will arrange a match for me before long."

"No, you mustn't say that. You mustn't."

"You must understand."

"I understand only this," Chang said, drawing the girl into his arms. "Since the heaven and earth were created, you were made for me and I was made for you and I will not let you go. It cannot be wrong to love you."

Meilan fled from his embrace and ran to her room.

The awakening of young love was a terrible thing. The more so when with it came the realization of their position, of the sweet poignancy of the unattainable. That night Meilan lay in bed thinking of what her mother had said and then what Chang had said. From that night on she was completely changed. The more they tried to stop the love that had been awakened, the more they felt themselves in its power. They tried not to see each other. After three days, the girl in humiliation came back to him and their excitement was increased by secrecy. Those were the days of young passions and tender regrets, temporary separations and renewed pledges, so sweet and so bitter, and both knew they were in the power of something greater than themselves.

They had no plans. They just loved. According to the customs of the time, Meilan's parents were already suggesting one young man after another for her but she kept putting them off. Sometimes she said she did not want to marry at all, which greatly shocked her mother. As she was yet young the parents did not insist and since she was their only daughter they were half-willing to keep her with them longer.

Meanwhile Chang was working and learning his trade. In jade work, Chang Po had found his natural element. Like a

born artist, he had made himself in a short time a master
of his trade. He loved it; he worked tirelessly until every
detail was perfect. The master of the shop was amazed by
him. The rich gentry began to frequent the jade shop with
orders.

One day Meilan's father decided to give a present to
the empress on her birthday. He wanted to find something
special and located an extraordinary large piece of jade of
very fine quality. At the mother's suggestion, the commissioner went to the shop where Chang Po worked and
explained what he wanted. Examining Chang Po's sculpture,
he was quite struck by its individuality.

"Son, here is a very special job for you. This is for the
empress, and if you do this job well your fortune is made."

Chang Po examined the jade. His hands traveled slowly
over the uncarved stone. He was delighted. It was agreed that
he should make it into a Kuan Yin, a goddess of mercy, and
Chang Po knew that he would make one of such beauty
as no man had set eyes upon before.

Chang Po permitted no one to see the statue until it was
completed.

When it was finished, the goddess was in the conventional
design and posture but it was a perfect work of art, exquisite
in its tender beauty. Chang Po had done what no other
craftsman had been able to do before: he had carved a pair
of freely revolving earrings on the goddess' ears; and the
ear-lobes themselves were so thin and well modulated that
they compelled admiration. The goddess' face was like that
of the girl he loved.

Naturally the commissioner was greatly pleased. This
piece would be unique even in the palace.

"The face is remarkably like Meilan's," the father remarked.

"Yes," replied Chang Po proudly. "She is the inspiration."

"Good. Young man, from now on your success is assured."
He paid Chang generously and added, "You ought to be
grateful to me for giving you this opportunity."

Chang Po's name was made. Yet what he wanted most he could not have. The success meant nothing to him without Meilan. He realized that the greatest desire of his heart was beyond him. The young man lost interest in this work. He would not accept lucrative offers. To the chagrin of his master, he just could not work.

Meilan was now approaching the scandalous age of twenty-one and not yet engaged. A match was being arranged with a very influential family. The girl could postpone no longer and her engagement was solemnized by an exchange of gifts.

Reckless with despair, the girl and the boy planned to elope. Assured of Chang's ability to earn a living, Meilan would take away some of her jewels and they could support themselves in some distant province.

The couple prepared to escape one evening through the back of the garden. As it happened an old servant saw them at the dark hour of the night and his suspicion was aroused, for the affair was known inside the household. Thinking it his duty to protect the family from a scandal, the servant held the girl and would not let her go. Chang had no choice. He pushed the servant aside. The old man tottered but would not let go and Chang gave him a blow which felled the poor man at the edge of the rockery. His head struck a jagged rock and he lay limp on the ground. Seeing the servant lifeless, they fled.

The next morning the family discovered the elopement and the dead servant. While they tried to hush the scandal, efforts to trace the couple proved completely fruitless. The commissioner was thrown into a fit of helpless rage. "I shall cover the earth," he vowed, "and bring him back to justice."

After escaping from the capital, the young couple traveled on and on. Finally, avoiding the big towns, they crossed the Yangtze and came down to south China.

"I hear that there is a good jade in Kiangse," Chang said to Meilan.

"Do you think you should work at jade again?" she asked hesitantly. "Your work will be recognized and betray you."

"I thought that was what we planned to do all along," Chang replied.

"That was before old Tai died. They think we murdered him. Can't you change your trade — make lanterns or clay dolls as you used to do?"

"Why? I have made a name for myself with jade."

"You have. That is the whole trouble," Meilan said.

"I don't think we have to worry. Kiangse is almost a thousand miles from the capital. Nobody will know us."

"Then you must change your style. Don't do those extraordinary things. Just do well enough to bring in customers."

Chang Po bit his lips and said nothing. Should he content himself with what a thousand mediocre jade workers were doing to remain safely unknown? Should he destroy his art or allow his art to destroy him? He had not thought of that.

But his wife's instinct was right. She feared it would be against her husband's nature to do cheap, commercial work. She sensed also, after they had crossed the Yangtze, that a mysterious force was dragging her husband toward the jade route in Kiangse, which led from the great mountain pass at Canton into the rich southeast plains. They did not dare stop at Nanchang, the provincial capital, and went on to Kian. The wife again brought up the question of change of profession. Kiangse produced the finest white kaolin and the finest porcelain. Porcelain would satisfy his artistic gift equally well. But Chang Po would not listen.

"Even if I did," said Chang Po, "I would make such porcelain figures that I would be recognized. Or do you want me to do cheap mediocre work? I am sure it is safe here to work in jade."

Against her woman's instinct, the wife yielded. "Then please, beloved, for my sake, do not make a name for yourself. We are in trouble, and if you do, we shall be ruined."

She said this because it was her belief, but she knew

it was unlikely that her husband would be satisfied with anything but the finest work his hands could produce. With his fine sense of beauty, his love of perfection, his pride in his work, and his passion for jade, what Chang Po really had to escape from was not the police, but himself. He sensed the tragic irony of his situation.

With his wife's jewels Change Po was able to buy a stock of uncarved stones of various qualities and set up a shop. Meilan watched him at work.

"Good enough, darling," she would say. "Nobody does any better. For my sake, please."

Chang Po looked at her and smiled ruefully. He began to make a number of common round earrings and pendants. But jade is a stone that demands its own expression and its own treatment; it would be wrong to cut up a stone for pendants which could be made into a lovely creation — perhaps a monkey stealing peaches. And so occasionally Chang made — at first stealthily and with a bad conscience — some ingenious and lovely things, strikingly original. These things, the work of his love, were snatched up as fast as he could make them and brought him far greater profits than the cheaper commercial goods.

"Darling, I am worried," Meilan pleaded with him. "You are getting to be too well known. I am expecting a baby. Please be careful."

"A child!" he exclaimed. "Now we are a family!" and Chang Po kissed away what he called her womanish fancies.

"But we are doing too well," Meilan murmured.

They were doing well indeed. After a year, the reputation of Paoho jade was established, for that was the name Chang Po had given his shop. All gentry came to buy his ware and the town of Kian itself became known as the city where people on their way to the provincial capital would stop and pick up some delightful jade objects.

One day a man walked into the shop and after looking

around casually at the display of goods, asked, "Are you not Chang Po, relative of Commissioner Chang of Kaifeng?"

Chang Po quickly denied it, saying that he had never been to Kaifeng.

The man eyed him suspiciously. "You speak the northern accent well enough. Are you married?"

"That is none of your business."

Meilan peeped from behind the shop. When the man was gone, she told Chang that the stranger was a secretary from her father's office. Perhaps his jade work had really betrayed them.

The next day the man came in again.

"I tell you I don't know what you are talking about," Chang Po said.

"Very well, I will tell you about Chang Po. He is wanted for murder, the abduction of the commissioner's daughter and the theft of his jewels. If you want to convince me that you are not Chang Po, will you ask your wife to serve me a cup of tea? I shall be satisfied when I see that she is not the commissioner's daughter."

"I am running a shop here. If you are trying to create trouble I must ask you to leave."

The man left the shop with a quizzical smile.

Hastily they packed their jadeware and precious belongings, hired a boat and left after dark, fleeing upriver. Their baby was only three months old.

Perhaps it was human perversity or perhaps it was in the divine plan of things. At Kanshein they had to stop, for the baby fell ill and they had run out of money after a month on the voyage. Chang Po had to take out one of his finest creations, a crouching dog with one eye closed, and sell it to a jade merchant named Wang.

"Why, this is Paoho jade," said the merchant. "No other shop makes such things. Absolutely inimitable."

"You are right. I bought it from Paoho," Chang Po said. He was secretly delighted.

Kanshien lay at the foot of a high mountain range. It was winter and Chang Po fell in love with the clear blue sky and mountain air. He and his wife made plans to stay. Their baby was better and Chang decided to open a new shop. Kanshien was a big city, and they thought it prudent to move farther out and settle in a town some twenty miles away. Chang Po had to sell another of his pieces.

"Why did you do it?" asked Meilan.

"Because we need the money to set up the shop."

"Listen to me this time," Meilan said. "We open a clay shop here."

"Why —" Chang Po stopped short.

"We were nearly caught because you would not listen. Does jade mean so much to you? More than your wife and baby? Later things may change and you can go back to your art again."

Against his wish Chang Po set up a shop making baked black clay figurines. He made hundreds of Buddhas but every week he saw the jade merchants from Canton pass this route and Chang yearned to handle the stone again. He would wander along the streets, stopping at some jadeware shop and anger would roll from his eyes. He came home and, seeing the wet clay figures on which he had been working, he crushed them between his fingers.

"Mud! Why should I work with this when I can chisel jade?"

Meilan was frightened by the fire in his eyes. "It will be your ruin."

One day the jade merchant Wang met Chang Po and invited him into his inn, in the hope of getting some more Paoho jade.

"Where have you been?" Chang Po asked.

"I just came back from a trip to Kian," Wang replied. He unwrapped a parcel and said, "You see this is the kind of stuff that Paoho shop is turning out now."

Chang Po was silent. When Wang produced a carnelian monkey, Chang shouted, "Imitation!"

"You are quite right," the merchant said softly. "There is no expression on the monkey's face. You talk like one who knows."

"I should know," Chang said curtly.

"Yes. I remember you sold me that marvelous crouching dog. I don't mind telling you that I made a hundred percent profit on it. Have you any more pieces of that quality?"

"I will show you what a real Paoho carnelian monkey is like."

At his shop, Chang Po showed him one that he had made in Kian and the merchant was able to persuade Chang to sell it. On his next trip to Nanchang Wang told some of his friends at the jade fair about the remarkable things he had been able to get from the owner of an ordinary clay shop in the south and added, "It seems strange that such a man should possess such lovely jade."

Some six months later three soldiers came with orders to arrest Chang Po and the commissioner's daughter and bring them to the capital. The secretary from the commissioner's office was with them.

"I will come with you if you will let me pack up a few things," Chang said.

"And there are things to bring for the baby," Meilan added.

"Don't forget he is the commissioner's grandson. If he becomes ill on the way you will be responsible."

The men had instructions from the commissioner himself to treat them well on the journey. Chang Po and his wife were allowed to go to the back of the shop while the soldiers waited in front.

It was a hard moment of parting. Chang Po kissed his wife and baby and jumped down from the window, knowing that he would never see them again in this life.

"I'll love you always," Meilan whispered softly from the window. "Never touch jade again."

Chang Po took a last look at Meilan as she stood before the window, one arm raised high to bid him good-by forever.

When he had disappeared, she withdrew and calmly entered the front of the shop to put down some of her things in a bag as if she were very busy packing. She told the soldiers to hold her baby and chatted with them as she went about packing. When the soldiers grew suspicious and searched the house, Chang Po was already gone.

Meilan returned to her home to find her mother dead, her father an old man. When she greeted him there was no smile of forgiveness on his face. Only a look at her baby son softened him a little. In a way the old man was relieved that Chang Po had escaped, for he would not have known what to do with him. Still, he could never forgive the man who had ruined his daughter's life and brought such misery to the whole family.

Years passed and no news had come of Chang Po. Governor Yang from Canton arrived one day at the capital. The commissioner gave a dinner in his honor and in the course of the dinner the governor revealed that he had brought a most precious statue which rivaled the Goddess of Mercy the commissioner had given to the empress and bore a remarkable resemblance to it in style and fineness of workmanship — in fact, it was far more beautiful. He was going to give it to the empress, for the statues would make a pair.

The dinner guests were skeptical and expressed the opinion that a better piece of workmanship than the empress' goddess was impossible.

"Wait till I show it to you," the governor said triumphantly.

When dinner was over and the table cleared the governor had a shining wood case brought in. As the white jade Goddess of Mercy was removed from its case and placed on the middle of the table, a hush fell upon them all. Here was the tragic Goddess of Mercy.

A maidservant hurried to inform Meilan. From behind a latticed partition, Meilan looked into the room and paled when she saw the jade figure on the table. "He has done it! I know it is he," she whispered. She pulled herself together to hear whether Chang Po was still alive.

"Who is the artist?" asked a guest.

"That is the most remarkable part of the story," the Canton governor replied. "He is not a regular jade worker. I came to know about him through my wife's niece. She was going to a wedding and had borrowed my wife's antique bracelets to wear for the occasion. They were identical, an intricate design of two intertwining dragons. My niece broke one of them and was horrified. It was really a pity, for the bracelets were unique and very difficult to replace. My niece insisted that she would have the one bracelet duplicated. She went to many shops but none would take the job, saying frankly that it could not be done these days. She advertised in teahouses. Soon after, a shabbily dressed man appeared and said he had come to answer the advertisement. The bracelet was shown to him. He said he could do it and he did. That was how I first heard about this man.

"When I learned that the empress would like another figure to match the Goddess of Mercy, I thought of this man. I ordered the finest piece of jade obtainable at Canton and sent for him. When he was brought in, he looked thoroughly frightened as if he had been caught as a thief. It took me a long time to explain to him that I wanted him to make a Goddess of Mercy to match one in the empress' possession. When I described to him the revolving earrings he winced but he said nothing. Gradually he approached the stone and examined it from every angle. 'What is the matter?' I asked 'Is it not good enough?' Finally he turned and said proudly 'This piece will do. It is worth trying. All my life I have been hoping to get white jade of this quality. I will do it, Gover nor, provided you do not pay me for it — and leave me in complete freedom to execute what I have in mind.'

"I put him in a room with a simple bed and table and installed all the equipment he asked for. He was rather a queer fellow. He talked to no one and was a bit rude to the servant who took things in for him. But he worked like one inspired. I was not allowed to see the statue for five months. Another three months passed before he came with the finished work. I was staggered when I saw it, as you see it before you. As he looked at his own creation, there was a strange expression on his face.

" 'There, Governor,' he said, 'I want to thank you. That statue is my life story.'

"He left before I could answer. I went after him but he was gone. He had completely disappeared."

The guests heard a scream from the next room, a woman's scream so striking and heart-rending that everybody was frozen in his place. Alone, the old commissioner rushed to Meilan, lying on the floor.

A guest who was a close friend of the family whispered to the bewildered governor, "That is the daughter of the commissioner. *She is the goddess.* I am sure your artist is no other than her husband, Chang Po."

When Meilan was revived, she approached the table before all of them. Slowly her hands raised to touch the statuette and then rested tightly on it, as if in seeing and feeling the statue she was in touch with her husband once more. And they all saw that the jade statue and the girl were the same woman.

"Keep the statue, my dear," the governor told her, when he had learned what had happened. "I can find some other present for the empress. I hope it will be some consolation to you. It is yours until you are reunited with your husband."

From that day on Meilan grew weaker, as if some mysterious disease was eating away her body. The commissioner was ready to forgive everything if his son-in-law could be found. By the following spring, word came back from the Canton governor that all efforts to locate Chang Po proved fruitless.

Two years later Chang Po's son died of an epidemic which swept through the city. Meilan then cut off her hair and entered a convent, taking along with her the jade goddess as her only possession. According to the prioress, she seemed to live in a world by herself. She would not permit another nun, not even the prioress, to enter her room.

The prioress told the governor that Meilan had been seen at night writing prayer after prayer and burning it before the statue. She let no one into that secret world of hers but she was happy and hurt nobody.

Some twenty years after she joined the convent, Meilan died. And so the perishable Goddess of Mercy passed away and the Jade Goddess remained.

5. CHASTITY

wwwwwwwwwwwwwwwwwwwwwwwwwwwwwwwwwwwwwwwwwwwwwwwwwwwwwwwwwwwwwww

This is developed from a short anecdote in popular books of jokes and anecdotes. The chicken story is in the original. The anecdote tells how a widow, on the eve of receiving a memorial arch erected in her honor, was tempted by a servant, lost the arch, and hanged herself.

BEYOND SUCHOW is a small town just between a range of tall blue hills, fairly denuded, and the beautiful Weishan Lake, fringed by marsh ground. A row of stone arches stands astride an old road. The sight is common enough in Chinese villages, cities and towns. Looking like decorative gateways they are monuments to men and women of the past: to scholars who achieved high honors or to women famous for their virtue. These are the arches of chastity, requiring a license direct from the emperor, celebrating widows who had lost their husbands while young and who had remained faithful to their memory for life. Men admire such constancy but how difficult it is this story will show.

"Come in, Meihua," shouted young Mrs. Wen to her daughter. "It is no way for a grown-up girl of your age to behave, standing around the street door."

Meihua came in, hanging her head shamefacedly. She was an extraordinarily pretty girl with gay red lips, white even teeth and a peach-blossom complexion. Frank, independent and stubborn, she was the type that could be produced only in the countryside. Although she hung her head and came in, her steps were reluctant and her heart still fluttered.

"Other girls are looking," she said to her mother in self-defense and then broke off.

A company of soldiers was marching down their street, seventy or eighty of them. The narrow street echoed with the thump of feet on the pebble pavement. Women, as well as men, had come out of their houses to watch and speculate where they were going. The older women came outside and stood against the walls. But the younger ones stayed behind the door screens of latticed split bamboo, which were a wonderful device for seeing without being seen.

But Meihua had gone outside the screen and stood on the raised stone curb outside her house, easily noticeable. The tall captain bringing up the rear, with an eye for a youthful feminine figure, had spotted her a few dozen steps away. When he passed, the young girl with the peach-colored skin gave him a slow smile. He looked and marched on, but not without turning his head for a second look at the girl's pretty face.

His brigade had come from Suchow some thirty miles south to root out a gang of bandits who had been hiding in the blue hills and making increasingly daring raids in the neighboring districts. In a small town like Hanchwang facilities for housing the soldiers were limited. Several temples were available but the officers would be billeted in homes where they could at least sleep in comfortable beds.

The captain had this on his mind and he could be excused if he turned his head to look at the girl and identify the house. Having provided for the soldiers, he appeared that afternoon at the girl's house and asked if he might impose on their hospitality. It was a house occupied by two widows, the girl's mother and grandmother, but he was unaware of this. He explained the situation. The campaign might last a couple of months and he would be away most of the time, but when he was in town he would appreciate it greatly if they could find a place for him to sleep. They exchanged names and the captain found, to his surprise, that there was not a man in the house.

The girl he had seen that morning was there, excited and waiting for her mother and grandmother to say yes. The grandmother was a wrinkled woman, about sixty, wearing a black velvet band around her head. The mother, young Mrs. Wen, was tall and a little thin, still a pretty woman, somewhere around thirty-five, with an unusually high, well-shaped nose and a small sensitive mouth. She looked like a refined and mellowed version of the young girl, with her youthful vivacity toned down and her emotional fire subdued — but not submerged — and carefully guarded and nurtured. She had drawn a veil of impassivity over her face, and if there was a quiver of a smile when the captain saw her, her lips immediately stiffened. Her quick intelligent eyes gave the captain the impression of a mystery that was worth fathoming.

It was a slightly novel idea for this family of three generations of women to take in a strange man but one look at the young officer made it easy for any feminine heart to entertain the idea. The captain was tall and slim, with broad shoulders, very regular features and a mass of jet-black hair. He was neither the burly, unlettered, spitting and loud-swearing, swashbuckling type one often finds in the army, nor was he prim and stiff and propped up with an artificial dignity as others were. A graduate of Peiyang Military Academy, his speech was cultured and his manners were well bred. His name was Li Sung, Sung being his personal name.

"I shall not bother you ladies for meals. All I need is a bed, a good place to wash up and now and then a cup of tea."

"This is not much of a house for you, officer," said the young Mrs. Wen. "But if you don't mind it we shall be glad to have you stay with us whenever you are in town."

The house was shabby enough and a trifle dark. The

furniture was genteel, but bare, the woodwork was discolored
from over-scrubbing, but the house was clean, orderly and
well managed. They could certainly provide a bamboo couch
in the front hall and Meihua would be sleeping in the inner
courtyard with her mother. The presence of the grandmother
would be guarantee against any gossip.

When the two widows saw the captain their first thought
was that here was a man for their Meihua who had already
arrived at an age to be married or engaged. She was a
striking beauty; she had her mother's well-shaped nose and
quick eyes, but not her mother's refinement of features. She
had many admirers and she knew it. She was known to be a
desirable girl of marriageable age. But there was a supersti-
tion about the unlucky males of this Wen family. There were
already two widows in the family, for both the grandfather
and the father had died shortly after marriage. Since it had
happened twice, it could happen a third time and the man
who was going to marry Meihua was practically planning
suicide. As they had no property except this house, people
were not interested. Young men interested in Meihua were
always discouraged by their parents when the question of
betrothing her was suggested. And so she had grown up to
be a buxom girl of nineteen and was still unspoken for.

There was a great change in the house of these three
women when Captain Li Sung came. He paid a great deal of
attention to Meihua and enjoyed the women's company.
He was courteous and respectful to the grandmother and
cavalierly charming to young Mrs. Wen. He was a good
talker and in love, showily jovial, entertaining and exuberant. He brought into the house of the widows a manly voice
and ringing laughter such as they had not known for years.
Certainly they hoped he would remain forever.

Back from the camp, the captain saw Mrs. Wen in the
inner hall. There was a small bookcase in which stood an

assortment of classics and literature. Some were very large volumes in old woodblock editions, boxed in faded blue cloth, and hardly seemed to be the reading for women. There were some cheap romances and dramas, and some children's books, and the collection was commonplace and undistinguished. Pointing to the volumes, he said to Mrs. Wen, "You have a fair collection of books."

"Oh, look at them, if you like. They belonged to my husband."

"What about the children's books?" There seemed to be more volumes of these than one would expect in a home without children.

The widow blushed a little. "I really had not much of an education. But I give lessons to small children and to young girls."

It was quite evident. There was a copy of *Girl's Analects*, several copies of the classic *Duties of Women*, by the woman historian Pan Chao of the second century, and three or four copies of *Models of Family Conduct* by Szema Kwang, just the kind of books used in the education of girls.

"Is that how you make your living? It is amazing. I was wondering how you mother- and daughter-in-law support yourselves."

Mrs. Wen laughed. "Oh, one always manages. When mother and I were younger, we used to do embroidery. Now I give lessons at home. The girls come and go. The lessons are very irregular; some last a few months, others a year or so. The families like to send their girls to me because they know I give them the right moral instruction, just what girls need to make good daughters-in-law."

He was opening the large set, *Collected Sayings of Chu Shi*, a favorite book of Confucian moralists but more philosophical than most, when Mrs. Wen said, "That belonged to my husband. It is not for us women. I told you I am not well educated. All a woman needs in the way of education is knowledge of the essentials; the duties of a mother, a wife, a sister, a daughter, and a daughter-in-law, and the principles of filial piety, obedience, chastity, and such."

"I am sure the girls taught by you would be well instructed in those principles. Your husband must have been a strict Confucianist."

The subject seemed painful to the widow and she said nothing. Her conversation, which was a mixture of modesty and pride, and her youthful looks and easy friendliness had produced a charming impression upon the captain. He was in love with her daughter, but he could see that the mother was the more refined and had in her the strength of patience, born of sorrow, and a true appreciation of the finer things which, by a happy balance, made her contented as she was. He had no idea as yet that the widows he was staying with had a unique position in the clan, and that a movement had been set on foot by their clansmen to obtain an arch of chastity for them.

After his return from Lincheng, the captain discovered that there was a vegetable garden at the back of the house, entered through the kitchen. One morning Meihua had gone out shopping and the captain did not see her.

He asked where the grandmother was, although he was thinking about Meihua.

"I believe she is in the back garden. Come and see it," said Mrs. Wen.

The garden was very spacious in proportion to the house. There were a few pear trees, some flowering shrubs and rows of cabbages, leeks and other vegetables. It was shut off by the walls of the neighbors' houses but on the east a side door led to a narrow alley. By the side door there was a one-room structure that looked like a guardhouse and beyond it was the chicken pen. The grandmother was sitting on an old wooden chair, enjoying the sun, and Mrs. Wen, dressed neatly in black, her hair set high at the temples in the fashion of those days, walked around the garden with the captain. On her face was a curious mixture of modesty and pride which was enchanting, and there was a soft glow in her eyes. He was quite sure that she could have married again any time she wanted to.

"Do you take care of this garden all by yourself?"

"No," replied his hostess. "Old Chang does it."

"Who is Old Chang?"

"He is our gardener. Sometimes, when we have melons and cucumbers and cabbages for sale, he markets them for good cash. He is the most honest man I know." Pointing to the guardhouse, she said, "He sleeps there."

At that moment the gardener appeared from the side door. He was bare to the waist, for it was summer, and his beautiful tanned muscles shone in the sun. He was about forty and his queue was wound round his head in peasant fashion. He had the kind of honest face that is distinctly likable in whatever station it appears. Moreover, it was free from worries, and his skin was fresh and firm.

The mistress introduced Old Chang to the captain, for that was the familiar name by which the gardener was called. Going to the curbed well, he hauled up a bucket of water and, taking a gourd, drank some, pouring the remainder on his hands by way of washing them. The simplicity of it was charming to see. As he was drinking and the sun shone on his clean beautiful brawn, the captain saw his hostess' sensitive lips quiver.

"I do not know what I would do without him," said Mrs. Wen. "He does not want any wages. He has nobody to support and all he needs are his meals and a place to sleep. He says he does not see what he wants money for. When his mother was living, she used to stay with us and he was such a good son. Now he is completely alone and without relatives. I have never seen anyone so clean and honest and industrious. Last year I made him a jacket and had to persuade him to accept it. He does more for the family than he ever gets from us."

After lunch, when the captain went back to the garden,

Old Chang was fixing the chicken pen. Li Sung offered to help. Later, he was amused to think that the chicken pen had so much to do with the future of Mrs. Wen, so significant are the little details of our life.

He got to talking with the gardener about Mrs. Wen.

"What a lady!" said Old Chang talkatively. "If it were not for her my mother would not have had such a comfortable and happy old age. They say Imperial Tutor Wen is going to get an arch of chastity for them. Old Mrs. Wen lost her husband when she was twenty; her only son got married to my lady. It is so long ago now, but I heard how he was combing his hair one morning and just fell dead on the floor. The young Mrs. Wen became a widow at the age of eighteen, and she was expecting a child, too. But it was a girl. You would not want such a young woman to enter widowhood for life. It would be inhuman unless she had a son to live for and carry on the family name, and unless she chose it. But she did not. The old lady wanted to adopt a baby boy for her daughter-in-law to continue the ancestral altar fire, but you know how it is with families. Some thrive and multiply, and have six or seven sons at a stretch; others just fizzle out. People say luck was running against the males of this family, and no one was willing to have his baby boy adopted by them. So my lady just kept the girl. I have seen Meihua grow up into such a pretty young one. Captain, why don't you marry her? She will make a wonderful wife for any man able to support her."

Li Sung smiled at the gardener's simplicity of manners. He did not have to have the gardener tell him about Meihua's charms.

"What is this arch of chastity?"

"Don't you know? The Hu family have the only chastity monument in town, and the Wen clansmen are a little jealous. They wrote Imperial Tutor Wen about these two widows of his own clan. The old widow has kept her widowhood already for forty years. They say that the imperial tutor will petition the emperor to have an arch of chastity erected in their honor."

"Is this true?"

"Why should I joke with you, Captain? Is this something to be joked about? For a woman to be honored by the emperor himself! They say the emperor usually grants a thousand taels of silver along with the permission for the arch. Then she will be rich and honored. And she deserves it, too. My lady is young and pretty and many men would like to marry her. She has chosen to stay in the Wen family for the sake of the old mother-in-law, to serve her in her old age, rather than marry again and leave her alone. You can't help admiring her for that. That will be the reason for the monument. And then she hopes that when Meihua marries, they will be able to keep up the altar fire of her husband's ancestors. Such a lady!"

The captain came and went, although he was more interested in chasing after Meihua than in chasing bandits. Meihua loved Sung as though no other girl before her had ever loved, and Sung was quite captivated. The girl did not try to conceal her love and admiration for him; she told him what she admired in him and why. It might have been artifice with other girls the captain had known, but one can sense it when a girl is wholeheartedly sincere, and the captain could not help feeling flattered. She was childish, vivacious, and sometimes frankly mischievous. All this made her extremely charming to the captain.

Their love was naturally made very clear to her elders by the girl's behavior and by the captain's more restrained but equally obvious attitude. Since Li Sung was twenty-seven and single, the grandmother was already convinced that this match was predestined.

Every precaution was taken of course against any impropriety. The grandmother slept in the western room and Mrs.

Wen and her daughter slept in the eastern room of the inner court. As soon as supper was over, the door of the inner yard was bolted and Mrs. Wen further took the precaution of bolting her own chamber door. But the mother was deceiving herself. Li Sung sometimes stayed at the camp so that he could meet the girl outside. Meihua sometimes disappeared in the afternoon and came back late for supper. Such irregularities always coincided with the days when the captain was supposedly not in the city.

Once she came home two hours after suppertime, for it was July and the days were very long. Following a road out of town, Sung and Meihua went on a shaded path skirting a large pond which led directly to a wooded hillside. It was a glorious afternoon and the sting of the noonday sun had cooled off and there was a delightful breeze in the spruce forest where stood rocks covered with shining green moss. In the distance, beyond the pond and its green banks, lay the beautiful lake. With the captain by her side life was complete for Meihua. They had already sworn to love each other forever. The girl told Sung how famous her mother was for her beauty in her youth, how many men had proposed to marry her but she had refused and, Meihua added, strangely to the captain's ears, "If I were in her place, I would have remarried long ago."

"Aren't you proud of your mother?"

"Of course I am. It is that I think a woman ought to have a home with a man, not like this. Perhaps I heard so much talk about Confucian ideas at home that I am sick of them."

Meihua was young. No example set by a sainted grandmother and a mother on her way to sainthood could shut out the spring in her young girlish heart.

"After all," said Sung, "it takes a virtuous woman to do what she has done."

"What do you think a girl is for?" answered Meihua quickly and spiritedly. "To get married and have a home and have babies, isn't it? It could not have been easy for Mother to lose Father so young, especially because we are so poor. I cannot help admiring her for it. But —"

"But what?"

"I don't believe in the chastity arches."

The captain roared.

"When I grew older, I thought about this. Mother is an ambitious woman and very stern with herself. There is a sort of distinction in being a chaste widow and I think Mother rather gloried in it. I don't know why I am talking like this."

Sung asked the girl about the arch of chastity which the clan had been expecting for her mother and grandmother.

"I am glad for Mother," said Meihua. "But after we are married we will be gone. And Grandmother's health is so frail. What will she do with a thousand taels, living all alone, with nothing to look forward to except another twenty years of lone confinement in glory, until she dies like a sainted carcass?"

Li Sung was much amused. How are you going to tell a young girl with her keen love of life that she is wrong? She had shared and watched the loveless life of the house of two widows and perhaps she knew what she was talking about.

Suddenly realizing that the sun was setting behind the hills, she said, "Oh, Sung! I must run. I did not know it was this late!"

During the captain's next period of absence, something happened. Mrs. Wen had heard from neighbors that the lovers had been seen together in town and once on the road leading to the wooded hillside west of the town. Nothing escaped the watchful eye of the mother. She questioned her daughter. Tearfully, the girl admitted her guilt and said the captain had promised to marry her. Mrs. Wen flew into a fearful rage.

"I never thought my own daughter would bring such disgrace to this house! Your grandmother and I have set an example to this town. Now you have sullied the name of the Wen family. How the neighbors will gloat over such a scandal when they find out! My own daughter!"

"I am not ashamed," said Meihua, wiping her tears. "No, I am not ashamed of loving him! I am of age to be married. If you do not like him find me one good young man, find me one! I am young and will not let myself rot in the loveless life of this house. As for you, Mother, I do not see anything in the hollow life you call your virtuous widowhood!"

Young Mrs. Wen choked with surprise and bewilderment.

"What are you saying, girl?" she gasped, reeling before her daughter's unexpected jab.

"Yes," said the girl. "Mother, why don't you get married again? You are still young."

"May the lightning cut out your tongue!"

No one but a complete child could have hurled a truth like a bombshell in that naked straightforward fashion. She had no idea how much she had hurt her mother, how deeply and unexpectedly her words had cut. The thought of the mother marrying again was horrible, shocking, unthinkable. "I have taught you all these years. Girl, have you no sense of shame?"

Mrs. Wen broke down completely and cried aloud pitifully. It is strange how much a sentence, a phrase, a mere word can do at times. All the torments she had endured and could tell nobody about for those long nineteen years now came out in those bitter salty tears. What had she not endured? And now her own daughter was laughing at her and taunting her years of sacrifice and self-denial whose price she alone knew. Not since Mrs. Wen was a little girl had she ever heard anyone question the virtue of a widow's chastity or the validity of her ideals. It was like questioning the sun. The idea of her remarrying was not really unthinkable, but truly unthought of for all those long years. It was a closed issue long ago. If she had ever had any idea of remarrying she had pushed it rigidly out of her mind. It was truly unthought of — until now.

Mrs. Wen ceased to scold her daughter. She had crumbled into a heap of misery. Meihua, frightened, had not said another word. But the mother seemed to break completely under her daughter's taunt. What Meihua said about the emptiness of a widow's hard life was only too true. The mother buried her head in her hands upon the table and continued to weep. She let her mind drift. Meihua's happiness with the captain was real and convincing. If she had met such a young man when she was young . . . It was such confusion.

Mrs. Wen decided that they had to wait till the captain returned to the house. He might be in the city now and the girl might go to warn him or even run away with him. She locked Meihua in her room.

When he returned three days later Sung was greeted by Mrs. Wen alone, somewhat sullenly.

"Where is Meihua?"

"She is all right. She is inside."

"Why doesn't she come out?"

"I was waiting for that question," answered Mrs. Wen in a grim voice, her lips tightening. "I thought you might be in the city and wondering why she did not come to have a rendezvous with you."

"What rendezvous?" asked Sung in surprise. "I came in only this morning."

"Don't pretend. I know all about it."

Her tone came as near a restrained feminine anger as he had ever heard from her lips. There was again that curious mixture of modesty and pride which had so charmed him.

The captain was silent. From the back of the house came Meihua's voice, crying frantically. "Let me out! Here I am, Sung! Save me, Sung! Let me out!" She broke into a howl.

"What is all this?" Sung shouted and dashed inside. He heard her pummeling the locked door and her pitiful crying.

Young Mrs. Wen had followed him to the inside hall and the grandmother had come out of her room. Walking slowly toward the captain, the old lady said with tears in her eyes, "Young man, will you marry her?"

Sung's face dropped in surprise. He understood now. The girl inside kept crying, "Sung, Sung, let me out!"

"Of course I will marry her. Now will you open the door and let me talk to her?"

The door was opened and the girl came out and fell into the arms of the officer, crying, "Take me away, Sung, take me away!"

Now it was the mother's turn to break down and cry. The captain apologized again and again and tried to comfort her, but it seemed that her crying had nothing to do with this, a thing which the captain could not understand at the time.

He spoke as if he knew clearly where he stood. He was very sorry for what he had done but he never had any other thought but marrying Meihua. He took all the blame on himself. He craved their pardon. But here he was, ready to marry Meihua, and he hoped to be their dutiful son-in-law. Meihua sat there, shocking her elders by her happiness.

Now that the crisis was over the match did not seem so bad after all. The captain's promise of marriage made it right with the family. The campaign against the bandits was soon over. Arrangements were made with the captain's family and Meihua was rather hurriedly married to her husband at Suchow.

The human mind is one of the most unpredictable things in this universe. The short and rather tumultuous romance of Meihua and the captain was ended. But it left a strange effect on Mrs. Wen.

Three months later the grandmother died. The captain came up alone to help with the funeral arrangements.

Mrs. Wen informed Li Sung that the granduncle of the clan had come to show her a letter from the imperial tutor, saying that he would make the recommendation for the chastity arch. It was almost a sure thing. The story had got about and excited the clansmen considerably, and now the whole clan seemed to have a vested interest in the two widows' chastity. Among the Wen family now, the two widows, living and dead, were already referred to as *chiehfu* — Dame Chaste — a term of great honor.

Curiously, Mrs. Wen told all this to her son-in-law without much enthusiasm and at times even with a suggestion of doubt.

"Why, it is wonderful!" said Li Sung, bubbling over. "Aren't you excited?"

"I don't know. How is Meihua?"

Li Sung gave her the news that they were already expecting a child. Mrs. Wen began to tremble. "Why did you wait to tell me? That is real news!"

"Oh, it is hardly so important as the honor of the arch to you, Mother," said the captain.

"The arch!" Mrs. Wen exclaimed contemptuously. "Let us not talk about it!"

Li Sung was surprised at her indifference to such a rare honor. He recalled what his wife had said about another twenty years of "lone confinement in glory." It was hard to believe that she herself would look at it that way.

"Do you think I should accept it?" Mrs. Wen asked, abruptly returning to the topic. What a strange question.

"It would be insane not to . . . " Li Sung's voice trailed off, as a doubt entered his mind. "Of course, after the arch is granted your widowhood would be sacred, as it were, in the emperor's keeping."

When the funeral was over, Mrs. Wen came back to her house alone. The front and back halls were still covered with hanging scrolls of condolence and stretching across the center of the hall was a white silk scroll, the present of the magistrate himself, with the four characters, "One door, two chaste."

Living alone in that house Mrs. Wen had plenty of time for thought of her future. As she looked ahead, she was a little frightened. Only a few months ago her mother-in-law, her daughter, and the captain had filled this house with gay laughter. Too many things had happened one after another — Meihua's romance and marriage, the grandmother's death, this sudden rise to a glorious but rather dreary height of fame, and the unborn child.

Old Chang had been wonderful throughout the funeral ceremony and now, seeing his mistress so sad, he came to be of even more help. He did the shopping in Meihua's place, he relieved Mrs. Wen of all household worries and of all things that had to do with the outside world and was able even to bring home some income from the sale of vegetables. From her kitchen she watched the faithful honest gardener at work and sometimes in sheer loneliness went out to the garden to talk with him. The garden was completely shut off and no neighbors could see them. A sort of intimacy developed.

But the granduncle called, bringing a hundred taels as a funeral gift from the imperial tutor. The granting of the monument and the thousand taels was now a practical certainty.

When the granduncle left Mrs. Wen had a difficult decision to make and she had to make it before it was too late. Old Chang congratulated her with all his heart. He was proud of his mistress and had never had any idea but that she would soon be a famous woman.

Several times Mrs. Wen wanted to open the question. But how was a lady, and a chaste widow at that, to propose to a man? Several times she went to the garden to discuss vegetables with him. But there were the blue sky and the white sun above, and her modesty and her long years of training prevented her from ever mentioning what was on her mind. She could not do it. Chang was so absolutely honest, so completely faithful. He never thought of her as a woman. He was desperate when it all happened.

When a baby girl was born to Meihua and the captain, they came to show Mrs. Wen the new grandchild. She was thrilled to hold the pretty little baby, plump and white and warm, close to her breast and croon to her. She had not held a baby for so long and she was so young to be a grandmother, which made her very happy.

"Meihua, I am so glad you are so happily married. You must be very proud of your child and your husband."

There were tears in Meihua's eyes. She thought her mother had become more human and had completely truly forgiven her. But during the first day of their visit Meihua saw her mother sitting silently alone and caught a worried expression on her face. She was no longer the self-possessed, contented woman Meihua had always known her to be.

Then the captain learned the astounding news. Coming to the garden the captain saw Old Chang tilling the ground. To his great surprise the gardener drew him to his sleeping quarters. On the gardener's face shone a strange light of happiness, excitement, and perplexity.

"Please tell me what to do, Captain. I am an uneducated man."

"What is it?"

Old Chang hesitated a second.

"It is my lady," he said.

"Is my mother-in-law in any trouble?"

"No. But, Captain, you alone can give me advice. I do not know what to do."

"Does it concern you too?"

"Yes."

"You must tell me what the trouble is. What happened between you two when I went away?"

The gardener was slow of speech, unused to fine conversation. As he told the story the captain could not believe his ears. Old Chang went on slowly and solemnly and then the captain understood how the highly correct widow that his mother-in-law was had gone about her problem in the most devious way, to suggest something which a young girl like Meihua could do with a simple gesture or a kiss.

The summer nights had been hot and Old Chang slept half-clothed on his mat. One night the week before, he woke up to hear his lady calling, "Old Chang!" The declining moon was in the western sky, shining directly over his bed, and he saw his lady standing at the door. Hastily he got up and asked whether there was anything she wanted.

"No," said Mrs. Wen. "You are indeed a heavy sleeper. I heard the chickens cackling and thought a mountain cat was stealing them."

In order to reach the chicken pen she had to pass Old Chang's sleeping quarters. It must have been three o'clock in the morning. The grass was wet with dew.

"Go back to bed," the widow said. "You may catch cold standing there without a jacket on." But Old Chang insisted on seeing her to the kitchen door.

Old Chang thought of the little wildcats that came from the mountains to prey on the poultry at night. But he never seemed to hear the chickens. He always slept soundly.

The next day Mrs. Wen said to him, "Close the pen well and see that nothing can get in there."

"Don't worry," he said.

This had never happened before, but on the third night it appeared that a wildcat got through the wire and made away with a black hen. Old Chang awakened when he felt someone covering him with a sheet and his lady was shaking him.

"What is the matter?" he asked as he sat up.

"I saw a wildcat. He jumped over the wall and got away."

Old Chang hastily threw on a jacket and they examined the pen and found a big hole in the mesh. His lady pointed out to him where she had seen the wild cat. They did not see any footprints but when they came to the spot they found, indeed, the black hen dead on the flower bed along the wall, with a gory gash in its neck. Old Chang apologized for his carelessness but the widow was kindness itself and said to him, "We have lost nothing. I can cook the chicken for supper tomorrow."

"How is it that you are such a light sleeper?" Old Chang asked.

"Oh, I often lie awake at night. I can hear the slightest noise even in my sleep," replied Mrs. Wen.

They went back to his room but his lady remained at the door. He saw spots of blood on his lady's dress and finger-tips. Throwing the dead hen to the floor he poured some water for her to wash her hands. He asked her if she would like to have a cup of tea. She declined at first but on second thought said she would; she was fully awake now and was not likely to go to sleep again.

"Shall I bring it to the house?" Old Chang asked.

"No," she said. "It is so beautiful out here."

"I won't be a minute."

"There is no hurry," said Mrs. Wen.

She sat on his bed and felt the mat and the bare boards and the ragged sheets he had for a coverlet and said to him, "Old Chang, I did not know that you have no decent coverlet. I shall give you one tomorrow."

The next day, when the bowl of chicken was served at supper, his lady reminded him again of the mountain cat. "Have you repaired the pen?"

He said that he had, of course.

"The same one may come tonight," she said.

"How do you know?"

"Why, he did not get what he wanted last night. He was too timid. He almost got the chicken but dropped it when he got scared. He wants the chicken and he knows where the chicken is. Then, if he is a sensible cat, he ought to come tonight. Isn't it clear?"

"So I was determined," continued the gardener with his story, "to sit and watch for the cat and told my lady not to bother. I turned the lamp low and brought out a stool behind the bush, with a heavy briar stick to cudgel the brains out of any mountain cat that dared show its paws in my garden. And the moon climbed to the zenith and there was still no cat, and climbed down again and there was still no cat.

"It was getting chilly and I decided to turn in when I heard my lady's voice calling softly, 'Old Chang!'

"I turned and saw my lady in white approaching from the house like a Fairy Maku. When she came close to me she whispered to me, 'Have you seen anything?'

" 'Not a thing,' I replied.

" 'Let us wait in your room,' she said to me.

"It was the most beautiful night I ever had in my life. We two sitting there, me and my lady, when all the world was asleep and silent around us. She had given me this new bed sheet that morning. It was so white and new that I had not the heart to sit on it and crumple it. Huddled there, we looked at the silvery moonbeams coming through the window. It was as if we had known each other for a long, long time.

"We sat and talked, or rather my lady was talking most of the time, of all sorts of things — of the garden, of life and toil and sorrow and happiness of heart. She asked me about my past and how it was I was not married. I told her I could not afford it."

"If you could afford it, would you get married?" Mrs. Wen asked him.

"Of course I would," Old Chang replied.

The widow looked rapt and dreamy and seemed unreal to the gardener, with the moonlight falling upon her pale face and her eyes bright like gems. Old Chang was almost frightened.

"Are you real or are you Fairy Maku coming out in a white dress in the harvest moon?" he asked.

"Old Chang, don't be silly! Of course I am real."

When she said that, she seemed more unreal to him and her eyes were looking at him and yet not looking at him. The gardener could not help looking at her.

"Don't look at me like that. Of course I am a woman. Touch me."

She held out her arm. Old Chang touched it and Mrs. Wen shivered.

"I am very sorry. Have I frightened you?" asked the gardener, feeling apologetic. "For a moment I thought you were truly Fairy Maku coming out on a moonlight night like this."

The widow chuckled and Old Chang felt relieved.

"Am I really as beautiful as that, Chang?" she said. "I wish it would always remain like this. Tell me, do you think that Fairy Maku would love and marry as men and women do on earth?"

"How do I know?" replied the honest Chang, still failing to catch the hint. "I have never met Fairy Maku."

Then Mrs. Wen asked a question which bewildered the gardener. "What would you do if you met her tonight? Would you make love to her? Would you prefer that I am Fairy Maku or that I am a woman?"

"Lady, you are joking. How dare I?"

"I am serious. Would you be happy if we lived always like this — like Meihua and the captain — as man and wife?"

"Lady, I do not believe you. I do not have that luck. What about the arch of chastity?"

"Never mind the arch of chastity. I want you. We can be happy together and live together till great old age. I do not care what the people say. I have had twenty years of widowhood and that is enough for me. Let other women have it." And she kissed him.

"Captain, what am I to do?" Old Chang cried in the same breath with which he finished the story. "Who am I to stand in the emperor's way? But my lady says it is all right. She asked me to marry her now or she would never be able to marry later on. Imagine my lady saying that! She said she would be happy with me and I could support her as we are now. Captain, what am I to do?"

The idea penetrated Li Sung's head very slowly, for he was bewildered at first and was intent on catching every syllable and nuance of the gardener's words. It was after some hard swallowing that he exclaimed, "What to do? You idiot! Marry her!"

He carried the news in a flash to Meihua. "I am so glad for Mother," said Meihua. And then she added in a whisper to her husband, "Mother must have killed the black hen herself! There ought to be an arch of chastity for men like Chang."

Late that evening, after supper, the captain said to Mrs. Wen, "Mother, I have been thinking. This baby girl of mine has been a great disappointment to you, I am sure. We do not know when we shall have a baby boy who could bear the name of Wen."

Mrs. Wen looked up. The captain continued solemnly, looking steadily at the ground, "I have been thinking. You must not laugh at me, Mother. Grandmother is dead and you are lonely living all alone. Chang is an honest man. If you will permit me to speak to him, I think he will be glad to adopt the Wen family name when he marries you."

Mrs. Wen blushed all over. She began to say, "Yes, the Wen family name . . ." and dashed to her room.

When her wedding to the gardener took place, it was a cruel disappointment to the Wen clansmen.

"You can never tell about a woman," the granduncle said.

6. PASSION (OR THE WESTERN ROOM)

The most celebrated love story in Chinese literature was written by the famous poet Yuan Chen. He wrote it down as a story which had happened to someone else, but it was clearly autobiographical. The dates, the events, the characters were too real and coincided too well with his own, and the writer's personal emotion was too deeply felt for it to be anything but an autobiographical account of his own romance. The thin disguise of the name "Chang" which he gave to the lover in the story did not deceive his friends, and the extraordinarily vivid story aroused a great deal of talk and curiosity. The author, who had become one of the two foremost poets of his day, was embarrassed, but he could not suppress the story or his feelings about it. And always, the word "Oriole" (Inging), which was the girl's name, slipped into his verse, when it was not disguised as Shuangwen, referring to the duplicated sounds in that name. The girl was his first love, but there were special reasons for his remembering it.

The version here faithfully follows Yuan Chen's own story until the point where the lover (Yuan Chen himself), abandons the girl and proceeds to make ridiculous excuses for himself. He makes the lover compare Inging to the historic beauties who ruined empires, and actually uses the word yaonieh, "evil spirit" born to destroy men, on his abandoned sweetheart. Yuan also says that the lover's friends who heard of the story commended him for "*stopping a mistake in time.*" Yuan Chen, although a brilliant poet and later a high official, was not generally respected for his character.

Many biographical details and poems of Yuan Chen make it certain that he was writing about himself. Among other things, I need only mention that his maternal aunt, also named Cheng as in this story, ran into trouble with looting soldiers and was saved by the nephew. There is too much evidence to present here.

In filling out the gaps in the original, I have depended upon Yuan Chen's own poems.

1. The original contains Inging's letter to her lover, which is considered a masterpiece, but omits the lover's letter to her. It merely says that the lover "*sent her a letter to explain*" his failure to return. I have taken lines from his "*Ku Chuehchueh Tzu*" (*Poem Severing Relationships in Ancient Style*) to fill in this important gap. Yuan Chen was actually casting suspicion on the girl's faithfulness to him. He was, in American terms, a "*heel.*"

2. The original gives Inging's poem inviting him to a rendezvous, but hides the poem he first wrote to her. I have taken some lines from his poem "*Ku Yen Shih*" about the floating petals, and so on.

3. The first paragraph about his sentiments in recalling the monastery bells twenty years ago is taken from his poem "*Ch'un Hsiao,*" or "*Spring Morn.*"

4. The line about "*a smile that was half a smile*" and the recalling of perfume is taken from his poem actually entitled "*On Inging.*"

5. Some other material about the rendezvous is taken from his long autobiographical poem sent to Po Chu-yi, in which the whole episode is told as a dream fantasy, followed by an account of his marriage to the Wei girl. Inging in the original was a girl who was shy and restrained in public and did not talk much, but who was

*clearheaded and practical. I believe the presentation was
true to life.*

*The friend Yang Chu-yuan was a real person, too, and
appeared also in the original.*

WHENEVER Yuan Chen stopped at an inn at Pucheng on
his official travels, the sound of the nearby monastery
bells, especially when heard in his bed at dawn, always touched
him to the quick and made him feel young and romantic
again. He was in his forties, a conventionally happy husband,
a popular poet, and a high official who had his many ups and
downs. He should have been able to forget, or at least calmly
reflect on, a love affair which happened so long ago. But he
surprised himself. Twenty years had passed, and the tolling
of those monastery bells in the early hours presaging the
break of dawn, their familiar pitch and rhythm, still evoked
in him a mood of infinite sadness, awaked some deep, hidden
emotion, intimate as life itself, and a sense of the strange
pathos and beauty of life which even his poetic pen could
only suggest. As he lay in bed, he recalled the sight of the pale
sky with its dim, shimmering stars, the suffocating emotions
associated with it, the strong perfumes, and the vision of a
smile that was half a smile on the face of the girl who was his
first love.

Yuan was then a young man of twenty-two, on his way to
seek literary honors at the capital. According to his own story,
he had never fallen in love before and had never had an affair
with a woman, for as a brilliant and highly sensitive young
man, he had set his mark high. He was not particularly
jovial or sociable, and the common, good-looking girls about
whom his young friends raved left him untouched, although
he confessed that when he saw a girl of distinguished looks
or talent, he was deeply moved.

In the days of the Tang Empire, scholars set out to

the capital months or even half a year before the national examinations, and took the chance to travel and see the country. His time was his own. When he passed Pucheng, at the bend of the Yellow River, he stopped to see Yang who was a schoolmate of his. Yang urged him to stop over, and he did. They often walked to the Puchiu Temple about three miles east of the city, where the hillsides were covered with plum blossoms in winter. The weather was cold, but crisp, sunny, and dry. Here one obtained a view of the wide expanse of the river and the distant Taipo mountains to the south, which rose on the other side.

Yuan was so enamored of the place that he made arrangements with the monastery to stay in one of the guest rooms provided for pilgrims. The temple had been built about fifty years before by the Empress Wu and was laid out on a grand scale, with glazed yellow roofs and gilt decorations. It was large enough to accommodate over a hundred pilgrims during the crowded spring season. There were cheaper rooms for peasants and their families, and some elegant suites in special courtyards reserved for the more important guests. Yuan chose a room in the northwestern corner for its quiet and seclusion. The tall trees at the back cast a cool green light over the court, while a covered corridor in front with its many hexagonal windows afforded glimpses of the great river and the mountains beyond. The room and the furniture were simple, but comfortable. Yuan was delighted, and with the few volumes of poetry which he always kept in his light luggage, he felt comfortably settled for a short and delightful vacation.

"You are romantic to choose a place like this," said Yang.

"Romantic about what?"

"The moon, the flowers, the snow, and the wind-swept hills. This is an ideal place for romance."

"Don't be silly. If I wanted to seek pleasures, I would go to the capital. No, I am going to be a monk and bury myself in books for a few weeks here."

Yang knew that his friend was highly temperamental, sensitive, and self-willed, and he let him have his way.

He had not been there a day before he discovered that on the west adjoining the temple wall there was a villa of some rich family, with a big orchard of flower and fruit trees at the back which he could see from his back window. The dark-tiled roofs, partly hidden by an apricot tree stretching across the wall, revealed a spacious building of several courtyards. He found out from the servant that the villa was part of the temple property and was occupied by a family by the name of Tsui. The father of the family, who was now dead, had been a patron of the temple and a great friend of the abbot, and used to come and live there whenever he wanted to get away from the city. After the father died, the family came to live there permanently because the widow, Mrs. Tsui, was a timid woman and said she felt safe there. The abbot permitted them to do so, partly because of their personal friendship and partly because the villa had been built by a large donation from the deceased father.

On the third night, the young man heard the sound of distant music, sweet and sad and low, played on a seven-stringed instrument. Heard in the silence of the night at a monastery, it was strangely exciting.

The next morning, his curiosity aroused, he walked around the temple grounds and found that there was a wall enclosing the villa so that he could not see much of the inside. A stream ran along the front of the house, which was set farther back than the temple, and the gate was reached by a charming red-painted bridge. The door was closed, and there was a sign of mourning in the form of a diagonal cross of white paper, old and torn, pasted over the red circle of the gate. A separate path ran for about fifty yards down and joined the main road at the temple outer gate. The air was fragrant with the many plum flowers in full bloom and a small stream ran from the inside garden through an opening in the wall and fell into the stream in front with the sound of frolicking children. Yuan was fascinated. He kept thinking of the family which lived in such beautiful seclusion and the player of the sweet melody he had heard the night before, who had never allowed herself to be seen. On coming back, he realized that the part adjoining his court was the back of the house.

He would not have paid more attention to his unknown neighbor had not something happened in the second week of his arrival. There was rumor of looting and riots in the city. General Hun Chan had died, and the ill-disciplined soldiery had taken the occasion of the funeral to stage a riot. They looted the shops and carried away women from the people's homes. The next morning, things seemed to get worse. Some of the soldiers, having looted the city, came toward the river. The village nearby was full of foot-loose ragged troops. Just before noon, when he was sitting in a rattan chair with his feet upon a table and a volume of Meng Haojan on his lap, he heard feminine voices and hurrying steps passing the corridor in front. He went out to see what had happened. He was the more surprised because his room was at the end of the passage. There was a door which was usually locked and which he had not noticed before. The door was now open and a middle-aged woman, about forty, and two girls were hurrying along the winding corridor toward the main temple rooms as fast as their feet could carry them. The woman, richly dressed, walked in front, while the daughter, who was about seventeen or eighteen, and a maid followed behind. The daughter wore a simple, old dark blue dress and her hair was down, gathered at the back with a large clasp. He was sure that it was she who played the music. The precipitate manner of the women showed that they were in fear of some trouble.

Rather enjoying the excitement, and attracted by the sight of the young girlish figure, Yuan hurried forward and followed them. There was a hubbub among the monks and the servants. A woman whose husband had been killed defending his daughter was weeping and telling her story. The young girl,

careless of others looking on, stood by and listened attentively.
She had a mass of beautiful black hair, a white neck, an unusually small mouth, and her face was slender and small. Her
mother looked terribly anxious and worried, evidently afraid
that the soldiers might come to their house, for it was believed
that they were wealthy. The abbot came out and told them
that in case of emergency he would provide a safe hiding
place for them. The rabble soldiers, out for loot mainly, would
not dare to desecrate the temple.

"Mother, I won't worry," said the daughter in a calm, but
chirping girlish voice. "We must stay in the house. It will
invite robbery to abandon it. Time enough when necessary
to escape through the back door and run into the temple."
The morning sun cast a white light over her pointed nose and
high forehead, which was the only thing unfeminine about
her, if it is true that brains and good looks should not go
together in a woman. The mother listened to her advice. She
seemed to rely a good deal on her daughter's judgment.

Being young, and cavalierly willing to help a young girl,
Yuan went up to the abbot and said with a correct and decorous countenance, not looking at the girl, that under the circumstances it would be wise to take all precautionary
measures for the ladies' protection. He said he had a friend
who knew the regional commander well, and who would be
willing to go and ask for the commander's protection. All
they would need would be half a dozen well-armed guards
stationed outside the house.

"That is sensible," said the girl, directing a pleading look
at him. The mother asked the young man's name, and Yuan
introduced himself.

Delighted at the chance to know the family, Yuan said he
would call on his friend Yang immediately. In the evening, he
came back with six soldiers and a formal notice signed by the
regional commander, warning the rabble off the Tsui house.
As a matter of fact, the sight of the red vests of these guards

was enough to deter any straggling ragamuffins from venturing into the villa.

Happy with his success, Yuan hoped to win a smile of gratitude from the charming young lady who had looked at him so pleadingly that morning. He went expectantly into an elegantly furnished parlor, but only the mother came out to see him. She said many pleasant things in appreciation of the trouble he had taken, and Yuan thought that being able to secure such official influence must have raised him in the mother's regard. But he could not obtain another glimpse of the girl and he returned to the temple, disappointed.

In a few days, the regional commander's own army arrived, order was restored in the city, and the guards were withdrawn. Mrs. Tsui invited Yuan to dinner in the central parlor, which gave the occasion an atmosphere of great formality.

"I wish to thank you for all that you have done for us," said the mother, "and I want to introduce you properly to my family."

She called to a boy about twelve, whose name was Huanlang (Joy) and bade him make his formal bow to his "elder brother."

"He is my only son," said Mrs. Tsui with a big smile, and then she called, "Inging, come out and thank the gentleman who has saved our lives."

The girl was long in coming out. Yuan thought that she was shy because this was to be a formal introduction, and girls of high families would hardly think of sitting at the same table with a strange young man. The mother called again impatiently and repeatedly, "Inging, I am asking you to come out. Mr. Yuan has saved your life and your mother's life. Is this the time to follow conventions?"

The daughter came out at last and made her bow, shyly, yet proudly. She wore a simple, tight-fitting dress, with a neat but modest makeup. Like a well-educated girl of a highly born family, she took a seat next to her mother silently, giving

Yuan the distinct impression that seeing her at all was a rare privilege.

According to custom, Yuan asked her mother, "How old is your daughter?"

"She was born under the present emperor, in the year *chiatse*. She is seventeen."

Though this was a home dinner and Yuan was the only guest, the daughter was perhaps overconscious of the young man's presence. She maintained a correct and distant manner throughout the whole dinner. Yuan tried several times to guide the conversation to familiar topics — her deceased father and her younger brother's studies — but he could not draw her into conversation. Any ordinary girl, even the most virtuous and least coquettish, would look and feel differently in a young man's presence, and her face and manner would show it. But this charming girl was a riddle to him, like a sphinx or a fairy princess who could not be touched by ordinary human emotions. Was she completely rigid and virtuous— which Yuan could not believe — or was that cold exterior a mask for deep passions within? Or was it an extra reserve adopted by girls brought up in the severe Confucian training?

In the course of the dinner, Yuan learned that the widow's maiden name was Cheng, the same as his own mother's, and being of the same clan branch, she was, in fact, an aunt by relationship. The mother was visibly elated at the discovery and she proposed a toast to the clan nephew. Only then did the daughter's face soften into a suggestion of a smile.

Yuan was both piqued and attracted by the girl's attitude. He had never yet met a girl who was so proud and reserved, and so difficult to approach. The more he fought against his feelings, the more he was fascinated by her and desired her.

He tried every excuse to call on the family, first to pay his return call, and then to talk with the younger brother. He made his presence felt in the family, and Inging must certainly have seen him, for girls of rich families observed and heard a great deal from behind the latticed partitions. But she was as shy as a deer at the approach of a beast of prey. Once he saw her playing in the twilight with her younger brother in the back garden, but upon seeing him, she darted off and disappeared. Oriole, Oriole, he cried, what an elusive oriole!

One day, he chanced upon the maid alone, on the path leading from the house to the outer gate. The maid, whose name was Rose (Hungniang), was a simple, direct girl, pretty and attractive in her own way, and wise in the ways of the world. Yuan took the opportunity to inquire after her young mistress. His face was crimson and Rose smiled a knowing smile.

"Tell me, is your mistress engaged?"

"No. Why do you ask?"

"Well, we are cousins, and I am interested to know more about her. We have been introduced, as you know, but I have never had a chance to talk with her. I should be so happy to have such an opportunity."

Rose was silent, and merely looked at him.

"Tell me, why does she avoid me?"

"How do I know?"

"She seems such a wonderful girl, so refined and well-behaved — I admire her greatly," Yuan said at last.

"Oh, I see. Why don't you ask to see her through the mother?"

"You do not understand. She hardly says a word when her mother is around. Is there a chance of my seeing her alone? Since seeing her, I have not been able to think of anything else."

"I see what you mean," said the maid. She covered her mouth in laughter and started to run away.

"Rose, Rose!" he called after her. When she stopped, he said, "Rose, I beg you. You must help me."

The maid looked at him steadily and said sympathetically, "I would not dare to bring such a message. She is very stern and proper. She has never spoken to a young man. Mr. Yuan,

you are a gentleman and you have done a service to the
family. I like you. I will tell you a secret. She reads and
writes poems, and often sits before her books, lost in thought.
You may write a poem to her. That will be the only way to
open her heart to you, if there is any way at all. And you'd
better thank me for the advice." She winked at him coquet-
tishly.

The next day, Yuan sent a poem through the maid.

> Green light suffuses the silent, deep courtyard;
> The twittering oriole is silent, too, hidden in the shade.
> The shut-out lover sees only flower petals
> Floating out with the garden stream, and feels lost.
> I watched the declining moon at dawn,
> My soul lost in thought of thy lovely face,
> And trembled with the fainting hope
> Of a kindly gesture, a gracious smile.

That evening, Rose brought back a poem by Inging, which
was entitled, "Full Moon Night."

> Some one waits in the moonlit night
> In the western room, with the door ajar.
> Across the wall, the flower shadows move —
> Ah, perhaps my love has come!

That was February the fourteenth. Yuan was overjoyed.
It was a clear invitation to a secret rendezvous. An appointment by night was more than he had hoped for.

On the sixteenth, he followed the hint in the poem and
climbed over the wall by the apricot tree and peeped inside.
He found, indeed, that the door of the western room was
left open. He climbed down and went into the room.

Rose was sleeping in the bed and he waked her. The
maid was surprised. "Why do you come here? What do you
want?" she asked.

"She asked me to come," Yuan explained. "Please go and tell her that I am here."

Soon Rose came back and whispered to him, "She is coming!"

Yuan waited ten minutes in unbearable suspense. When Inging appeared, there was a mixture of excitement and confusion in her face, but her deep, black eyes were veiled in mystery. The momentary wave of bashfulness passed and she said, rather stiffly, "I have asked you to come, Mr. Yuan, because you said you wanted to see me. I am grateful for what you have done to protect my mother and our family, and I want to thank you personally. I am glad that we are cousins, but I am surprised that you sent such a love poem through the maid. I could not, and would not, expose it to my mother, for it would be unfair to you, and I thought I had better personally see you to ask you to stop this." She paused in confusion. It sounded very much like a rehearsed speech.

Yuan was aghast. "But, Miss Tsui, I was only asking to have a talk with you. And I came because of that poem you sent me."

"Yes, I invited you," she replied resolutely. "I took the risk and I did it gladly. But you would be wrong to think I am making an appointment for anything improper. Do not misunderstand."

Her voice shook with suppressed emotion. She turned and left hurriedly.

The disappointment and shame made Yuan angry. He could not believe it, could not understand it! Why should she write that obviously suggestive poem, instead of sending a simple reply through the maid, and then take the trouble to come and lecture him? Or had she changed her mind only at the last moment, afraid of what she was about to do? What womanly caprice! He could not understand women. Now she appeared to him more like a marble-cold princess than ever. His love almost turned into hatred because he thought she was making fun of him.

Two nights later, Yuan was asleep in his bed when he felt some one shaking him in the dark. He sat up and lighted the lamp. Rose was standing before him.

"Get up. She is coming," she whispered, and left the room.

Yuan sat up in bed, rubbing his eyes, not quite sure that he was awake. Quickly he threw a robe around himself and sat up and waited.

Soon the maid brought Inging into the room. The girl's face was flushed, shy, uncertain, and she looked as though she was leaning on her maid for support. All her pride and haughty self-control was gone. She did not apologize, nor explain. Her hair was let down over her shoulders, and she looked at him with a deep, dark look in her wonderful eyes. No explanation was necessary.

Yuan's heart palpitated. This sudden surrender of herself of her own free will in his room was even more surprising than her cold repudiation of him on the previous occasion. But all his anger had dissolved at the sight of the girl he loved.

The maid had brought a pillow and, quickly depositing it on the bed, she withdrew. The first thing the girl did was put the light out, still without uttering a word. Yuan walked up to her and, feeling the warmth of her body close to his, he took her in his arms. Just as quickly, the girl's lips found his, and he felt a quiver go over her whole body and heard her quick intake of breath. Again without a word, she sank softly on the bed in a natural gesture, as if her legs were too weak to support her.

Too soon he heard the matin bells of the temple. Dawn was breaking and Rose came to urge her mistress to leave. Inging got up and dressed in the pale light of the dawn.

After adjusting her hair roughly with her hand, she left with the maid, a languorous expression on her face. The door closed without a sound. She had not spoken all night. He had done all the talking and when he spoke of his adoration for her, she answered only with sighs and the warm, wet pressure of her lips.

Yuan sat up suddenly and wondered if it had not all happened in a dream. But her strong perfume still lingered in his room and he saw the rouge marks on the towel. Yes, it was real. This sphinx-like girl, who had seemed so aloof and impassive, had given way to a passion beyond her self-control. Was it passion — or was it love? She had come to him shamelessly. He remembered the intense emphasis with which she had said previously, "You would be wrong to think I am making an appointment for anything improper. Do not misunderstand." What did she mean by that? It was enough that she had come. He had not believed it possible only the day before.

He had never known such happiness; he was transported into a new world, with unknown frontiers of beauty and delirious happiness before him. He waited hourly for the coming night when, like a luminous pearl or warm, glowing jade she would again transform his humble room into heaven, by the magic of her love. She had made no sign that she would come again the following night.

It is entirely believable that the girl had decided to come to him in a moment of passion. It is also possible that after the first night, she wanted to take time to think over the romance which she had so rashly begun. Yuan stopped trying to figure out women. Night after night he waited, with the blood pounding in his veins, hoping for another visit from the fairy princess. Was this suspense another caprice of the girl? Had she come to him merely to satisfy her whim and desire?

He sat alone in his room every night. He had bought coils of incense, in preparation for her visit, and he watched the cold cinders fall silently into the container. He tried to take his mind off what seemed to be vain, hopeless waiting by reading a light romance — for he could not read anything serious, prepared to sit up at the slightest noise of footsteps or the faintest creak of the door. Once he went to test the passage door like a thief, but it was firmly locked.

During the first few days, he avoided going to her home, for having had a secret meeting with her, he thought it would be wise to show himself in the house as little as possible. After the third day, however, he could not stand it any longer and he called on the mother. She was as cordial as usual and asked him to stay for lunch. Inging came to the table, again with that cold, correct look on her face, which would not betray their intimacy by so much as a gesture. He waited for a sign, but the girl was a master in the art of deception. When he looked boldly at her, her eyelids did not even flicker. He thought that perhaps her mother's suspicion had been aroused and she was being extra careful. There *had* to be some reason for her silence.

Two weeks passed uneventfully. He did not mention the affair to Yang, and when his friend asked him to stay overnight, he always insisted on returning to the temple, for fear of missing her visit. He could not tear himself away from the place. He composed a poem of sixty lines, recording his strange experience of meeting a fairy, and telling of the heights of his ecstacy and the depths of his longing. "And the seas were wide and the clouds were high, and the fairy did not return."

One evening, past midnight, as if in answer to his prayer, he heard the passage door creak. Quickly he rushed to open it and found Rose standing there. She confided to him that her young mistress had had a key made for the lock so that they could meet in the western room. She had arranged it so that the padlock would appear to be in place, but he could push it open and reach the western room by a short passage. Even in his delirium, Yuan was impressed with the cunning and audacity of his lover's meticulous plans for their meeting.

After that, Inging came to meet him in the western room every other night, or as often as she could get away, and she always sent a message through the maid when she could not. She nearly always came after midnight and returned to her room before dawn.

Yuan was deliriously happy. The girl opened her heart to him, loved him passionately, and they pledged to be true to one another no matter what happened. It was difficult to believe that there was so much love in her small body. Inging had a mature mind and was interested in all that he was doing or planning to do. They lay together in the dark and talked in whispers, for there was the danger of discovery even though Yuan's ears were always on the alert. On the other hand, she never showed the slightest regret for what she had done. The only explanation for her conduct, when he asked her, was a passionate kiss and a murmur, "I cannot help it, I love you so."

"What if your mother finds out? he asked her once.

"Then she will have to make you her son-in-law," replied Inging with a smile. Her nerves were as good as her brains.

"I will speak to your mother when the time comes," Yuan said, and Inging did not press the question further.

The time of parting had to come. Yuan told Inging that he must leave for the capital. Inging was not surprised, but remarked calmly, "Go if you must. But the capital is only a few days' journey from here. You will come back in the summer. I want you to." She was so sure of herself.

The night before his departure, he was fully prepared for their usual rendezvous, but for some reason Inging did not come.

He returned in late summer for a short visit, just before the autumn imperial examinations. There was no indication that Inging's mother knew about the affair. She was as cordial as usual and invited him to stay at their house. Perhaps she had an idea that she might marry her daughter to him.

Yuan was pleased with the idea of seeing Inging in the daytime. They had a wonderful week together. She had lost her shyness before him and sometimes he could see her playing with her younger brother, tying blades of grass into a boat to sail down a small stream in their back garden. He was very happy about their secret love.

Yuan's happiness did not escape Yang. When Yang came to visit his friend at Inging's home, he sensed the situation without being told.

"What is going on here, Weichih?" Yang remarked, calling him by his courtesy name, and Yuan smiled.

The mother saw it, too. The day before Yuan left, she asked Inging about the young man, and the girl said with a wholehearted confidence, "He will come back. He has to go and take the national examinations."

That evening, they had an opportunity to be alone. Yuan looked miserable and sad, sighing at her side, but Inging had full confidence in his love. There was another side to her character. The girl who trembled in his embrace was clear-headed and unsentimental in a crisis. She did not utter useless words. Calmly, she said to him, "Do not look as if this were good-by forever. I shall be waiting."

The mother gave Yuan a farewell dinner, and after supper he asked Inging to play the *chin* for him. He had once chanced to find her playing the music alone, but when she discovered that he was listening, she had stopped and refused to continue, in spite of his pleading. That night, however, she consented. Seated before the instrument, with her curls hanging over her bent head, she struck notes slowly and pensively, the *Prelude to the Cloud Cape Dance*. Yuan sat entranced, absorbed in the beautiful player and her exquisite melody. Suddenly she lost control and broke off and dashed inside. Her mother called her, but she did not come out again.

The lovers only saw each other once more. Yuan failed at the examinations. Perhaps he was too ashamed of himself to come back and ask for her hand, but she was waiting for him and there was nothing to prevent him from paying her a visit. At first he sent her letters; then the intervals between them became greater. The capital was only a few days away, but Inging could always find reasons for his delay, and she never gave up hope.

At this time, Yang came to see Inging and her mother rather frequently. The mother spoke to Yang about Yuan, for he was an older man and married, and she showed him Yuan's letters. Yang knew something was wrong. He had an idea that his friend was leading a new life in the capital, for Sian was full of distractions. He sent Yuan a letter, and the reply only increased his worries. The girl persuaded her mother to put the best complexion upon the matter and assured her that he was hiding until he passed the examinations the following autumn. Then he would surely come.

Spring had come round and summer was approaching. One day Inging received a poem from Yuan, phrased in the most equivocal language. He spoke of their past happiness and his longing for her, yet the meaning between the lines was clear. It was a poem of farewell. He sent her some gifts and spoke of his torture in their yearlong separation, comparing it to that of the Cowherd and the Spinning Maid in Heaven, who were permitted to meet across the Milky Way only once a year. But, he went on, "Alas! in this yearlong separation, who knows what may happen on the other side of the Milky Way? My future course is as uncertain as that of the clouds, and how can I be sure that you will be as pure as snow? When a peach flower blooms in spring, who is to prevent admirers from plucking its rosy petals? I am happy that I was the first to receive your favor, but who will be the lucky one to take the prize? Ah, a year to wait, and how long will it seem before another year is out? Rather than endure this endless waiting, would it not be better to part forever?"

Read carefully, what the poem implied was utter nonsense — it was an outright, unjustifiable insult on the girl's character. When Yang saw Inging with the letter lying in her hand, her eyes were swollen. Yuan must have gone out of his mind, or he was simply trying to extricate himself from the situation. What was there to prevent him from coming to see her if he loved her? And he did not have to impute to her what he was guilty of himself. Yang made up his mind.

"Miss Tsui, I am going to Sian on some business. I shall look him up, and shall be glad to take a letter for you."

Inging looked at him. "Will you?" she asked calmly. Yang was surprised by the matter-of-fact tone in which she said it. "And don't worry about me. I am all right," she added. "Tell him I am all right."

Yang went back and packed up for the trip to Sian which he had really undertaken for the girl's sake. He would like to find out what was happening and perhaps give Yuan a piece of his mind. As a man of honor, Yuan should have married her, though Inging was the last girl to demand it of him. He would have liked to bring Yuan back if it were possible.

Three days later, he set out for the capital. He brought with him a letter from Inging which he gave to Yuan. It was as sincere and to the point as it was dignified in her self-defense:

"I am delighted to receive your last letter and touched by your loving remembrance. I am excited and happy to receive the box of hair ornaments and the five inches of rouge. I appreciate these thoughtful gifts, but of what use would they be to me in your absence? They bring you closer to me and only increase my longing to see you. I am glad that you are well and able to pursue your studies at the capital, and I am only sorry for myself, shut up in this small town. There is no use grieving about Fate. I am prepared to take what it has in store for me. I miss you so much since your departure in autumn. I try to appear happy and gay when there is company, but when I am alone, I cannot restrain my tears. I have dreamed often of you and we are so happy together like old times, and then I wake up, clinging to the half-warm quilt with a sense of desolation. I feel you are so far away from me.

"A year has passed since you were gone. I am grateful beyond words that in a gay city like Changan, you have not forgotten your old sweetheart entirely. But I shall always be true to our promise. We were formally introduced by my mother, but under the circumstances I lost my self-control and completely surrendered myself to you. You know that after our first night together, I swore I would never love anyone but you, and we would be true to each other for life. That was my hope and our promise to each other. If you keep your promise, all is well, and I shall be the happiest woman in the world. But if you discard the old for the new and think of our love as a casual affair, I shall love you still, but shall go down to my grave with an eternal regret. It is all up to you, and I have nothing further to say.

"Take good care of yourself, please. I am sending you a jade ring, which I wore in my childhood, hoping it will serve as a souvenir of our love. Jade is a symbol of integrity, and the circle of the ring signifies continuity. I am also sending a strand of silk threads and a tear-stained bamboo tea roller. These are simple things but they carry the hope that your love will be as spotless as jade and as continuous as the ring. The tear stains on the bamboo and the skein of threads will be reminders of my love and my tangled feelings for you. My heart is near you, but my body is far away. If thinking would help, I would be hourly by your side. This letter carries with it my ardent longing and my desperate hope that we may meet again. Take good care of yourself, eat well, and don't worry about me."

"Well?" Yang watched his friend's face turn from red to white while reading the letter. After a pause, Yang said, "Why don't you come and see her?"

Yuan stammered some excuse about his studies and his being unhappy with himself. Yang saw through it all.

"You are not doing right by her," declared Yang. "Tell me what is the matter."

"I am not ready to marry. I have my scholastic career to attend to. It is true, I had an affair with her. She came to me — I do not think that a youthful folly should interfere with my career."

"Youthful folly?"

"Yes. Don't you think that when a young man has done something he should not have done, the only thing to do is to end it?"

Yang was angry. "It may be a youthful folly to you. But what about the girl who writes you that letter?"

Yuan's face showed great embarrassment. "A young man can make mistakes, can't he? And he shouldn't waste his time with women. He should — "

"Weichih," said Yang, "if you have changed your mind, don't try to moralize about it. Let me tell you what I think. I think you are the most moralistic and the most selfish person I have known."

Yang was convinced his friend was not being honest with him, that there was some other reason. He stayed at the capital for about a week and had time to learn what Yuan was doing. He was having an affair with a Miss Wei of a very rich family. In utter disgust, Yang returned to Pucheng.

He had a difficult job in breaking the news to the girl. He was afraid it would hurt her terribly. He told the mother first.

"Well," asked Inging, when she saw him, "have you brought a letter for me?"

Yang remained silent. He couldn't say it, and while he was trying to find words, he saw the girl's countenance change. In that moment he saw the deep, dark eyes of Inging become bright and penetrating, like those of a woman who understands not only her situation, but all life and eternity; or like one who has been forsaken not by one lover, but by ten. Her eyes burned, and Yang instinctively lowered his lashes.

"Well," he said finally, "that poem he sent you was a poem of farewell."

Inging stood there motionless and speechless for a full five seconds. Yang was afraid she was going to collapse. But something proud and hard was in her words as she said, "So be it!" She turned abruptly to leave the room. Just as she reached the chamber door, Yang heard her hysterical laughter. Her mother rushed after her, and for five minutes Yang could still hear that laughter inside.

Yang was greatly worried, but the next day he found out from the mother, to his great relief, that the girl was all right, that she had been proud and silent as a queen after the moments of hysteria. She had given her consent to marriage with a cousin of her mother's family, by the name of Cheng, who had been soliciting the match for some time. The following spring, Inging and Cheng were married.

One day, Yuan came to her home and asked to see her, as a distant cousin. Inging refused to see him, but as Yuan was preparing to go away, she stepped out from behind the screen.

"Why do you come to bother me? I waited for you and you did not return. There is nothing to be said between us. I have got over it, and you should, too. Go away!"

Yuan left without a word, and Inging collapsed on the floor in a heap.

7. CHIENNIANG

~~~~~~

From T'aip'ing Kwangchi, No. 358, written by Chen Hsuanyu (766-775). This popular story was dramatized by a great Yuan playwright, Cheng Teh-hwei. The drama version follows the general outline. A later, expanded version by Chu Yu in Chienteng Hsinhwa brings in a complication. In this version, there were two sisters, the elder one being engaged to the lover. The lover returned to find his fiancée already dead. The ghost of the dead sister borrowed the body of the younger sister, making it appear that the latter was in love with him, and eloped to live with him for a period. The younger sister, deprived of her soul, lay sick in bed. Later the elder sister's soul returned to the younger sister, who woke up, not recognizing the lover, but later married him, according to the departed elder sister's wish. This expanded version is also found in P'ai-an Chingch'i, No. 23. I prefer the simple first version.

WANG CHOU, a young boy of seventeen, had lost his father and was now alone. Steady and more mature than his age indicates, he was old enough to shift for himself. His father had told him on his deathbed that he should go to live with his aunt, who was living in the south at Hengchow, and had reminded him that he was betrothed to his cousin. This was a promise between his father and the father's sister when the babies were being expected; they had said that in

case one was a boy and the other a girl, they would be
betrothed to each other. Wang Chou disposed of the house
and set out to the south accordingly. The young boy's mind
was enlivened by the hope of seeing a girl cousin whom he
had not seen since the age of six when his father received
an appointment in the north. He wondered how she had
grown and whether she was still the fragile, affectionate
child who used to cling to him as a play companion and
wonder at all his doings. He had better hurry, Wang Chou
thought, for a girl of seventeen might be betrothed to someone else if he did not show up. But the voyage was slow, and
it took him a full month to come down the Hsiang River and
then the Tungting Lake and finally reach the mountain city
of Hengchow.

His uncle, Chang Yi, ran a shop dealing in herbs and
medicinal products. He was a broad-jowled, heavy-voiced
man. Every day for the past twenty-five years, he had gone
to the shop as regularly as a clock, and he had never traveled or taken a holiday. Cautious, thrifty, and conservative,
he had slowly built up his business until he was now quite
well-to-do. He had expanded his shop to do wholesale business, added to his property, and built a new house. When
Wang Chou saw him at the shop, the uncle growled, "What
do you come here for?"

Wang Chou told him. He knew his uncle was a simple
and timid man at heart, who wanted only to pay his taxes and
have the good opinion of his neighbors. Sober and unimagina-
tive, he had never relaxed from his stern appearance as an
elder, having enough trouble keeping himself in the straight
and narrow path.

He was taken to the uncle's new house, and announced
himself as a relative from Taiyuan. The aunt was away at
the moment.

Soon he saw a young girl in a blue dress come into the
parlor. Chienniang had grown up into a beautiful girl with
a very slender figure; she wore a braid of black hair over

her shoulder. Her silken smooth face flushed at the sight of her cousin. After a moment's hesitation, she let out a small scream and cried, "You are brother Chou!"

"You are sister Chien!"

The girl was so excited that her eyes filled with tears. "How you have grown!" cried the young girl, eyeing her handsome cousin.

"And so have you!" exclaimed Wang Chou.

Wang Chou looked at the girl with unconcealed admiration, especially with his father's dying words in mind. Soon they were lost in a busy exchange of news of the families and random recollections of their childhood. She had a younger brother several years her junior, who was greatly surprised to see a total stranger who called himself his cousin. They had been separated so long that the family hardly ever spoke of him.

When the mother came back, she gave a hearty, warm welcome to this son of her deceased brother. She was a woman with clear-cut features, a very delicate complexion, and graying hair. A shy, sensitive woman, her lips constantly quivered when she smiled. He informed her that he had finished the district school, and did not know what he was going to do next, and she informed him in turn that his uncle's business was doing well.

"I can see that. You are living in such a beautiful house," said the nephew.

"Your uncle is a very funny man. It took a long time of persuasion on my part and that of the children to get him to move into the new house after he had built it. He is even now regretting how many dollars he is losing by not renting it out. You stay with us. I will ask your uncle to give you a job at the shop. Do your part and don't be afraid of his big voice."

The uncle never came home until evening, and when he did, he was as gruff and as uncommunicative as he had been that morning. The death of his brother-in-law did not

seem to concern him, and Wang Chou felt very much like a
poor relative and an orphaned young man to be put to the
test of apprenticeship. But the aunt was kind and a gentle
creature. She was much better educated than her husband
and seemed to look upon her husband's businesslike and
authoritative attitude with light amusement, although she
always obeyed his wishes. She had seen to it, too, that
Chienniang received a perfect education through private
tutoring. There was just nothing to talk about at dinner,
because the mother and daughter did not understand business, and the father was not much interested in anything
else. With his stern appearance and his naturally big voice,
he had established himself as the head of the family.

In time, the nephew settled down as a permanent member
of the family. Nothing was said about the promised betrothal which was of course verbal between the aunt and
her brother when they were both expecting babies. To Wang
Chou, the girl in the blue dress would be his choice even if
there had been no such promise. Chienniang found Wang
Chou's quiet and reserved disposition very much to her liking,
too, and as they were thrown into each other's company,
before long she had given her heart completely to him.

The mother saw the new happiness on Chienniang's face.
When Chienniang cooked something special for the family,
she felt as if she was cooking for Wang Chou alone, and a
new happiness and pride welled up in her heart. Step by
step, she forgot her youthful bashfulness and took over the
mending of his clothing and looking after his laundry; she
assumed a sort of prior right to take care of him. There was
no definite division of jobs, for the daughter was being trained
to look after the general household although they had several
maids, but the business of cleaning his room and looking
after his comforts fell naturally to her. Chienniang would not
even permit her younger brother to upset things in his room.

The mother knew that she loved him. One day she said

to her daughter dryly, "Chienniang, I see that our dishes are getting more and more salty these days."

Chienniang blushed, for Wang Chou had several times complained that the dishes were not salty enough.

Wang Chou had never dreamed that life could be so sweet and beautiful. He did not mind putting up with his gruff uncle at the shop; he would do anything for the sake of Chienniang and to be near her. Loving Chienniang, he loved all that was connected with her. He felt toward his aunt as if she were his own mother and played with the little boy as if he were his own brother. The father seldom talked at dinner or indulged in jokes with the family, but he was away all day, and was often invited out to business dinners in the evenings.

The Hengchow climate was changeful, varying to extremes between sudden storms coming over the mountains and a scorching heat when the sun was out. Once Wang Chou fell sick and found it so comfortable to lie in bed all day at home, served by his cousin, that he stayed in bed longer than was necessary.

"Now you must go to the shop, or my father will be angry," Chienniang said to him.

"Must I?" asked Wang Chou reluctantly.

One day Chienniang said to him, "You must put more clothing on. I think it is going to rain. If you get sick again, I will be angry with you."

"I would love to," replied Wang Chou impishly, and she understood what he meant.

"Don't be silly," said Chienniang, pouting her lips, and she made him put on extra clothing.

One day Chienniang's elder aunt, the wife of her father's brother, arrived from Changan for a visit. The brother was an extremely wealthy man. He had helped Chang Yi, the girl's father, found the shop with his money; their property was not yet divided and Chang Yi still retained that devotion to his brother which amounted to fear and servile respect for the head of the family. The aunt was royally treated. Family devotion, and Chang Yi's timid nature and natural respect for wealth, both could account for his attitude toward this elder aunt. The best dinners were served every day, and Chang Yi talked and joked at dinner and tried to make himself pleasant to the elder aunt in a way that he had not talked and joked with his wife.

The elder aunt found nothing more pleasant and agreeable than to arrange a match with a rich family for her niece. One day returning from a party with the wealthiest family of the town, the Tsiangs, she said to the girl's mother, in the girl's hearing, "Chienniang is a sweet girl and she is eighteen. I am arranging a match for her with the second son of the Tsiangs. You know of course who the Tsiangs are, and I mean *the* Tsiangs."

"My dear sister-in-law, I have betrothed Chienniang to my brother's son," replied the mother.

"You mean that nephew staying with you? But your brother is already dead."

"That does not make any difference. They seem wonderfully suited to each other." Chienniang, hearing her mother taking the nephew's side, blushed.

The elder aunt broke into loud laughter. "You are crazy! What has he got? I am talking about a respectable match with a decent family with some social standing like ourselves."

Chienniang rose from her seat, left the room, and slammed the door.

"What an ungrateful girl!" the elder aunt shouted after her. "She does not realize what I am doing for her. You have never seen their garden home. Don't be a weak mother. You will thank me when you see the inside of their house. Why, their mistress wears a diamond ring almost as big as mine."

The mother did not reply, and excused herself. But the elder aunt, having thought of this match as her best recreation during her stay, would not give up. An engagement would mean dinners and parties, her holiday would be filled with social activities, and she would be happy to have accomplished something memorable during her short stay. But if the mother resisted her suggestion, the elder aunt found in the father of the girl a ready, appreciative, and delighted listener. Chang Yi could not conceive of anything more gratifying to his social ambition and purpose in life. He had always envied one family in the city and that was the Tsiangs. They were an old family and old Mr. Tsiang had been an official in the capital. He had wanted to move in the circle of the Tsiangs and had not been once invited by them. The result was that Chienniang's betrothal to the second son of the Tsiang family was celebrated over the protest of the mother, while the girl lay in bed on a hunger strike.

"No good will come of this," said the mother to her husband. "It is against the girl's wish. You should have gone in and seen the girl crying her heart out in bed. It is her life we have to consider. You have fallen for the Tsiang money."

In time Chienniang was persuaded to eat and get up from bed. She went about the house like one condemned.

The young lover did not care what happened now. He took leave and disappeared for three weeks, trying to drown his sorrow in the Heng mountains. After three weeks, he could not resist the idea of coming back to see his love. When he came back, he found Chienniang suffering from a curious, unknown disease. The day after his departure, the girl lost her memory and did not know who she was. She lay in bed and refused to get up. She did not recognize her own mother and father or her maid. She mumbled words which they did not understand. They feared she had gone out of her mind. But there was something worse. She had no fever, no pains, but she lay in bed all day without food, without drink. They tried to talk to her but her eyes were blank. It was as if her soul had departed from her body, and the body, without the master, stopped functioning altogether. A white pallor settled over her face and the doctors confessed that they had never seen a case like this, and did not know what it was.

With the mother's permission, Wang Chou rushed in to see her. "Chienniang, Chienniang!" he called. The mother watched anxiously. The girl's blank eyes seemed to focus again, her eyelashes moved, and a tinge of red returned to her cheeks.

"Chienniang, Chienniang!" he called again.

Her lips moved and parted in a glad, sure smile.

"It's you," she said quietly.

Tears filled the mother's eyes. "Chienniang, your spirit has returned. You know your mother, don't you?"

"Of course, Mother. What's the matter? What are you crying about? Why am I lying in bed?"

The girl apparently did not know all that had happened. When her mother told her that she had been lying in bed and had not recognized her own mother she could not believe it.

The girl became strong again in a few days. When she was sick, her father had been really frightened, but seeing that she had recovered, he settled back into his authoritative manner again. When the mother described how color returned to Chienniang's cheeks — which she had seen personally — when the nephew came to the girl's bedside, he said, "A fake! The doctors have never seen such a disease. Not knowing her own parents! I do not believe it."

"My dear husband, you have seen the girl lying in bed without food and drink for days. It is in her heart. You should reconsider the engagement — "

"The ceremony is over. Besides, you don't mean that I should break the engagement with the Tsiang family. They will not believe the story. I don't believe it myself."

The aunt who was still staying with them was heard to make sarcastic remarks, implying that the girl's sickness was feigned. "I have lived for fifty years and have never heard of a person not knowing her father and mother."

The father refused to reopen the question. The lovers were

miserable and saw no way out. Wang Chou found the situation intolerable. There was nothing he could do. Chagrined and in despair, he informed his uncle that he was leaving for the capital, to be on his own.

"Maybe that is a good idea," replied the uncle curtly.

The night before his departure, the family gave him a farewell dinner. But Chienniang was heartbroken. She had been lying in bed for two days and refused to get up.

Wang Chou had the mother's permission to go into the girl's room and say good-by. She had not eaten for two days and she was really ill with a high fever. Touching her gently, he said, "I am leaving and have come to say good-by. There is nothing we can do."

"I will die, brother Chou. I have no desire to live when you are gone. But I only know this — living or dead, my spirit shall always be with you wherever you are."

Wang Chou could find no words to comfort her. They parted in tears, and the young man started on his way with an open wound in his heart, believing he should never come back to the house.

His boat had gone about a mile. It was about supper time, and the boat was anchored for the night. Wang Chou lay in bed, sad and lonely, and shedding futile tears. Toward midnight, he heard footsteps drawing nearer and nearer on the bank.

"Brother Chou," he heard a girl whisper. He thought he was dreaming, for he knew she was ill in bed. He peeped out over the gunwale and saw Chienniang standing on the bank. In utter amazement, he jumped ashore.

"I have run away from home," said the girl weakly and fell into his arms. He carried her into the boat quickly, unable to understand how she could cover that distance in her condition except by a superhuman will power, and then he discovered she had come barefooted. How they cried together for joy!

Lying close to his body, caressed with kisses and restored

by the warmth, she soon recovered. "Nothing can stop me
from following you," she said to him, when she opened her
eyes again. It was as if she had completely recovered, and
now that they were together and sure of each other, nothing
mattered.

It was a long voyage, and during the whole trip, Chienniang expressed only one regret: she felt very sorry for her
mother who would be heartbroken when she found that her
daughter had disappeared.

They finally arrived at a town in distant Szechuen, where
Wang Chou found a small job with a salary barely large
enough to support them. In order to make both ends meet, he
rented a room in a farmhouse about a mile from the city, a
distance which he had to cover on foot daily to and from his
office. But he was unbelievably happy. Chienniang washed
and cooked and she was contented and happy with him. He
looked at his small room, furnished with rustic chairs, a table,
and a simple bed, and said that he had all he wanted in life.
The farmer who let him have a room upstairs was a simple
man and his wife was kind to them. They offered them vegetables from their garden, which helped them to save money
for food, and they in turn offered to help in the garden.

Then winter came and Chienniang gave birth to a baby
boy, sweet and plump. When spring came, Wang Chou
would return to find his wife holding the fat baby in her arms,
breast-feeding him. His cup of happiness was full. He never
apologized to his wife for making her live like a poor man's
wife, for he knew he did not have to. Nevertheless, he knew
that she was used to more comfortable living, and was surprised that she had adapted herself to the circumstances
so well.

"I wish I could earn more money and hire a maid for you."
His wife stopped him with a soft pressure on his cheeks.
It was a complete answer. "You didn't ask me to come. I
ran away to follow you," she said simply.

Then they went through that delightful period when every

week revealed something new and amazing in their child. The baby was adorable. Now he could grab what he wanted; now he could point to his nose and grab his ear and twitch it. Then the baby learned to crawl and smack his lips, and to say "mamma" and demonstrate those daily miracles of growing intelligence. He was an endless joy who filled their lives. The farmer couple, who were without children, loved the baby and helped Chienniang take care of him.

There was only one thing which marred their happiness. Chienniang kept thinking of her mother and little brother, though she cared not much for her father. Wang Chou was so much in love with her that he could sense her thoughts.

"You are thinking of your mother, I know. If you wish, I will take you home. We are married now and have a baby, and there's nothing they can do about it. At least, it will make your mother happy to see you again."

Chienniang wept with gratitude for his kindness and solicitude for her happiness.

"Let us do it. My mother must have gone crazy thinking that I am lost. And I have this beautiful grandchild to present to my parents."

They started out on the voyage again. After a month on the boat, they arrived at Hengchow.

"You go up first and prepare my parents to receive me," said Chienniang. Taking a gold hair brooch, she gave it to him and said, "Bring this as a token, in case they are still angry and deny your entrance or refuse to believe your story."

The boat anchored on the sandy bank. With Chienniang waiting in the boat, Wang Chou trudged the short distance to her home.

It was about suppertime and the father was at home. Wang Chou knelt on the ground and implored his forgiveness for running away with his daughter. The mother was there and seemed glad to see him, though she looked older, and her hair had turned completely white. He told them that they had now returned and their daughter was waiting in a boat.

"What are you talking about?" replied the father. "Forgive you for what? My daughter has been ill in bed for this entire year."

"Chienniang has never been able to leave her bed since you were gone," said the mother. "It has been sad this long year. She was so ill that at times she went without food for weeks. I could never forgive myself. I promised her that I would break off the engagement, but she was so weak she didn't seem to hear me, as if her spirit had already departed from her body. I was daily hoping for your return."

"I assure you that Chienniang is well and in the boat at this moment. Look, here is her token."

He presented the gold hair brooch. The mother examined it closely and recognized it. The family was greatly confused.

"I tell you she is in the boat. Send a servant to come along with me and see."

The parents were puzzled, but a servant was sent to go with Wang Chou and a sedan chair was ordered. The servant came to the boat and recognized the girl who looked exactly like Chienniang.

"Are my parents well?" the girl asked.

"They are well," replied the servant.

When the family was thus held in suspense and confusion, waiting for the return of the servant, a maid had taken the hair brooch and gone in to see the sick daughter. When the latter heard that Wang Chou had returned, her eyes opened and she smiled. She saw the hair brooch and said, "Indeed I have lost it," and put the brooch in her hair.

Without the maid's notice, the girl got up from her bed, walked out of the house silently like a somnambulist and went straight toward the bank, with a smiling face. Chienniang was leaving the boat already. Wang Chou was holding the baby, waiting for her to get into the sedan chair. He saw the girl on the bank, come steadily nearer, and when the two girls met, they merged into one body and Chienniang's dresses became double.

The family was greatly excited when the maid reported that the sick daughter in bed had disappeared. When they saw Chienniang step out of the sedan chair, healthy and well and holding a plump baby in her arms, they were not more delighted than they were astonished and bewildered. They understood then that the girl's spirit, her real self, had gone to live with him. For love had wings which broke prison bars. What they had seen in the sick daughter lying in bed was no more than an empty shadow left behind, a body without a soul, from which the conscious spirit had wandered away.

The incident happened in the year A.D. 692. The family kept the story of this strange happening a secret from their neighbors. In time, Chienniang gave birth to several other children, and Wang Chou and Chienniang lived to a happy old age, loving each other more the older they grew.

8. MADAME D.

~~~~~~

This was taken from Ch'ingchunlu, *by Lien Pu of Sung Dynasty, who said he personally knew of the story when he was a student at the university in the capital. I have filled in the details about the students' movement for recovery of national territory, which are well-known facts in history, based on such works as Chou Mi's* Kweihsin Tsachih.

THE Lantern Festival on the fifteenth of January in the capital of Hangchow in Southern Sung Dynasty was, all things considered, the gayest festival of the year. It rivaled in gaiety and magnificence the lantern festival in Kaifeng before North China was lost to the invaders. Hangchow turned that night into day. From the Yungchin Gate to the Sea Wall, the city was packed with holiday makers. Thieves and burglars were out, and young lovers met on the shores of the lake. The city gates were not closed. Usually some incident occurred on such a night.

The biggest crowd centered around the Liupuchieh, or the Street of Six Ministries, where the best lanterns were to be seen. The place was brilliantly illuminated. The emperor himself gave a display of fireworks for the benefit of the city population. He had built for the occasion a gigantic tower fifty feet high, called "turtle mountain," covered with multicolored silk festoons and lights which formed different characters. The officials' families had their own booths, partitioned off by curtains, where they displayed their lanterns of novel designs and watched those of others. Men, women, and children jammed the streets, and when the high-ranking ladies moved about to see the show, their servants held a "portable brocade screen" around them. The ladies, bejeweled and dressed for the gala occasion, walked inside these bands of silk, free from the jostling crowd, while their men companions preferred to walk outside. They stopped to chat for a moment with those they knew, complimented them on the beauty of their lanterns, or merely smiled a greeting.

One booth was still empty, guarded by two menservants. It was that of an imperial censor, the husband of Madame D. — reputed to be the most beautiful woman of the capital. Moreover, it was a title indirectly conceded by the pretty women themselves. It was said that when some of the society women got jealous of each other, one of them would say, "She thinks she is Madame D. Absurd!" Or, "That fantastic coiffure might look well on Madame D., but not on her fat, overpainted face." She was the daughter of a scholarly family and seldom allowed herself to be seen in public.

Soon Madame D. appeared, greeting this one and that one on the way. She arrived at her place, accompanied by her maid and her lovely children, a boy of eight and two twin girls of ten. She was only twenty-eight.

Madame D. was dressed in a simple black gown of the finest material, with no jewelry except a crescent of pearls on her hair. Perhaps she had better taste than the others; perhaps she knew she was like a work of art which required no gilded frame. She wore no heavy make-up. Other women ascribed it to her vanity, and they were not far wrong. No woman can be blamed for being vain about her beauty when she is as truly beautiful as Madame D. Having a naturally fair complexion with smooth, white skin, her face looked like a piece of sculptured jade which glowed with a soft, warm luster. There was a sweet expression about her lips, which revealed white even teeth when she smiled. If there was a slight defect, it was only that her ear-lobes were thin and proportionately small. Her shoulders were round and she had a slim, well-molded figure, revealed to advantage by her unembroidered, black satin dress.

The ladies rather envied her. People thought she was one of the luckiest of women — a young mother of beautiful children, and a wife whose husband had risen rapidly to become an imperial censor at the age of thirty-three.

"Mamma, why is Papa not here?" asked the boy.

"Hush, Papa is very busy. He will be here in a minute."

There was just a sign of annoyance on Madame D.'s face, hardly visible to others except to her maid Hsianglien. Her husband had said he would join them here, but it would not be surprising if he did not show up. Hsianglien understood. She had been Madame D.'s maid and girlhood companion, and she had come with her mistress when she married. She was a few years younger than her lady and was her loyal *confidante*. Opposite them and around them, the fathers and husbands sat with their families as was usual on this annual occasion. Madame D. was bred in the old tradition and she never allowed herself to show her feelings about her husband in her friends' presence.

The crowd of passers-by looked at Madame D. and not at the other bejeweled ladies. Young men filed past, laughing and joking, guardedly snatching glimpses of the attractive and usually secluded lady. There was generally a thicker crowd around her section than elsewhere, and the metropolitan guards hung around, perhaps to keep the crowd moving, and perhaps to look at Madame D. themselves. Her gorgeous, silky hair and her black gown set off her white face to great advantage. The effect of her beauty was enhanced by the lanterns, and with the lights and the full moon and the notes of flute and string instruments of the imperial orchestra coming from the distance, she seemed to be a fairy from another world.

Madame D. laughed and talked with her children and her maid.

A lady from the Ministry of Justice in the next stall asked, "Why is your husband not coming?"

"He will be," replied Madame D. sweetly. "He will not miss the fireworks unless he is unavoidably delayed. My husband enjoys them as much as the children."

The husband still did not appear. Madame D. saw a nun coming up, Sister Huicheng whom she knew well. The nuns of the capital often visited the home of the rich matrons who were their patronesses. In those times, having privileged access to the ladies in their deep seclusion, they were often useful in running errands and passing messages, and had come to know many family secrets.

"Come in, Sister Huicheng," said Madame D.

"I will, for a moment." The servant lowered the silk band for the nun to pass through.

"Sit down for a minute." She pointed to the vacant seat reserved for her husband. Hsianglien stood behind the lady.

"Oh, no, I shouldn't. But that crescent of pearls looks beautiful on you!"

Madame D. insisted, and the sister sat down and enjoyed looking at the lantern show and the moving crowd passing in front of them.

"Is your husband not coming?" the nun asked.

"He said he would. He had dinner somewhere with one of his friends. I don't know where he can be."

Nothing escaped the sharp eyes of the sister. "I am sorry," she said softly.

"I tell you he will be here."

Soon they heard a commotion in the square and everybody tried to find out what had happened. It turned out that some university students had been arrested. Some one had thrown leaflets in the square with the words, "Traitors, appeasers, resign!" One leaflet demanded the resignation of the prime minister. It was the time of the Southern Sung

Dynasty when the whole of North China was under foreign occupation, and the court had moved its seat of government to Hangchow. The people demanded the recovery of national territory, but victorious Chinese generals had been summoned back from the field of battle and murdered in prison to appease the enemy. Passions ran high. Those in power, secure in their position and their luxurious living, so long as their policy of appeasement was unchanged, had to take forceful measures to suppress public opinion. The incident passed, and the holiday makers went on milling about and enjoying the display of lanterns on the "turtle mountain." Fireworks would soon begin.

"I must be going," said the nun and arose. "I do not want your husband to see me sitting here. But that crescent of pearls I bought for you is really divine."

"I kept it for today. If you see a good necklace, you might bring it to me, too," remarked Madame D. casually. Madame D. had a weakness for pearls. She had on two huge pearl earrings which subtly covered up and offset her small earlobes.

When the fireworks were nearly finished her husband finally arrived.

He was long and a little thin, and his brows were constantly knitted in concentration. Like the scholars of those days, he wore a mustache. He was impeccably dressed, and with the mustache and his tall hat, he was not bad-looking, though he could hardly be called handsome. People knew that he was capable and ambitious and were not surprised that he had married such a beautiful wife, for the match was the union of two old families. He had been attracted by the girl's beauty and had begged his mother to arrange the match. The girl's mother was dead, and the fathers of the couple were officials of the same party and old friends. The girl disliked the match but did not have much to say in the matter. Like the fortunate sons of rich families, he had a regular degree and a good political career marked out for him. He was devoted to her, and their first few years of marriage were quite happy. Then their affection cooled and he began to take interest in actors and handsome boys. People could not understand how he could neglect such a beautiful wife at home, and when they complimented her on her husband's promotion or envied her for her happiness, she did not know exactly what to say. She, however, always managed to appear happy. Tonight, he had been to see his disreputable men friends, she was sure. Her maid knew and the nun knew. But she said nothing when he came, and they enjoyed the rest of the fireworks together, greatly admired by the spectators.

She did not ask her husband where he had been on their return home, but she was annoyed and a little upset. The husband and wife slept in separate rooms, but he followed her for a few words before retiring. When she had taken off her pearls, she remarked, "You know some students were arrested this evening before you came. Leaflets were thrown on the streets demanding the resignation of the prime minister."

"Serves them right! Those cheap, contemptible, rabble rousers!" her husband replied. It was a sore subject between them.

Madame D. flared up. "Rabble rousers, indeed! It should have been your job and your duty. Rabble rousers are demanding the recovery of national territory and the resignation of these dead-alive officials because people like you won't."

"Women should leave politics alone!" shouted her husband. He banged the door and went to his rooms.

Madame D. remembered that her affection for her husband had cooled first. She had discovered a streak of greed, something hard and selfish in his character, which changed her opinion of him. Her father had been a great radical, the terror of the appeasement party when he was living. Because her husband was a young man, it was strange that he went along with the ruling clique, but she knew that he was a conservative only because it was the easiest and surest way to get ahead and secure the patronage of those in power. The wife saw the inner soul of the man as no one else could.

One day she read in a court bulletin that one official had sent a memorandum impeaching the prime minister and had been sentenced to exile. Another brave official had done the same thing and, knowing the fate awaiting him, had hanged himself before he sent in his petition to the palace. Madame D. was profoundly moved and shed tears.

"What are you crying about?" her husband asked. "He is a fool. You don't know the story. The prime minister had offered him a high post in the Military Council if he would stop the impeachment and come into his camp. It was one of the best jobs a man can hope for in this life."

Madame D.'s mouth opened wide. "You cannot understand why a man wants to sacrifice his life for his country when it is necessary, can you?"

"Honestly, I cannot."

"Even Hsianglien can." Turning to Hsianglien, she asked, to be spiteful, "You do understand, don't you?" Hsianglien dared not express her opinion.

With her husband's appointment as imperial censor, Madame D. lost all hope in him, and with it all love and respect. The censors were the voice of criticism of government policy, and the prime minister would naturally pack the imperial censorate with his henchmen to impeach any one he liked. The young man was active, hard-working, and competent in his own way. One day he came home to announce with great enthusiasm that he had been made imperial censor. Madame D. snickered.

"Why, you don't even congratulate me on our good fortune. I don't understand what you want in life."

"Don't try to." She was curt.

After all, to be an imperial censor was a very high honor. The husband's vanity was wounded. He now constantly

boasted of his new friends and their positions, and his knowledge of important persons. She had the habit of ignoring
him. She had been born to power and wealth and she was
not impressed. She had come to see in her husband an unscru-
pulous, selfish individual who was interested only in his
personal advancement. It hurt her personal pride. When he
continued to brag at home, she tolerated it, and either smiled
or showed total indifference. She had begun to despise him,
and he felt it.

Madame D. had come to regard her husband as a bore,
but she was resigned to her fate. After the boy was born,
she gave birth to no more children. She left her husband
alone because there was nothing she could do, and she centered her interest in her lovely growing children. She was
rarely seen in public except on such occasions as the Lantern
Festival and the Dragon Boat Festival, apart from visits to
the temple. No gossip had ever been whispered against her.
When she went out, her sedan chair was always carefully
closed with fine bamboo screens. She would have lived comfortably and contentedly, if nothing had happened. Something
had happened on that night of the Lantern Festival, however,
without her knowledge, and it was to change the course of
her life.

A few weeks later, Madame D.'s husband left for another
province on an official tour which would keep him away
for six to ten months. One day she received a visit from the
sister, Huicheng. She brought her a pearl necklace, which was
valued at three thousand dollars.

"Why, I can't pay that sum! My husband is away," Madame D. said.

"The party will part with it for half that price — perhaps
even less."

"In need of cash?"

"No, he wants to beg some favor from you, Madame."

"What favor?"

"He has been removed from his office. Though your husband is away, his relatives can put in a good word for him."

Madame D. hesitated for a moment. "I shall have to consider it. You must take back the necklace."

"I should advise your ladyship to keep it and take time to give a reply. He might offer it to someone else. I will come tomorrow for your decision."

The next day when the nun came again, Madame D. told her that she would take the necklace and would do what she could for the owner.

"How much does he want?"

"Madame, the necklace is to be a present, if you will help him. There is only one thing which I dare not mention, except with your permission. I have to satisfy the young man."

"A young man!" said Madame D., as her face reddened.

"Yes. He has entrusted this necklace to me. But it is a thing of such value that naturally he wants to have some assurance that everything is all right. He must know whom he is dealing with. The young man begs to see you."

"What can I do?"

"Why don't you come to the temple, and I will arrange for you two to meet accidentally."

"No, no, that won't do!" said Madame D. emphatically.

"But he is only begging to be given back his position. Of course, if you don't approve, there is an end to it."

Madame D. coveted the beautiful pearl necklace. After careful thought, she replied, "The day after tomorrow will be the anniversary of my brother's death. I will come to the temple. But I will permit only a few words with the young man. I do not know what kind of person he is! I wouldn't mind, you know, if he were old."

"Madam, you are wrong," replied Sister Huicheng with a smile. "I am sure you will like him when you see him. He is so tall and handsome." She looked at Madame D. and saw a light color come into her cheeks.

"Don't be silly," replied Madame D. severely. "I know

you nuns. I am a married woman and the mother of children. Take the necklace back. I do not want it."

"Ah, madam, you have misunderstood me. If he were not a perfect gentleman, I would not have dared to suggest this meeting. He only wants a favor. You must give the young man a chance. He is so well-bred and well-spoken, and he is from a very good family, as you can see from these pearls. You go and meet him, and if I am wrong, you can deny me entrance to your house from now on."

"You devil," answered Madame D. with a laugh. "Oh, well, I will see him — but only for a minute."

"Omitabha!" cried Sister Huicheng.

It was not without a sense of novel adventure that Madame D. went to her appointment at the convent. She brought only her maid Hsianglien with her. After all, an appointment with an unknown young man was something which she had never permitted herself. When she arrived, there were only five or six old women at the temple. She asked Huicheng with some excitement, "Is he here?"

"You would not want to see him here. I will take you to him by and by."

Madame D. was surprised. She had thought they would meet accidentally in the temple.

Prayer was said for her deceased brother and paper money was burned for his benefit. Sister Huicheng made a suggestion, as if it were a happy thought, for one of the younger nuns to accompany Hsianglien to a grotto in the valley, and it was arranged.

"Now you come with me," said Sister Huicheng. She took Madame D. to a house not far away. When they arrived, she said, "The handsome young man is inside." There was just a hint of pleasant excitement in her voice, indicating that there was something involved besides business.

They went into a room on an inner courtyard, which had a back door leading to a small rock garden with many peach and pear trees in it. The parlor was severely but elegantly furnished with plain lacquered tables, some shelves with books in them, and two hexagonal windows looking out on the yard and the garden. The place had an atmosphere of perfect seclusion. It was May and the air was filled with the subtle fragrance of lilacs. Nobody was in the room. On the table were laid wine cups, some fruit and nuts, and a few dried delicacies.

"Why, what is this for?" asked Madame D. in surprise.

Pouring a cup of wine, the sister said with an artful smile, "Let me drink a cup to your health and happiness."

Madame D. was excited. "Where is the young man? I don't want to tarry too long. Let us get through with the business."

"Be seated. I will fetch him immediately," said Sister Hui-cheng and went out through the back door of the yard. Madame D. soon saw her in the garden with a young man. They were talking together. She sensed a conspiracy between them. "The daring of this young man!" she thought to herself. The young man wore a high Tang hat and a becoming gown of purple. He walked with easy, comfortable steps, gracefully swaying a little in his gown. His face was flushed, and he had a high forehead, straight nose, and remarkable eyes. "I ought to die," she thought to herself. "What am I doing here?" She felt she was doing something wicked. Yet from the first look, she liked him, as Huicheng had predicted.

The nun came in first and introduced them. "Mr. Tseng, Madame D."

The young man made a deep bow, and Madame D. acknowledged it with a smile.

"Be seated, both of you," said the nun. She began to pour wine into their cups, and then said, "You have business to talk about and I shall not be in your way."

"No, you stay," said Madame D. a little desperately, but the sister had lifted the bamboo screen and disappeared into the front rooms.

For a moment the two looked at one another, and it was

instantly clear to her that this was not a business meeting.

"May I drink to your health?" said the young man, lifting his cup.

"And I will drink to you," replied Madame D. instinctively, as she would to a gentleman. Then she remembered herself and said, "I understand you wish to speak to me about some business." She meant to be severe and decorous but her voice shook a little.

"Yes," said the young man, looking at her for a minute. "I do not know where to begin." His voice was a mixture of tenderness, confusion, and bashfulness.

"I understand you want my help."

"Yes, very much so, madam, if you will be so gracious."

"What was the office which you lost?"

"I had no office."

Madame D.'s heart jumped a little. She looked at him in surprise for a moment, and said, not unkindly, "I thought that was why you wanted my help. If not, what was the present for? The necklace is beautiful."

"It is a token of my esteem. It is worthless, compared with the chance to meet you and speak a few words with you."

"You are too bold," Madame D. said reproachfully. She stood up. "You know I am married and have children."

"Pardon me, madam. I beg you to listen to me, and if what I say does not please you, you can dismiss me and I shall consider myself scolded by the most beautiful woman in the world. I shall treasure these few moments for the rest of my life. It is indeed reckless of me to hope to speak a few words with you. But you commanded me to come. I had no choice."

"I commanded you?" said Madame D., seating herself slowly again. His words intrigued her. "Be brief."

"Yes, your spirit left me no rest. Since I saw you at the lantern festival, your image has stayed in my mind day and night. I have dreamed of you, thought of you. I said to myself I would die happy if I could be near you and see you just for a moment and talk with the most beautiful woman in all the capital. Then even if I should go about the streets as a beggar, I shall be the richest man in the world, for I shall carry with me the treasure of your memory and of these brief, golden moments." His voice was manly and his eyes were afire.

Madame D. looked at him with interest. "Does this meeting really mean so much to you?"

"Yes. I must confess that I have been presumptuous and reckless I would risk my very life to see you. When Sister Huicheng told me you would come, I dared not believe my own luck."

"You must have bribed her heavily," remarked Madame D. with a smile.

"Frankly, I have. I searched the city to find out who would have approach to you. I was lucky. You see, it was your own fault. Other women might permit themselves to be seen in public, but not you, for to see you is to love you. Madam, you don't know how happy you make me. I have waited for this hour. Now you can send me away and I am content. But please say something for me to remember you by."

Madame D. could not resist his flattery. She had changed her mind, for it was pleasant to hear him talk. "Please stay. Since you are here and have taken so much trouble, tell me about yourself. Who are you?"

"A scholar at the university."

"Oh, I see. In politics?"

"We university students are all in it. But it is not politics; it is a question involving the honor and independence of our country. It is everybody's concern. It is wrong to speak of a war party and a peace party. The choice is between national honor and dishonor. Who does not want peace? But offer me peace with dishonor and I will choose war."

Mr. Tseng spoke with force and passionate conviction. He was a leader of student demonstrations against the appeasers. In those days the university students, numbering thirty thousand, had repeatedly demanded a positive policy toward the northern invaders, and because they had made themselves the voice of the people, they were greatly feared by the government leaders. Student leaders like Chen Tung had been killed and then posthumously honored because public sentiment had demanded it. Mr. Tseng spoke out of his heart, while Madame D. listened with admiration. The more she listened, the more she felt he was voicing with clarity and great force what she had thought in her own mind. She felt a sense of elation.

"Pardon me," he paused for a minute. "I have been carried away."

"On the contrary. My father used to say the same things. It is in the family tradition. Li Kang was my granduncle on my mother's side."

"No!" The young man almost jumped up in surprise. Li Kang was the central figure of a war party, around whom the storms of political battles had been fought two generations ago. He was next to God in the eyes of the university students.

They drank a toast to Li Kang. Madame D. felt completely at home and safe with the young man now. Mr. Tseng was frank and easy. The meeting turned out better than he had dared to expect. They felt they had something intensely in common, and Madame D. forgot all her pretensions to rank and spoke as a woman does to a man who fascinates her. She had never before felt such intoxication. With none of her husband's friends had she ever had such a conversation. All her youthful life seemed to flow back to her again, as if a dam had been broken. Her happy girlhood, her great and forceful father, the innocence and joys of belief, which she had suppressed and forgotten for so long, came back to her in those brief moments, and with them some of her youthful gaiety and irresponsibility.

"Madam, you cannot blame me for admiring you," said

Mr. Tseng, as he sought her hand. She permitted him to do so, feeling weak inside.

Suddenly she pulled herself together and said, as if with an effort, "Mr. Tseng, I am glad to have met you. We can be friends, I hope."

"I would die of happiness if you would permit me."

There were footsteps outside. When the nun came in, she asked, fixing her eyes on both of them, "Well, have you finished your business?"

"Yes," replied Madame D. She made a gesture toward leaving. "I did not know it was so late." She stood up, her face flushed. Then suddenly a change of expression came over her face, and she bent over, falling to her chair again, groaning in pain.

"Why, what has happened?" asked the sister.

"I do not know. I feel ill."

Sister Huicheng rushed over to her. "Come into the next room," she said. "Lie down there and have a good rest."

The nun helped Madame D. into the inner room. When she was laid in bed and properly covered, she said to Huicheng, "Send some one to go home with my maid. Tell her to come with the sedan chair for me tomorrow morning. Tell the people at home that I have had a sudden spell of pain and am too weak to go home tonight."

As Huicheng went out through the parlor, she passed Tseng and whispered to him, "Congratulations, Mr. Tseng!"

The next morning, when Madame D. bade good-by to Mr. Tseng, she said to him, "If I had not met you, I would have lived my life in vain."

Madame D. became reckless. Engaged at the age of seventeen, she had never known the joys of courtship. No man had ever made love to her like that, and Tseng, as we have seen, was a great lover.

For a lady of her position to have a paramour was dan-

gerous. Though she was mistress of her household, with only
her husband's old mother living with them, who was most
of the time confined to bed, she could not possibly allow her
lover to meet her at her home, and she could make no
movements without the knowledge of the servants and the
sedan-chair carriers. Her days were long, and she waited
patiently for some proper excuse to go out. Two or three
times she met him again. She could no longer keep the
affair from the knowledge of her maid Hsianglien, but
Hsianglien shared the mistress' abhorrence of the master.
Once, Madame D. could not resist the temptation to feign
sudden illness again and pass a passionate night with her
lover.

When her husband returned to the capital in autumn, he
saw her pearl necklace and asked her where she had got it.

"I bought it from a private family," replied his wife. "I
have not paid for it yet, and promised to pay when you are
back. It costs six thousand dollars."

The husband looked at the necklace and admired its
beauty.

"It is worth the price," said the wife. "In a few days, they
will come for the money."

The husband said nothing, and when the nun appeared a
few days afterward, he paid accordingly. Mr. Tseng would
not take the money, but Madame D. insisted on his taking it,
she loved him so much now.

All winter her husband remained in the city. Madame D.
had as much fear of her husband as she had of public gossip.
Happy with her new lover, she wanted to make amends, but
the husband was cold and unresponsive. They hardly spoke
to each other outside of routine household affairs.

Madame D. took extraordinary risks. On one occasion she
was invited to the home of the metropolitan magistrate (who
was also police commissioner) for dinner. It was a ladies'
party. She made an arrangement for her maid to come during
the dinner and tell her that the grandmother was ill, and the

lady and her maid went off to their rendezvous and returned home at midnight. Such were the risks she was willing to take, but they could not be repeated too often.

Then Madame D. fell ill with a cold. Everything seemed wrong and she felt miserable. She told her husband that she wanted to go to her mother's home at Yuchien, a journey which could be made in one long day. When she arrived at her home, she sent the sedan chair back, telling the carriers to come back for her in a fortnight. Her parents were dead now, and as a lady from the capital she could do pretty much as she pleased. She went off with Hsianglien to meet her lover at the Tienmu Mountain. They spent ten delirious days there, walking over the mountainside in the old forests of giant pines which were centuries old. Nobody asked any questions, and they left happily.

Word had reached the husband's ears, however, that when the wife was returning home, the sedan-chair carriers had seen a young man in her company who came back on the same day. They had even stopped to lunch together on the way. The husband grew suspicious, but in his methodical way, he said nothing.

When the wife showed signs of morning sickness, she was horrified. She tried to cover it up before her husband by dismissing it as something of no importance, but the husband knew the symptoms too well and his suspicion was increased. Again, however, he did not question her. Madame D. was desperate. To outsiders, there was nothing surprising in her having another child. But the husband and wife knew between themselves that it was impossible. She kept up the pretense that it was perhaps something other than pregnancy, but her waistline was growing perceptibly.

"Tell me who is the man?" her husband demanded one evening.

"Don't be silly. I do not think I am with child, and if I were, whose child could it be but yours?"

"That is impossible, and you know it."

"You were drunk one night. You did not know it yourself," said the wife, looking straight at him. The husband looked at her out of the corner of his eye. It was, of course, theoretically possible, but he was unconvinced.

"Drunk or not, I would not have slept with you," he said cruelly. "And I think a child conceived in your mother's home had better be born in your mother's village."

How she hated him then! "You are outrageous!" she cried.

The suspicion never left the husband's mind. He wanted only to find out who her lover was. He treated her now with a cold contempt even as she had treated him before. She stopped all communications with Tseng. The baby was already five months old in her body.

Everything would have gone well but for a political storm which again threw the court into a turmoil. One official who had sent a petition to the emperor demanding the dismissal of the prime minister had been flogged, which was considered a very unusual form of punishment for officials, and then sentenced to exile. Incensed by this and supported by public opinion, over a hundred students and some of the officials staged a great demonstration before the palace gate, demanding to be heard. They were joined by tens of thousands of the populace. The previous day, the prime minister had been met with angry shouts of "Resign! Resign!" while passing through the streets in his carriage. Disturbed by the menacing crowd, a eunuch was sent out to read an imperial order promising consideration of their demands. The crowd was dissatisfied, and after the edict was read, the eunuch was beaten up and several palace guards were killed, trampled by the surging mob.

Some of the student leaders were caught and thrown into prison, and Madame D.'s lover was reported among them. The news of the arrests spread quickly through the teahouses, and Tseng's name was on everybody's lips. Madame D. was terrified. She did not know what to do.

That night when her husband returned, she approached him gently and tried to persuade him to effect the release of the students.

"Those students are only wanting to help the nation," she pleaded.

"It was nothing but a mob," her husband replied coldly.

Madame D. pleaded again and again. Her voice trembled and her face was white. The husband kept quiet for a moment, and then asked:

"Why are you so anxious? I hear the government is determined to put a stop to these mob demonstrations. The arrested will be killed."

Madame D.'s teeth chattered with fright, and she collapsed. When she recovered, she broke into tears and mad entreaties.

"You must stop the murders!" she cried desperately.

"What can I do? Tell me, whom are you trying to save?"

During repeated questionings, Madame D. refused to divulge her lover's name. The husband left the house in anger.

Madame D. trembled for the fate of her lover. She could not sleep all night. She saw the expression on her husband's face as she went out in the morning. As soon as he left the house, she sent her maid to find out from the university the names of the arrested. She knew that once his suspicion was aroused, the lives of those arrested would be worthless. Hsianglien came back to report that Tseng was missing. Some said he had escaped.

She knew that her husband would not return for lunch. By noontime, Madame D. was waiting in suspense for more exact news, and thinking of means to send Tseng warning, when a man came to the house who reported himself to be a cousin-in-law of Hsianglien from the country, to call on the maid. Hsianglien went out to see him and saw him dressed as a rustic with a countryman's bag on his shoulders. She came to report to the lady, with happiness in her eyes.

"If he is a close relative of yours, ask him to come up." Tseng was soon ushered upstairs.

"How did you escape?" Madame D. gasped as she recognized him through the disguise. "This is no place to meet."

"I am going away. I had to see you before I went. I broke away during a commotion when another tried to escape."

"You must flee at once. My husband's suspicion is aroused, and he means to kill you. He will go after the leaders and you are too prominent."

Madame D. went to her room and took out the pearl necklace.

"Here, take this," she said. "Go far away until the situation changes. You will need money on the way. I do not know when we can meet again." Her eyes were veiled with tears. "As for me, I shall always live in the memory of you, and pray for you. Do not worry about me. I have the child to live for. I shall love him as I love you." She put the necklace in his bag.

"I have money," he protested. "What if he finds out?"

"Leave that to me. It can be lost or stolen. I never wear it and he will never know. The necklace is the cause of our meeting and perhaps it will enable us to meet again."

"Better days may come," he said to her. And then he left hurriedly.

When her husband came home that night and told her that the arrested would be killed, Madame D. merely remarked, "Kill all the patriots. That is your job, is it not?" Her husband was surprised at her calmness.

They did not speak to each other again for a long time.

"I will go and have the child born in my mother's village," Madame D. announced to her husband one day. She could not stand living with him any longer.

"You might as well," replied the husband.

Madame D. knew that he would never risk the scandal of a divorce. She knew all his thoughts and was certain that he cared most for his social position. Besides, she was of a high official family and her brother was still living. Divorce would be difficult and rather unusual under the circumstances, and the husband had no evidence.

The baby was born in her mother's home, and Madame D. continued to live in the country apart from her husband. It was a boy, and Madame D. loved him perhaps just a little bit more than she did the other children. Tseng seemed to have completely disappeared.

Three years later, the emperor died, and the new emperor reversed the government policy. Radical officials in exile were called back. It was now the husband's turn to be exiled, for he was condemned for his cruel murder of student leaders. He died of an apoplectic stroke on the way.

One day, when Madame D. had returned to live in the capital as a widow, Sister Huicheng appeared and asked her if she would like to buy a pearl necklace. She knew that Tseng had returned, and the excitement of their meeting under the new circumstances was all the greater when Tseng told her that he had received a high post in the Ministry of Ceremonies, in charge of civil service.

Her three years of mourning being over, she was married to Tseng, and Hsianglien was married to a clerk in Tseng's office.

Years later, at the time of the Lantern Festival, Madame D. was once more "Madame Imperial Censor." Times had changed. She had grown plumper, and there were many new faces, but there were the same crowds, the same lanterns, and the same fireworks. She sat in the same section with her husband, and the boy who was now ten, but there was a more mature beauty in her face. She did not laugh so much, nor was she as gay, but there was a look of serene happiness on her face.

"Look, there is Auntie Huicheng!" cried the boy.

The nun came up and said, "The necklace looks beautiful on your ladyship. It has brought you luck, madam."

Ghosts

9. JEALOUSY

~~~~~~

From the Chingpen T'ungshu Shiaoshuo, *Sung Dynasty, author unknown. This is probably the type of horror story that the teashop audience enjoyed. The story is so built up that, toward the end, not one person, but a whole group of persons connected with the story are re-revealed one by one as ghosts, to create a climax of horror. The same collection has another ghost story in which the same technique of gradually revealing suspicion is used. "Jealousy" was expanded and incorporated in a later Ming collection,* Chingshih T'ungyen. *I have omitted the ending where a Taoist priest is called to exorcise the spirits.*

W u HUNG, a derelict sojourner at the capital, had a curious feeling of contented solitude when the students at his private school went home. He did not mind brewing his own tea. He did not even mind drinking tea alone. His bachelor's quarters on the inside courtyard had a secret charm for him. There were feminine touches in them, for his bedroom was furnished with a dressing table, an old toilet case with a collapsible mirror on top, and various articles of known and unknown feminine use. There were needles, ribbons, and hairpins in the drawer, the bottom of which was smeared with powder. He smelled a subtle perfume in the room every time he entered it. He recognized it as the exciting fragrance of musk which had settled permanently in the room, though he

167

could not locate any visible sign of it. All this boudoir atmosphere rather intrigued his bachelor's fancy. Being of an imaginative turn of mind, he liked to picture to himself the kind of woman who had lived here. Was she tall and slender? What would her voice be like? All he needed was a woman in the flesh to make himself believe that he was living in a home.

In a big city like Hangchow, he mused, there were so many mysterious creatures, sweet and charming. This was the reason why he had chosen to stay, instead of returning to his home in Foochow, after he had failed to pass the national competition in scholarship and literature. He had merely convinced himself that the journey would be long and expensive, and he would remain there till the next examinations came around. Unlucky in literature, lucky in love. As a marriageable, handsome young man, the city owed him something. He was quite ready to marry, provided he could find the right girl. He would pick a plum from the devil's own orchard if it struck his fancy.

"Oh, if I could find a woman who was beautiful and rich, unattached and alone!"

The house he had found for himself was like his mind. It had an unwhitewashed earthen brick wall outside (and he paid a ridiculously low rental for it), but what charm in its interior! Of course it was cheap because it was situated in an isolated district, far from the center of town. But that could hardly be the whole story. He was familiar with so many stories telling how a lonely scholar, sitting in his studio in the quiet of the night, raised his head and saw a bewitching apparition of a woman standing before him, smiling at him in the lamplight; such a woman would come to visit him night after night and live in secret with him, save him money, serve him in sickness — all in all a wonderful dream-life come true. He told himself that he would like to commune with the ghost of the woman who had lived in his room. There was no reason why he should think of the woman as dead, except that he wanted it so. He thought he could hear her voice at times when he was alone at night. But when he listened carefully, it turned out to be only a neighbor's kitten. Such disappointment! Why not marry a real woman?

There was indeed a certain advantage in being a lone bachelor and a stranger in a city. Many parents would like to marry their daughters to a man without a big family of relatives. One day, Wongpo came. She had known him when he was staying at Chientang Gate before he moved to the present house. Being a professional matchmaker, she had tried to make a match for him, but at that time he was busy with his examinations and the first excitements of arrival at the capital. Now he was feeling settled. With an interesting gesture, the old woman whispered that she had something important to talk to him about, and signaled the teacher to follow her inside. Her thin grayish hair was in a small bun at the back of her neck, and Wu noticed a red kerchief wrapped high around her neck even though it was April and the weather had been warm. He thought she must have a cold in her throat.

"I have an interesting proposition for you," said the old woman romantically. She had an irresistible smile and a pleasant way of talking, both of which were assets in her profession — the profession of romance.

Wu asked her to sit down, which she did and then pulled her chair close to him. He asked her how she was getting along. It had been almost a year since they had seen each other.

"Don't talk about me. I remember you are twenty-two. She is twenty-two, too." She pulled at her red kerchief a little, as if her neck had been hurt — perhaps from slipping over one of those smooth leather pillows while asleep, Wu reflected.

"Who?"

"The girl I am going to speak to you about."

"Any girl you are speaking about would be twenty-two," replied Wu in a tone of depreciating disbelief. "I am in no hurry to marry, not unless you find me one of those sweet mysterious creatures that Hangchow must be full of." Wongpo had suggested several matches which he had found upon investigation to be very common and uninteresting. "You matchmakers are all conjurers with words. You would call a crescent moon the hopeful beginning of a full moon and defend a dark moon by saying, 'You haven't seen the other side yet.' I want the full moon."

It was true that Wongpo's business was to see all the marriageable young men and girls at the capital paired off — not always happily, but paired off anyway. To her, a marriageable bachelor of twenty-two was an offense in the sight of Heaven.

"What kind of woman do you want?"

"I want a young woman, of course, pretty and understanding, and living all alone."

"And who perhaps would bring you a thousand dollars and a maid, huh?" Wongpo added, smiling triumphantly as if she knew he was captured. "She is all alone, with no relatives."

Wongpo drew her chair still closer and whispered in his ears, although there was nobody else in the room. Wu listened with keen interest.

She named a very desirable young lady, a famous flute player who had recently left the house of her former employer. Her master was no other than the third son of the all-powerful imperial tutor, Chin. Such rich families always kept a complete troupe of actresses and musicians in their mansions. People called her Li Yonia (roughly the equivalent of "Mademoiselle Artist Li") because she was a professional artist. Miss Li was independent and free and had only a foster mother who did not need her support. She had a thousand dollars of her own and would bring her own maid.

"This sounds very interesting," said Wu. "But why should she want to marry a poor scholar like me?"

"She has money of her own, as I told you. She wants only

to marry a scholar, living alone, without in-laws. Let me tell you, I am doing you a favor. A wealthy merchant has already made an offer to take her, but she would not marry a businessman. I have tried to persuade her, but she is stubborn. 'No,' she said to me, 'make me a match with a scholar. No in-laws, no parents.' Not many persons can qualify in that respect. That is why I thought of you and came all the way to tell you about it. I wonder if you realize how lucky you are."

"Where is she?"

"She is living with her foster mother at the White Crane Pond. If you want to see her for yourself, it can be arranged, too." There could be no fairer proposal.

A few days later, Wu went to a certain restaurant by appointment. There he was introduced to Mrs. Chen, the foster mother. Her hair, for some reason, was wet, and water was dripping down her skirt even though it was a bright clear day. "You must excuse my appearance," explained Mrs. Chen. "I had the bad luck to bump against a water-carrier on our way here."

"Where is the young lady?" asked Wu.

"She is in the next room. The young girl you will see with her is her maid, Chin-erh. Quite a maid, too. She can cook and sew and do everything around the house."

Mrs. Chen said good-by to Wu and went into the next room, leaving curious, wet footprints on the floor. Wongpo remained with Wu, who wet his finger on his lips, made a hole in the papered lattice partition, and peeped through. He saw the foster mother bending over a pretty young woman and whispering to her. He could see the straight tip of her nose. Suddenly she raised her head, smiled, and blushed consciously. He saw her dark deep-set eyes against an extremely white face, framed by a mass of black hair. A young maid, between fifteen and sixteen, seemed keenly interested in what was going on. Wu was amazed.

"It cannot be!" he exclaimed to himself.

"What is the matter?"

"If she will marry me, I shall be the happiest man in Hangchow."

He seated himself at the table for dinner, and he could hear the women's voices in the next room, mixed with gay laughter. Evidently the company in the other room was having a good time. Once he looked up and saw an eye behind the hole in the partition, which immediately withdrew, to be followed by a quick shuffling of feminine feet and a loud giggle, which he imagined must have come from the maid.

"To tell the truth," remarked Wongpo with a smile, "I have made the appointment because the young lady wants as much to see you as you want to see her. She won't buy her husband sight unseen. She is bringing you a thousand dollars and you are getting her for nothing."

Arrangements were made for Miss Li to come in a fortnight. It was agreed that since the bridegroom was a stranger in the city, there was no point in making a show of the wedding. Miss Li would be very happy to come and live with him, bringing her maid with her.

It never occurred to Wu to inquire why Miss Li had left the house of her former master.

Wu could not wait for the day to come. But good fortunes, like misfortunes, do not come alone. The following week, another woman appeared to suggest a match for him. In order to save himself trouble, he told her he was already engaged to be married, but she was persistent.

"Who is the lucky lady?" inquired the woman, who called herself Widow Chuang.

Wu told her the name of his fiancee. The widow appeared to suppress a great shock of disapproval.

"What is it?" asked Wu.

"Oh, nothing. Since you are already engaged, I do not want to say anything."

Wu's curiosity was aroused. "Do you know her?"

"Do I know her! Well," she said after a pause, "I thought I was going to propose another match for you. The girl I have in mind is all that a man can wish for in a wife, pretty as a flower, sweet-natured and hard-working, and good at cooking and needlework. She would make a lovely little wife for a gentleman like you. I do not mind telling you that the girl I am speaking for is my own daughter. I should not interfere, but I think a poor man's daughter would make a better wife for you. Do not listen to match-makers."

Wu was getting impatient. "I have seen the young lady myself. I am sorry but I am engaged." He showed Widow Chuang to the door and said good-by to her politely, only because he thought he had seen the last of her.

On a rainy evening, Miss Li came in a sedan chair with her maid, her foster mother, and the matchmaker, old Wong-po. The sedan-chair carriers did not stop to demand tips and a bowl of noodles, as they usually did on such occasions. When the bridegroom thought of it, they were already gone in the dark. The maid, Chin-erh, did everything, from un-packing the lady's clothes to fetching water and making tea. The bride had brought a whole set of musical instruments which Chin-erh at once proceeded to lay out carefully on the table. Chin-erh was as playful as a kitten and knew her way about without being told. The women seemed to have ap-propriated the house, and the bridegroom had nothing to do except enjoy himself.

They had a simple wine dinner. Mrs. Chen's hair was wet again, but this was not surprising for it had been raining very hard. Wu thought, too, that she smelled of duckweed. The seat of honor was given to old Mrs. Wong as the go-between. She still kept her wrap around her throat although the April evening had been stifling with dampness and heat.

"Swear to me that you will love no other woman but me," said Yonia that night, and it was very easy to make such a promise on the wedding night.

"Are you very jealous?"

"Yes, I am. I cannot help it. I intend to make this my love nest, but if you should be untrue to me — "

"Would you be jealous if I fell in love with a woman in a dream?"

"I would!"

The wife and the maid made a very happy home for Wu. It was too good to be true. For once, a go-between's words could be trusted. He felt as if he was living in a dream. Yonia was as accomplished as Wongpo had claimed her to be. As an artist, she could read, write, drink, and play cards. She played the flute wonderfully in the evenings and sang little love songs to him. She was also very clever and good at figures. She could tell him instantly that a piece of cloth eleven and a half feet long, at seventy-three cents a foot, was $8.39½. It was uncanny. She and Chin-erh also loved to play the most intricate wire puzzles, like the nine-dragon-loop, whispering all the time.

"What the devil are you two up to?" Wu would ask.

"M-hm! A gentleman does not use that word!" admonished Yonia.

"What are you up to, then?"

"That's better." For the tenth time she had corrected him. She would not permit him to say "what the devil" or "how the devil" and felt offended if he did.

At first he resented the intimacy between the mistress and her maid, and was suspicious to hear them constantly whispering together. But it always turned out to be a conspiracy for his benefit. They always seemed to be thinking up new dishes and made delicate white buns, stuffed with onion and mutton, for his breakfast. What was a still rarer gift, bordering on the uncanny, was that Yonia could anticipate his wishes and did the things for him without being told, as if she could read his thoughts. When he remembered his bachelor days of taking a basket to market in the morning, he laughed.

One day, however, after they had been married about a month, he came in from town and found his wife weeping. He tried his best to comfort her, and asked her what he had done to displease her.

"It had nothing to do with you," replied Yonia.

"Is it somebody else?"

Since he could get nothing out of her, he asked Chin-erh, who seemed to know but would say nothing.

Two days later, he came back from the streets just before supper and heard his wife screaming aloud, "Get out you, get out!" He rushed in to find her panting with rage. Her hair had fallen over her forehead and there was a light scratch on her face. Chin-erh was standing by her, panting and puffing like her mistress.

"Who was here?" he asked.

"Someone — someone has been bothering me." said Yonia reluctantly.

The husband could see no one in the house, not even a shadow. There was a side alley leading from the court to the street, but he had not heard a thing.

"You are perhaps seeing things," suggested the husband.

"I, seeing things?" said the wife, breaking into great laughter. The husband could see nothing to laugh about.

That night in bed he asked his wife, "You must tell me who is bothering you."

"Someone is jealous of me, that is all."

"Who?"

Under repeated questioning, the wife finally said, "It is an old girl friend of mine."

"But who?"

"One Miss Chuang. You would not know her."

"You do not mean Widow Chuang's daughter?"

"Do you know her?" The wife sat up in surprise.

Wu told her how the widow had come to propose a match

with her own daughter a week after they had become engaged, and she had, in fact, discouraged his marriage with Yonia. It is said that a woman in jealousy is more to be feared than a tigress in anger. The wife started to curse with a string of profanity which he had never expected from her lips.

"You have nothing to worry about," said her husband. "We are married and she has no right to come here to bother you. Next time she comes, you just call me in and I will thrash her before your eyes."

"You love me more than her, do you not?" asked the wife.

"Yonia, you are talking foolishness. I never saw Miss Chuang even. I only saw her mother one time."

In spite of himself, he was a little upset. He had the feeling that his wife had a secret which she was not willing to confide in him.

Miss Chuang did not come again, however, and the husband and wife passed their days happily. Hangchow, he thought, was a wonderful city. He lived in an enchanted world.

It was the time of the Dragon Boat Festival. According to custom, Wu closed school and suggested that they go out, either to the city or the surrounding mountains to visit temples. The wife had never left the house since their marriage and she declined, saying he should go alone. She did ask him, however, to take her to spend a day with her foster mother at the White Crane Pond. He left her there and went on toward Wansungling, stopping on the way to look at the Tsingtse Temple. On his way out of the temple, a servant from the wine shop opposite came up to him and said, "A gentleman from the shop asked to see you."

When Wu went in, he saw a young man he had met during the examinations, by the name of Lo Chisan.

"I saw you go in and thought I would like to have a chat with you. What are you doing today?"

Wu replied that he was taking a holiday and had no idea exactly where he was going. He also informed him that he had recently married.

In playful revenge for keeping his marriage a secret from him, Lo thought to himself that he would like to hold the bridegroom for ransom for a day, just to see how uncomfortable he would be.

"I say, I am going to visit my family cemetery up Wansungling. How about coming with me and making a day of it? The azaleas are still in bloom and I know a good wine shop out that way which has the best wine I ever tasted in my life."

Wu readily agreed as he was happy to find a companion for the day. They came out of the wine shop and crossed the lake by the Su Tungpo Embankment where they could see a full holiday crowd of men, women, and children strolling on the broad willow-covered walk. There they hired a boat from Nanshin Road and went ashore at Maochiapu. The family cemetery of his friend was situated up a steep rocky mountain called the Tuohsienling. It took them an hour to go up and after passing the peak, they went down on the other side for half a mile and reached their destination. The day was mild and the hillsides were a profusion of pink and red blossoms. They were so enchanted with the place that the afternoon went by without their knowing it.

Wu's friend then took him to the wine shop. To do this, they had to go down to the valley, following a winding brook, charmingly shaded by trees. They passed a wooden bridge, at the head of which, on the other side, stood a big banyan tree, rarely seen in this region, throwing its long branches almost horizontally about ten or fifteen feet from the ground. Long tassels of roots hung down like beards from the branches, in a seeming effort to reach the ground. About fifty feet from the tree stood a cottage with a piece of square cloth on a bamboo pole, the familiar sign of a wine shop.

"There it is," said Lo. "I know the widow. The last time I came here, I had a most wonderful time talking with her daughter. A wonderfully sweet girl."

Wu felt his heartbeat thumping in his head.

Widow Chuang stood in front of the shop to welcome them, as if she had seen them coming. She was all smiles.

"Why, if it is not Professor Wu!" said the widow. "What wind blew you this way? Come in, come in!"

She showed the men inside, moving chairs and patting cushions in an energetic show of hospitality. "Sit down, gentlemen. I did not know that you knew each other."

"Li-hwa!" shouted Widow Chuang. "Guests are here, come out!" This was her daughter's name, which meant "Pear Flower."

Soon a tall, slender girl of eighteen or nineteen appeared, in a purple dress with a broad black trimming. She had very long eyebrows and wore a perpetual smile on her face. She curtsied to the guests without the shyness of city girls.

"Warm up the best wine for our guests," the mother ordered.

While Li-hwa went to a corner of the shop to take out some wine in an earthen pot, Widow Chuang said to Wu, "What did I tell you about my daughter? Is she not pretty, and such a good girl too? I would not know what to do without her. Yes, she makes me very happy. She might have been yours. Well!"

Widow Chuang stopped as the girl came back, pot in hand, and a deepened color in her cheeks. She set the pot of wine over the fire. Her eyes shot several sparkling glances at Wu and she smiled, not brazenly, but gaily and consciously, as a girl of her age would smile at a handsome young man. She stood, fanning the stove, shaking her body a little and now and then brushing back some curls which had fallen forward as she stooped. Wu sat silently, looking at her back.

Every one of her movements seemed exquisite. The charcoal having burned to a bright red, she left the stove and began washing some pewter cups, which she then laid on the table, looking at Wu as she did so.

"Put down four," said Widow Chuang.

Li-hwa got two more cups, repeated the ablutions, and then stood idly at the table. Then she went back to the stove to see if the wine was ready and pour it into a pewter pot.

"Mother," she called, "it is ready.". She poured the wine into the gentlemen's cups.

"You sit down first. I will be with you in a minute."

After brushing her curls back from her forehead with a white arm she patted some ashes off her apron and sat down.

The widow soon came to join them and the four of them sat drinking and chatting. The widow asked Wu how he was getting along and inquired about his marriage. Wu told her how happy he was. He restrained himself a little because he remembered the incident at his home. He could not believe that this sweet, pretty girl could have attacked his wife. But he was almost sure that there had been something between the two young ladies.

"All the same," remarked the widow, "now that you have seen Li-hwa, you can see what you have missed.

"You have every right to be proud of your daughter," replied Wu, glad to pay a compliment to the girl. Li-hwa blushed a little.

The men said they wanted to leave, but the widow would not hear of it. "Stay for supper. You do not know what carp tastes like till you let Li-hwa show you what she can do with it."

Wu thought of his wife and said it was late already.

"You cannot reach the city tonight anyway. The Chientang Gate will be closed by the time you reach there. It is four or five miles from here."

Wu consented because what she said was true, but not without a guilty conscience. He knew, however, that his wife would be waiting for him in her foster mother's home, and she would be safe.

The fish, fresh from the brook, was unsurpassable, and the warm wine caressed the throat and made him relaxed inside. Wu felt very happy.

"What *did* you do to the fish?" he asked.

"Nothing," replied Li-hwa, very simply.

"There is magic in it. I swear I never tasted carp like that before."

"What did I tell you?" said the mother. "Did I not tell you the truth about my daughter? But you would believe the words of a professional matchmaker."

Wu resented the insinuation and said with obvious annoyance, "What is wrong with my wife?"

Li-hwa seemed to be bursting with words, but her mother silenced her with a look and said, "We know her very well. Your wife was a frightfully jealous woman. Otherwise, why would such a talented musician be thrown out of her master's house?"

"What did she do? You said she was a frightfully jealous woman!"

"Yes, she was. She could not stand anybody prettier or who played the flute better than herself. She pushed a girl off the veranda and killed her. It was only because she had the protection of the all-powerful Chin family that she escaped a charge for manslaughter. However, you are married to her and I do not want to say anything more. Do not bring this up when you talk with your wife. Pretend that you do not know."

Under the influence of the wine, Wu's friend flirted foolishly with Li-hwa, looking at her goose-eyed. Li-hwa tolerated him good-naturedly, as one does a drunken man, while she smiled understandingly at Wu. Soon Lo was so drunk that they assisted him to a couch where he lay snoring.

Wu was now all the more confused about the mysterious woman he had married. He saw, too, that Li-hwa, without

Yonia's glamour, was the sincere, sweet, and cheerful kind of a girl who would make a man very happy to live with her. In spite of her complete simplicity, she was very good to look at. The words of her mother, "You don't know what you missed," kept coming into his mind. His meeting her here tonight in a roadside wine shop, his recent marriage, and all the happenings of the past month seemed like a weird succession of unreal events.

Darkness had fallen, and fireflies were flitting through the window. The woman and her daughter closed up shop while Wu strolled outside. There was not another single cottage in the whole valley. Birds had settled in their roosts and all around them was silence, broken now and then by an owl's screeches and the faraway eerie cry of some night-prowling animal. A pale crescent moon with its horns pointing downward stood over the hilltops in the western sky, transforming the trees into tall black specters shaking in the wind, and giving the valley a phantom beauty.

Li-hwa stood in the doorway. She had changed into a white dress and her hair fell in graceful curls. She came toward him, flute in hand. She gave him an ingenuous smile and said simply but expressively, "Look at the moon."

"Yes." Wu gulped down the rest of his feelings.

"We will go to the brook. There is a nice spot there where I love to sit and play the flute in the evening."

When they came to the place, she chose a big boulder by the brook for them to sit on, and began to play a soft, plaintive, heart-rending melody. There was just enough moon-light to show the indistinct outline of her oval face, her hair, and body. It seemed she played even better than Yonia; and to hear the flute played in a secluded valley in the moonlight by a beautiful girl, and feel its notes mingle with the music of the brook, float over the treetops, and echo back from distant hills, would be an unforgettable experience for any man. It was so for Wu that night. It was so beautiful that it inflicted a kind of pain. Wu was seized with a great anguish.

"Why look so sad?" Li-hwa asked him.

"Your music makes me feel that way," he said, looking at her white ghostly beauty in the starlit night.

"Then I will stop playing," Li-hwa said with a laugh.

"Please go on."

"No, not if it makes you sad."

"Are you happy here?"

"Yes. Is there a prettier place in all the world than this — the trees, the brook, the stars, the moon?"

"Do you not feel lonely here?"

"Lonely?" she replied, as if she did not know the word. "I have my mother and we love each other very much."

"Don't you want a man — I mean — "

Li-hwa laughed. "What do I want a man for? Besides, good men are difficult to find. My mother told me about you. She likes you very much. If I had been able to marry a person like you, I would be very happy and I would have babies to play with."

She breathed a warm sigh.

"Li-hwa, I love you," said Wu, his voice hoarse with emotion. "You fascinated me from the moment I saw you."

"Don't be silly. You are married now to that she-devil and you have got to take it. Come, we will go in. I bet she will kill me if she ever finds out about your spending the night with me here."

Wu felt as if he were in a trance, so great was the magic influence of the place and the music and the lovely girl's voice upon him. It was true then that the two girls he loved had been enemies.

As they walked along the bank toward the cottage, the moon emerged from the clouds and printed the beautiful white oval of her face upon the dark surface of the night. A white flower was just above her head. Wu seized her in his arms and kissed her passionately. The girl submitted, then broke into a sob.

"She will kill me!" she said with a sudden horror.

"What nonsense! Who?"

"Yonia! She will kill me!" Her voice shook.

"She will never know. I will not be so foolish as to tell her."

"Yes, she will know."

"How?"

"Well, can you keep a secret?" Wu felt her hot breath upon his face as she drew very close. "Your wife is a ghost. She hanged herself when she left her master's house because she was expecting a baby. She haunts human beings. My mother could not tell you the truth. It is against the principles. She warned you, but you were under her charm."

A chill went down Wu's spine as he listened. "You mean I have married a ghost?"

"Yes, you have. Her ghost haunted me when I was in the city."

"She haunted you?"

"Yes, I had had a quarrel with her because she was jealous of me. Why do you suppose we mother and daughter have chosen to live so far out? Just to get away from her." The girl paused and added, "Now I am completely restored and we are happy here. She does not know. There are always tourists passing this way and my mother is saving up a lot of money, and we do not care to go back to the city. Some day, I hope my mother will find a nice handsome man like you for me." The girl told her story as if it were a common, everyday experience.

"You will, a pretty girl like you. But what am I to do?"

"How do I know? But you must never mention to Yonia that you have met me here or anywhere else. Do not tell my mother that I have told you. If you love me, keep absolutely quiet about your visit today. Do not ever let Yonia know where I live." Her voice shook as she said this.

All his man's instincts made Wu want to protect this sweet

girl. He promised, and then tried to kiss her again. But the girl turned her head and said, "We must go in. My mother will be waiting for us."

Wu went in to find his friend snoring in his sleep, and the girl holding a candle in her hand. She bid him good night. He was getting in bed ready to sleep when Li-hwa appeared again at the top of the staircase and asked sweetly, "Are you all right?"

"Yes, so many thanks."

The girl went up. He heard her footsteps above him. Then there was silence. He tossed in his bed all night.

The next day the two friends returned to the city. Before parting, Widow Chuang said, "You must come again." Li-hwa cast a lingering look at him.

Wu parted with his friend at the Chientang Gate, not daring to tell him what had happened between him and Li-hwa. He thought of her all the way. He was confused, but he knew he wanted to see her again. He said he had something to attend to at the gate and told his friend to go ahead. What Li-hwa had told him — that his wife was a ghost – was fantastic, but he was upset and hesitated to go home.

He recalled several instances, now, of Yonia's uncanny gift for reading his mind. Once he was writing a letter and, not finding any envelope in his drawer, was going to call for Chin-erh when he saw his wife standing before him, holding an envelope. He remembered also that one day he was thinking of going out to the streets after school, which he seldom did. It was raining. Exactly at half past four, his wife brought an umbrella and left it against the wall. He looked up, bewildered. "You are going out, are you not?" she asked, and went in. These might be natural coincidences, but the more he thought, the more he became frightened. He remembered how she did not permit him to say the word "devil" or "ghost" in the house, and how not only she, but Chin-erh, too, had an uncanny ability to locate things in the dark.

He decided to call on Wongpo and find out the past history of Yonia. When he arrived at her house, he saw the door sealed up by official order, with the words, "Human heart like iron; the emperor's law like fire." He made inquiries of the neighbors and was informed that Wongpo had been hanged six months ago for seducing young girls for illicit purposes.

Now he was thoroughly frightened. What Li-hwa had told him was true, then. His heart warmed at the thought of her. She was such a sweet girl. He kept thinking of her white face, her simplicity, her good cheer, and sense of humor. It would have been so much better if he had married her.

He must see Li-hwa and solve the mystery once and for all. But he also remembered what a good wife Yonia had been to him, and he was afraid of making a mistake. The longer he stayed away from home, the harder it was going to be for him to explain his absence. His mind was so confused that, after spending a night at the Chientang Gate, he did not get started toward the Tuohsienling till three o'clock in the afternoon. When he got into a boat, the thought of seeing Li-hwa already made him feel safer and better, and he could not wait to see her face and hear her voice again. The boat made slow progress against a steady head wind. Dark clouds formed in the northwest and it looked as if a June storm was coming up. When he looked up at the Western Hills, he saw the clouds covering their peaks. He had not brought an umbrella, but he was undeterred. He almost welcomed a storm, thinking it might relieve him of his mental oppression.

He knew the route well and had no difficulty in finding his way across the Tuohsienling. When he stood on top and looked down, his pulse quickened as he thought of Li-hwa's cottage by the brook. The sky had already darkened so that he could not judge the exact hour of the day but it must have been five or six o'clock already. The wind whistled through the bending forest. On the middle of the slopes, below the big rocks, stood a number of public and private cemeteries, old and new. He hurried down the steep stone steps which led to the bank below, partly from impatience and partly in the hope of reaching the wine shop for shelter before the storm broke.

Down on the level, he began to run. About a hundred yards from the wine shop, the storm caught up with him. Thunder cracked and lightning flashed, and big drops of rain the size of peas came pelting down. He noticed a small, solitary, square building nearby, which stood at the entrance of a cemetery, and quickly took shelter there. A sixth sense told him to bolt the door and he pulled the latch all the way back. We do not know how we sense these things, but he had a distinct feeling that he was the only human being in that valley. The June storms never lasted long and he was glad to keep himself dry until it was over.

When he had caught his breath a little, he saw some one push at the door. He held his breath.

"It is locked," said a girl's voice which sounded like Chin-erh's. "Shall we slip in through the chink?"

"He cannot get away anyway." It was his wife's voice. "Coming to see that little devil on such a day. Never mind, I will settle accounts with that wench first. If he escapes, time enough to deal with him when he comes home." He heard their withdrawing footsteps.

Wu was quaking all over. The first fury of the rainstorm had abated but the intermittent flashes of lightning illuminated the room as if to punctuate his misery. He went to the back of the room and saw it was an old public cemetery mostly consisting of ancient tombs. The tops of some mounds had fallen through, leaving gaping holes in the ground. Suddenly he heard a woman's terrible scream from the direction of the wine shop.

"Help! Help! Murder!"

All Wu's pores opened and his hair stood on end. There was a great cursing and swearing and screaming as if three or four women were fighting together. They were clearly female voices, but inhuman, ghostly, octaves higher than the human voice.

Wu saw the tall muscular shadow of a man jump over a hedge from the keeper's house into the graveyard, calling, "Chu Little Four! Do you hear the cry?"

A shabby figure with long unkempt hair crawled out from one of the graves. His back was bent and he was coughing hard. "That ghost looks as if he had died of asthma," thought Wu to himself.

"There's murder, let's go!" the tall figure shouted in the dark. The two ghosts dashed out like a gust of wind. In the drizzle he could hear the man's voice shouting, "Quiet! All of you! How can I hear you when four women start talking all at once?" Over and against it he heard distinctly — he was sure of it — Li-hwa's cries and moans. Soon the voices stopped and he heard the sound of beating and of chains dragging across the wooden bridge. The noises steadily approached. Wu was unnerved. His hands were clammy. They were coming toward the door.

There was a low wall, five feet high, around the cemetery. He could not see what was happening, but he heard a clank of chains and a thump on the outside. "Ai-yoh!" a woman's cry was heard. It was his wife's voice.

"Your face is not familiar," said the man's voice. "Why do you come here to disturb the peace? Don't you know better than to come to my territory?"

Whack! Whack! Yonia's ghost screamed.

"I came to find my husband," she said. "I trailed him here. He is somewhere around." It did not help Wu any in his hiding place. "Officer, we are properly married. He is bewitched by this girl. He came here on Dragon Boat Festival and has not returned home. I came out with my maid to look for him."

"I didn't do anything! I didn't do anything!" protested Li-hwa, still crying. Wu felt as if his heart would break. Even if she was a ghost, he loved her more than ever.

"Oh, yes, you did!" answered the angry wife. "You should be chopped to death with a thousand knives." It was as if she were tearing at Li-hwa's hair and Li-hwa screamed again.

"Stop it!" shouted the ghost keeper of the cemetery.

"We mother and daughter have been living peacefully." It was Widow Chuang's voice. "We have done no harm to anybody. This woman killed my daughter and would like to kill her again if you had not come."

"I know, I know," said the ghost officer. "Li-hwa is a good girl and a dutiful daughter. Even if she stole the affection of your husband, you should have come to me and not taken the law into your hands and tried to strangle her. You know it would not work. I shall have to report you for this. Where is your proper abode?"

"At the Paosu Pagoda."

"You say you are properly married. Who was the go-between?" asked the man ghost.

"Wongpo of Chientang Gate," his wife replied.

"Do not lie to me!" Whack! Whack!

"I am telling you the truth," pleaded Yonia pitifully.

Wu suddenly remembered that at any time he might be discovered. He pulled the bolt back silently and slipped out of the temple and began to run for his life. Luckily with the beating and crying of women, no one had heard him. He ran past the bridge, made for the banyan tree, and looked round. The wine shop was gone. On the spot where it had stood, he saw two tombs, but he was too afraid to stop and read the inscriptions.

A cold perspiration broke out all over his body. The more he ran, the more frightened he became. All around him were shadows in a valley of ghosts. He hazily remembered that the last time he and his friend had got out of the valley by following the stream. The road was dark and slippery. At the bend of the path he saw two women standing near a clearing in the woods. The old woman's red kerchief around her neck was clearly recognizable, and it would have been remarkable if the other woman's hair was not wet that night.

"Where are you going, running like this?" said Wongpo and Mrs. Chen the foster mother. "We have been waiting for you."

Frightened out of his wits, he ran again and he heard the women laughing after him.

He must have gone half a mile when he saw a light in the distance near the mouth of the valley. Never did a light look more comforting than it did that moment to Wu. As he approached, he saw it was a small wine shop with hardly any furniture in it. A gaunt couple, like skeletons, were sitting over a table under an oil lamp. The husband, a man over fifty, wore an apron smeared with blood like a butcher's.

Wu asked for a drink of wine. "Four ounces, and make it hot."

The man looked up without leaving his chair. "We serve only cold drinks here," he answered gruffly.

Wu realized he had run into another pair of ghosts. Without a second word he got up and ran. It was almost eleven o'clock when he reached the Chientang Gate. He went to a hotel restaurant and squeezed in a teashop downstairs as close to a table of six or seven men as he could.

"You look as if you had seen a ghost," remarked a fellow near him.

"Yes, I have. A whole pack of them."

He went home and found his door locked. He was afraid to go in and turned in the direction of the White Crane Pond. When he reached the house of his wife's foster mother, he found the door standing ajar. He went in. The appearance of the house had changed. Where there had been green curtains before, the windows were now empty, flapping lazily against the wall. Instead of the bright green, the paint had come off. He was beyond surprises now.

Having nowhere to go, he went into the nearest wine shop.

He gulped down a cup of wine. When he recovered a litt.c, he asked the waiter quietly if he knew anything about the deserted house.

"That house has been abandoned for over a year now. It is so haunted that nobody wants even to steal the furniture, and it's good wood, too."

"Haunted?" asked Wu, in a tone of affected incredulity.

"Yes. There used to be terrific noises inside at night. The sounds of footsteps thumped up and down the stairs as if some women had been chasing one another. Chairs flew and frying pans crashed. Some heard the screams of female ghosts. The noises always began at midnight, lasted a quarter of an hour and then stopped."

"Who lived in it?" asked Wu, honestly glad to hear the story, as if it were all news to him.

"The owner was a woman by the name of Chen," said the waiter. "She had a pretty foster daughter, whom people called Yonia. They were quite well-to-do. She was a wonderful flute player, and the third son of the imperial tutor Chin heard about her and offered a big sum of money to the foster mother and took her into his household. Then we heard that she had been thrown out of the house because she had killed a girl in a fight. She was expecting a child and came home and hanged herself. It seemed as if the two ghosts were fighting it over again every night. Yonia should have been satisfied because she was buried at Paoshu Pagoda with a complete set of musical instruments. After she died, the woman Chen was one day washing laundry by the pond and fell into the water and was drowned. It was a shame, for her body was hidden by the lotus leaves and was not discovered till two days afterwards. When she was hauled up, it was bloated and all covered with duckweed. Her own little girl — we called her Chin-erh — was left alone, crying day and night, until Mrs. Chen came and took her along."

"What do you mean by that?"

"Well, it was the first night that the neighbors heard

the female ghosts fighting in that house. The next day they found Chin-erh dead in her bed. She must have been frightened to death. You would not believe the story, would you? But it was true."

"Who said that I would not?" replied Wu enigmatically.

Wu decided that the capital was no place for a lone bachelor. Next day, he set out on his journey home.

10. JOJO

wwwwwwwwwwwwwwwwwwwwwwwwwwwwwwwwwwwwwwwwwwwwwwwwwww

From Liaotsai, *by P'u Sungling (1630-1715). About one third of the over 450 stories in* Liaotsai *have been translated by Professor Herbert A. Giles under the title* Strange Stories from a Chinese Studio. *Unfortunately, some of the best are not included. Readers who are interested may read "The Picture Horse" and "Laughing Girl," in that book. The original name of Jojo is "Hsiao Hsieh," which I have altered because it means so little to English readers.*

I DON'T believe in ghosts," said Tao, a young man of thirty and a recent widower. He spoke in a tone of cocky confidence. His friend Chiang who knew him quite well did not mind it at all. He knew Tao was eccentric and brilliant. Tao had come to ask if he could live in his friend's house. It was summer, and his own house, which consisted only of one room, a kitchen, and a very small garden, was hot and oppressive. Flies swarmed around the place. Chiang had a garden residence in the suburb which was cool and shaded, but which had been abandoned because it was haunted.

"Now look here," said Chiang with a kind smile, "worthless as you are, I love you too much to want you to risk your life. In two and a half years, three successive caretakers have died."

"It could be a coincidence."

193

"No, no, don't tell me that. One or two deaths could be a coincidence, but not three."

Tao produced from his pocket an essay, entitled "An Expansion on Yuan Chan's Theme Disproving the Existence of Ghosts."

"Read it," he said. "I have lived thirty years without seeing a ghost and, if there is one, I would love to meet her. The ghosts I read about are usually so charming anyway."

Chiang glanced at the paper. The gist of it was that there is an occult world of the spirits and a human world, and that the two worlds, while undeniably existing side by side, do not move in the same orbits. Practically considered, therefore, the question of the existence of ghosts is academic. Ghosts avoid the daylight and are as much afraid of men as men are of them. Something keeps them apart. Normal men leading a normal life do not see ghosts, and if some do, it is because they are mentally abnormal. Certainly some people have died of fright at seeing a ghost, but it was the fright, and not the ghost, which killed them. Or in the case of charming female ghosts, to whom so many handsome and strong men have succumbed and died, it was again the temptation in their own hearts which was their own undoing, and not the charming apparitions of women they saw in their heated imaginations. It is true that, while ugly, cruel, and vengeful ghosts are more frightening, the beautiful, charming devils in female form are more difficult to resist, and being gentle, soft, and seductive, are more deadly in the long run. If a man can conquer his own fear and his own carnal desires, no ghosts can do anything to him.

"Your handwriting is very fine. That is all I would say," said Chiang with a rueful smile, and handed the paper back to him. "I would not let you live in the house. It is a beautiful theory, but let us not argue about it."

"I am not arguing about it. I am trying to find a house to live in. My home is unbearable in this summer heat and I should appreciate enjoying the cool of your great mansion.

Perhaps I shall drive away the ghosts for you. Please say yes."

"All right, if you want to seek your own destruction. You are a strange man."

Tao was one of those young men who at thirty look as if they should be a success, but somehow are not. He dressed in good style, had a deep voice, and walked with a manly gait. It is difficult to account for his outward failure — he was unemployed; perhaps he could not stick to any one thing for long or settle himself down to a job. He had a charming air of nonchalance. He was avid for knowledge and was many-sided. He was poet, connoisseur, occultist, and amateur doctor in succession. He had delved into Taoist lore about the occult world and come out as a rationalist. In that occupation he had experimented, too, with the secret art of love, taught by the Taoists as a method of harnessing the sex force and building up an eternal flow of health to prolong life. He had had many experiences with women during this period and then had dropped them — as he had dropped many other things — as if he had come to his own conclusions about women. Chiang, the owner of the mansion and an official, liked and respected him. Tao had been once an overnight guest at the mansion when it was still occupied. At dinner, he talked and flirted gaily with the maids, but Chiang had occasion to find out later that when one of the maids went to him at night, she was repulsed. Chiang could not quite make out what sort of man Tao was.

One day at sundown Tao moved in. He did not admit to himself that he secretly desired to find and perhaps meet one of those pretty seductive creatures. He had brought twenty-odd volumes of books, and went back to fetch other personal things, but on his return, he found the books were gone. This puzzled him greatly. He went to the kitchen to prepare a light supper, and after supper, lay down on his couch, waiting to see what would happen.

A strange aura in the house made him feel uneasy. He kept very quiet and soon heard a rustle of curtains and feminine dress. His nerves became taut. Two feminine voices were heard in the next room. Raising himself a little, he looked in. The door opened gently and two pretty young girls, holding the volumes in their arms, came and laid them on his desk, arranged them nicely in order, and looked at him with amusement. They were obviously delighted with the presence of the guest.

"We have come to return your books," one of them said.

The elder one looked about twenty and had a long face, and the younger one, about seventeen or eighteen, was plumper and had a round face. The latter was a little shy and merely looked at Tao with appraising eyes, while the elder one walked to his bed, seated herself familiarly on the edge of it, and said, "I have never seen you before," smiling boldly at him. Tao stared at the two girls without a word. Then the elder one, placing one bent leg on the bed, moved closer to him and the younger one giggled. She wriggled her toes against Tao's body and her companion covered her mouth in laughter. Tao quickly sat up in a gesture of self-defense. Steady, he thought to himself. The girl brushed his hair back with her right hand, and with the fingers of her other hand lightly stroked his whiskers and patted his cheek with an artful, enticing smile.

Tao pulled himself together and shouted, "How dare you! Why don't you keep to yourselves, you ghosts!"

The two girls ran away, abashed. Tao blew out a deep breath. He realized he had asked for it. He was sure they would come again and he would not be able to sleep all night. He thought of moving right away, but felt it would be too embarrassing if his friend found out, and decided to stay. He would try to keep his presence of mind and control himself. The feeling of a strange presence remained in the room. He thought he saw moving shadows in the dark and heard whispers and tripping steps. It was the strangest experience of his life. Anybody else would have jumped out of bed, but Tao was a queer soul and rather delighted in it. He remembered what he had said about conquering fear, turned the lamp bright, and went to sleep.

The moment he had fallen asleep, he felt his nose itching. Some one had tickled him. He sneezed, and heard the sound of suppressed laughter somewhere in the room. He said nothing and pretended to be asleep. Out of his half closed eyes, he saw the younger girl crouching and moving slowly on her soft slippers. She was holding a paper rolled up into a thin point and approaching his bed. He sat up and shouted, "Go away!" and the shadow disappeared. He had not fallen asleep long before he jerked up again with some one tickling his ear. It was a restless night, to say the least, but his theory had worked so far. Only after the cock's crow did all disturbances stop, and he slept soundly till noon.

Nothing happened during the day. As soon as Venus appeared in the west and he lighted his lamp, he heard sounds again. He would hear light knocks at his door and would shout at the ghosts to go away. "Don't bother me, you ghosts!" But that did not stop them. The door would creak again and he would raise his head and see them peering at him. This happened several times. It was most distracting, and he decided to sit up all night. Ignoring their presence, he went out to the kitchen to make himself a pot of tea and get some cold meat. On coming back to his room, he found the girls standing over the table, looking at his books. Seeing him enter, they put the books back, wiped some dust off the table, and stood looking at him.

"Well, sit down, if you insist on keeping me company. But I have work to do. I have borrowed the house from the master and I intend to live here. Behave like good girls."

The girls obeyed him and loitered around, but now talked only in low whispers. Twenty minutes had passed when he saw a white arm resting on his table and felt a woman's hair brushing his cheek.

"What are you reading?" It was the elder girl.

"Leave me alone." He turned to her. She straightened

herself up and looked disappointed. "Leave me alone, will you?" he repeated more softly.

"Why are you working so hard?" the girl asked in evident disapproval. Tao did not reply, but his face showed that he did not mind their company. The younger girl now came and stood opposite him, pressing her body against the table. Her dark lashes were beautiful to see in the lamp light. She was quieter, but she had the look of a young girl who was deeply interested in a young man. Tao was quite moved. He pressed down his hands desperately on his book and tried to concentrate. Then the younger girl slipped behind him and covered his eyes with her hands. She touseled his hair and then ran away and laughed. He ran after her and, as he was reaching for her, he grasped his own hand.

"Now you charming ghosts," he said as he came back to his desk, "if I ever catch you, I will kill you!"

"You cannot!" shouted the younger one and laughed.

The girls would not go away, nor were they afraid of him.

"I know what you two want. I am afraid I cannot oblige you. No use tempting me." The girls only laughed again. Tao heard the night watchman striking the third watch.

"Are you hungry?" the elder one asked. "How about our making you something warm?"

"I do not mind."

The two ghosts trotted off to the kitchen and soon came back with a steaming hot bowl of congee. Tao looked up and said, "That is fine. Thank you, young ladies."

He saw that there was only one bowl and one pair of chopsticks.

"Are you not eating?"

"No."

"How can I thank you for your service?" he said, with real appreciation.

"You can thank me afterwards," replied the elder girl. "But be careful. I put arsenic in it." She gave him a wistful smile.

"You would not. Why should you want to poison me?"

Tao took up his chopsticks and finished his bowl, while the two girls stood ready, vying with one another for the chance to give him a second helping. Before he had quite finished, the younger one ran to the kitchen and brought him a hot towel.

While wiping his face with the towel, Tao said to the girls, "Thank you, young ladies. We might as well get acquainted, since it looks as if we are going to share the house for some time." He asked their names.

"My name is Autumn-Mien and my surname is Chiao," replied the elder one, and, pointing to her companion, "Her name is Jojo and her surname is Yuan."

"What a funny little name!" said Tao with a laugh. "Tell me about your family — your parents and grandparents."

"Why should you ask?" answered Jojo. "You are not going to marry us. You would not dare show yourself in bed with a woman. I do not think you can marry!"

"Now, young ladies, I must speak to you," replied Tao seriously. "I am not unconscious of your feminine charm. In fact, I rather like you both. But you are aware, I am sure, that a physical union with a being from the nether world is destructive to a man. I am not running away from you and intend to stay on. If you do not care for me, why should you want to sleep with me? And if you do love me, why should you want to cause my undoing? Listen, why can we not go on as we are, as friends?"

The girls looked at one another as if they were ashamed of themselves. They seemed quite moved.

"What you say is right. We like you, too. Let's be good friends," said Autumn-Mien.

They still made no move to leave him. "Why don't you go to sleep?" asked Tao.

"We sleep plenty in the daytime."

From that time on, they did not try to tempt him, or suggest carnal relations with him. Tao began to like their company and thought it not at all a bad arrangement. He would work at night with the girls for company, and sleep in the daytime.

One day he went out of the house, leaving some copying work unfinished. On his return he found Jojo sitting over his desk, trying to complete the work for him. On seeing him, she threw the brush down and looked up at him with a smile. Tao looked at it and was agreeably surprised to find that her handwriting, immature though it was, was quite good for a girl of her age.

"I did not know you could do this!" he exclaimed enthusiastically. "If you are interested, I shall be glad to teach you."

He made Jojo sit on his lap and enclosed her hand in his, trying to guide her wrist and fingers in the formation of characters. At this moment, Autumn-Mien walked in. There was a look of jealousy in her eyes when she found them in that position. Tao understood.

"I have not practiced the script since my childhood when my father taught me," explained Jojo. "I hardly know how to handle the brush now."

Autumn-Mien said nothing. Tao pretended not to notice anything and offered her his chair, saying to her, "You try. I would like to see what you can do."

Autumn-Mien sat down, wrote a few characters, and got up.

"They are wonderful," remarked Tao, trying to soothe her. Only then did she smile.

Tao then cut two pieces of paper, lined them properly in squares, and said, "Why don't you two take this seriously? You sit over there practicing your script, while I work here."

An extra lamp was brought in, and placed on another desk. It was a very good idea to find them something to do, leaving him free and undisturbed, and Tao was glad to see them so interested in their work. When they had finished, they brought their papers and stood before his desk, asking for his criticism.

Of the two, Jojo was the better educated, and Autumn-

Mien sometimes made characters with wrong strokes in them. She was conscious of her mistakes and felt ashamed. Tao was gentle with her and encouraged her.

The girls seemed to like this arrangement, too, and now treated him as their teacher, and were quite devoted to him. Like students at a private school, they fetched things for him, made tea, and cleaned his room. Their personal devotion included scratching his back for him and massaging his legs when he was tired, but everything remained on a platonic basis.

One day, Jojo presented some handscript which showed remarkable progress and received enthusiastic praise from the teacher. Suddenly he heard Autumn-Mien weeping over her desk. He went over to her, raised her tear-stained face, and patted her kindly. "She had a better start," he said to her. "You have to work harder. You are so intelligent, I am sure you will catch up with her in no time." Then Autumn-Mien was satisfied and smiled.

Autumn-Mien did very well indeed. There was no question but that she was doing her best to please her teacher. Whatever Tao said to her once, she would remember and take to heart. And so the room was transformed into a night school, filled with the sweet sounds of two girl students reading aloud. They went on from the elementary books to a classic, and before they had got through with the classic they asked to be taught the elements of versification. Jojo secretly asked Tao not to teach Autumn-Mien, and Tao promised. Autumn-Mien also asked him not to teach the secrets to Jojo, and he promised her, too.

Then it was October, the time for the local examinations. Tao prepared to leave, but Autumn-Mien said to him, "I see trouble ahead. Why do you not say you are sick and excuse yourself?"

"I must go," replied Tao. "My friends will laugh at me. It is a poor excuse."

Tao left, and as the girls predicted, he ran into trouble in

the city. Someone he had offended with his outspoken tongue
had him charged at court, arrested, and thrown into jail,
accused of misconduct with women and disgracing the
scholars' profession. Tao was at his wits' end. He knew that
he had in previous years been too free with women, but that
was years ago and he could not remember exactly what he
had done. He had no friends and no money and had to beg
for food from the jailor.

On the second night in jail, he was awakened from his
sleep to find Autumn-Mien standing before his bed, holding
a basket.

"Do not worry," she said. "Here is some food for you and
some pieces of silver from the jailor. I will get you out of this
at whatever cost."

He started to thank her, but the shadow disappeared.
That day, while the magistrate was passing through the
streets, a woman stopped his sedan chair and, kneeling before
it, presented a plea for Tao. It gave the details of the case,
showing that Tao had been falsely accused for private revenge, and it was signed by Autumn-Mien. The magistrate
accepted the plea, but when he wanted to question the person
who had submitted it, she disappeared in the crowd. He read
it and put it in his coat pocket but, on reaching home, found
it was gone.

The next day, Tao was summoned for trial. "I received
a plea for you yesterday," said the magistrate. "Who is Autumn-Mien? It is clearly a woman's name."

Tao pretended that he had never heard of such a person.

"What are you trying to hide from me?" said the magistrate in anger. "You are charged with philandering with
women. This seems to prove the charge of misconduct, unworthy of a scholar. I am going to — "

Suddenly the magistrate felt an acute shot, as if someone
had stuck an awl into his ear, and he left the sentence
unfinished.

"That was years ago, Your Honor," explained Tao.

"This is not all. As a Confucian scholar, you are also accused of studying Taoist black magic — "

Before the magistrate had finished his sentence, the clerks saw his face turn greenish pale, his breath became short, and the whites of his eyes rolled as if someone were trying to strangle him. Tao was amazed along with the rest. The magistrate put his hand across his forehead and complained of a splitting headache. His face was the color of water and he ordered the case postponed until further notice.

Next day the magistrate sent for Tao to have a personal talk with him. He told him that he had had a strange dream during the night in which a woman had appeared before him and spoken on Tao's behalf. He would dismiss him with a reprimand, and he urged him to reform. His tone was now courteous and he talked to him like a fellow scholar. He wanted to know who this Autumn-Mien was — was she a ghost?

"No, no," replied Tao. "I do not believe in ghosts." He went into the reasons why he did not believe that ghosts exist, mentioning the fact that he had, in fact, written an essay on this topic.

"On the contrary," said the magistrate, "I believe that they do exist."

Tao was happy to be released and said good-by. When he reached the haunted house, he found nobody at home. A little past midnight, Jojo and Autumn-Mien appeared, dragging their legs along and leaning on one another. Both of them limped. Jojo assisted Autumn-Mien to the bed and went to make a cup of tea for her.

"Autumn-Mein ran into such trouble," Jojo said with a sigh. Tao was informed that Autumn-Mein had been arrested by the City God on her way back for abusing her spiritual powers and interfering with the magistrate in the lawful execution of his duty. She had been thrown into the jail of the City God's court and subjected to considerable mistreatment by the little devils. Jojo had gone a long way to explain the case to the

City God, telling him that Autumn-Mein had done all this not for herself, but to help a poor scholar, and that he as the City God should be pleased that justice was done in his territory. Autumn-Mein was then released, but they had to walk thirty miles all night and their feet were blistered.

Happy now to be reunited with them, and deeply touched by what they had gone through for him, Tao felt a passionate love for them. He could not control himself and wanted to make love to them both.

"I do not care. I love you so. I do not mind death itself," said Tao, throwing all caution to the winds. But Autumn-Mein said to him, "Please, Mr. Tao. Once we had other intentions but you yourself opened our eyes. How can we bear to sacrifice you for our own gratifications?"

It seemed that after the trouble, during which the two girls had helped one another, Autumn-Mien and Jojo had forgotten their mutual jealousy entirely. A change had come over them. They no longer cared for their studies. They were as affectionate and devoted to him as before, and patted him and kissed him, but they denied him against his entreaties. On the other hand, they appeared in their pyjamas, were free and easy with him, and curled up in their seats as if no man were present. Living so intimately with girls whom he now loved so passionately, it was difficult for him to control his desire. He did not know what to do with himself.

"We love you too much," said the girls. "We will not do to you what we did to the three caretakers."

Tao's soul was in torment. "Then I must leave," he said.

The girls wept on hearing this, and Tao could not tear himself away. In desperation, he went to see a Taoist whom he had befriended before, and told him the whole story and the dilemma he was in.

"These, then, are good ghosts," said the priest. "You must be true to them. I will help you."

He gave Tao two pieces of paper with a magic formula written on them and instructed him as follows: "You take these home and give one to each girl. When they see a coffin pass by, they should put the piece of paper in a bowl of water and drink it and rush out. Whoever arrives at the coffin first will have the privilege of borrowing the body of the deceased and come back to life. It is a matter of luck who wins."

After a month or so, they heard a funeral procession passing by the house. Both girls rushed out, but Jojo dashed out without remembering to drink the charmed water first. She could do nothing and saw the wraith of Autumn-Mien disappear into the coffin. Sadly, Jojo turned back into the house, weeping.

Tao was watching outside the gate and saw what had happened. The family of the deceased girl saw a double enter the coffin and soon they heard a noise inside. In bewilderment, they ordered it opened, hoping to find the daughter of the family revived. The body in the coffin was breathing, at first feebly and then regularly, and the girl's eyes opened. In their joy, the Ho family quickly had her carried out of the coffin into the house and laid her on Tao's bed. She was white and plump and her voice was rounder than Autumn-Mien's. When they were ready to take her home, Miss Ho refused. She said to her parents, "I am Autumn-Mien. I am not your daughter." She looked at Tao, and although her face was different, she smiled at him, not as a stranger, but as a lover and old friend.

The parents were hardly prepared to believe what their daughter said, but the girl flatly refused to go home, and insisted on remaining where she was.

"I love him, Father, if you are my father," the girl said.

"If that is the case," said the father to Tao, "I shall leave my daughter with you. If she insists, I have no other course but to accept you as my son-in-law."

The funeral was canceled and the parents returned home. The next day they sent a personal maid who brought bedding and wedding gifts to the house. As Tao talked with the girl, he tried to get used to her appearance. But of course she was Autumn-Mien herself. Her smiles, and ways of talking and walking, all revealed it. They were happy together beyond words.

But on the wedding night, they were constantly distracted by a girl's weeping voice. It was Jojo, sulking in a dark corner by herself. Tao took the lamp and went to talk with her and tried to comfort her, but her dress was wet with tears and she would not be comforted. They were so troubled that they could not sleep that night.

The same thing happened the following night and for six or seven successive nights. Always they heard Jojo's weeping in a dark corner, and were unable to consummate their marriage. Tao and Autumn-Mien took great pity on her, but could only try and comfort her with words. Jojo seemed so lonely.

"Why don't you ask the Taoist again?" said Autumn-Mien. "He might be able to do something for her."

Tao went to the Taoist again and was told at first that nothing more could be done. Tao begged him and told him how pitiful it was to leave Jojo in that condition. If he saved one, he should save both.

"I am very sorry for her," said the priest. "I will use every means in my power. I will try, but I cannot guarantee success."

The priest came to the house with Tao and asked for a quiet room, where he could meditate and use his psychic powers. He told Tao to ask no questions and to leave him completely alone. For ten days and ten nights, he sat in that room without taking a drop of water. Tao peeped in and saw him sitting with his eyes closed and motionless, like one in sleep.

On the eleventh day before noon, a sweet young girl lifted the curtain and entered Tao's room. Her eyes glowed with a soft radiance as she said with a tired smile, "Oh, I am so exhausted after walking all night. I had to trudge over thirty miles before I found the house. The priest is following with her, and when they arrive my duty will be done."

Toward sundown, Jojo arrived. The girl who had been waiting rose to welcome her. As she embraced Jojo, the two became one and the girl fainted on the floor. Now the priest came out of his room, told Tao everything would be all right, and took his departure.

Tao sent the priest to the gate and on coming back to the room found that the girl had recovered sufficiently to open her eyes. He carried her and laid her on the bed. In a little while, she was completely well, and only complained that her legs were sore from the night's trip.

"Oh, I have come back to life!" said Jojo. She was so happy that she shed tears. She and Autumn-Mien talked as if they had known each other from childhood, now joined in their love for Tao.

Tao was very happy to live with his lovers who had now become normal, charming human beings. There might have been some question as to who should be the wife and who the concubine, but it was easily settled — for Autumn-Mien was older and the first to come back to life.

There was a classmate of Tao's by the name of Tsai Tse-ching who came to visit him one day on business. Tao asked him to stay for a few days, and he accepted. When Tsai saw Jojo he rushed quickly after her, but she ran away. She complained to Tao about the visitor's behavior. Tao was surprised, but he would not mention it.

Later in the day, his guest said to Tao, "I must speak to you about something which puzzles me greatly. It is most embarrassing, but with your permission, I would like to ask you a question."

"What is it?" asked Tao.

"I lost a sister about a year ago. On the second night of her death, her corpse mysteriously disappeared from her bed. It has remained a complete mystery to my family. I just saw a girl here who looks remarkably like her. Is she a relative of yours?"

Tao told him. He said that, as they were old classmates, he would be glad to introduce his concubine to him. He took his friend inside to meet Jojo and made Jojo put on the same dress in which she had come.

"Indeed, you are my sister!" Tsai exclaimed when he saw her. Tao had to explain how it had happened, and the friend said, "I must go home quickly to inform my mother that my sister has come back to life."

After a few days, Tsai's mother and family came to see Jojo and they recognized her as their daughter, even as the Ho family had recognized Autumn-Mien.

Juvenile

II. CINDERELLA*

The story is found in Yuyang Tsatsu, *by Tuan Ch'eng-shih who died in 863. Tuan was a zealous recorder of strange tales. Folklorists have studied the migration of this universally loved fairy tale, and it is interesting that the earliest record in writing of this tale is found in Chinese. This Chinese version has both the Slavonic feature of an animal friend and the Germanic feature of the lost slipper. Tuan recorded that this story was told him by his servant who came from the aboriginal tribes of Yungchow in modern Kwangsi. The earliest known European record of this story is by Des Perriers in his* Nouvelles récréations et joyeux devis, *published in 1558. Because of the historic interest of this piece, I have made here as exact a translation as possible.*

ONCE, before the time of Chin (222-206 B.C.) and Han there was a chief of a mountain cave whom the natives called Cave Chief Wu. He married two women, one of whom died leaving him a baby girl named Yeh Hsien. She was very intelligent and clever at working on gold and her father loved her dearly, but when he died she was maltreated by her stepmother who often forced her to cut wood and sent her to dangerous places to draw water from deep wells.

One day, Yeh Hsien caught a fish more than two inches long with red fins and golden eyes and she brought it home

*Reprinted from *The Wisdom of China and India* by courtesy of Random House, Inc. Copyright, 1942, by Random House, Inc.

and placed it in a basin of water. Every day it grew bigger and bigger until the bowl could not hold it any longer, and she placed it in a pond back of her home. Yeh Hsien used to feed it with what she had saved from her own food. When she came to the pond, the fish would rise to the surface and pillow its head on the bank, but if anyone else came to the water's edge it would not appear.

This curious behavior was noticed by the stepmother who often waited for the fish, but it would never come up. One day she resorted to a ruse and said to the girl, "Are you not tired from work? I will give you a new jacket." Then she made Yeh Hsien take off her old clothing, and sent her off to a distance of several hundred *li* to draw water from another well. The mother then put on Yeh Hsien's dress, and hiding a sharp knife in her sleeve, went to the pond and called to the fish. When the fish put its head out of the water, she killed it. The fish was by that time over ten feet long, and when it was cooked, it tasted many times better than any other fish. And the mother buried its bones in a dunghill.

Next day, Yeh Hsien came back, and when she arrived at the pond, she saw that the fish was gone. Thereupon she wept until a man with disheveled hair, dressed in a ragged garment, descended from the sky and comforted her, saying, "Do not cry. Your mother has killed the fish, and its bones are buried under a dunghill. Go home and carry the bones to your room and hide them. Whatever you shall want, pray to them and your wish will be granted." Yeh Hsien followed his advice, and it was not long before she had gold and jewelry and finery of such costly texture that they would have delighted the heart of any young maiden.

The night of the Cave Festival Yeh Hsien was told to stay at home and watch the fruit orchard. When the lonely girl saw that her mother had gone a long distance, she arrayed herself in a green silk jacket and went to the festival. Her sister who had recognized her said to the mother, "Is that girl not strangely like my elder sister?" The mother also seemed to recognize her. When Yeh Hsien became aware of their glances she ran away, but in such haste that she dropped one of her slippers, which fell into the hands of the cave people.

When the mother came back home, she found her daughter sleeping with her arms around a tree. She put aside any suspicions she may have had about the identity of the finely dressed girl.

Now near the caves there was an island kingdom called T'o Huan. Through its strong army, it ruled over twenty-four islands, and its territorial waters covered several thousand *li*. The cave people therefore sold the slipper to the T'o Huan Kingdom, where it found its way to the king. The king made the women of his household try it on, but the slipper was an inch too short even for those who had the smallest feet. Then he had all of the women of the kingdom try it, but the slipper would fit none of them.

The king suspected the cave man of getting the slipper from dubious sources and imprisoned and tortured him. The unfortunate man could not tell where the shoe came from. Finally it was placed by the roadside and couriers were sent from house to house to arrest anyone who had the other slipper. The king was greatly puzzled.

All houses were searched and Yeh Hsien was found. She was made to put the slippers on, and they fitted her perfectly. She then appeared in her slippers and her green silk dress, looking like a goddess. Then a report was made to the king, and the king brought Yeh Hsien to his island home, together with her fishbones.

After Yeh Hsien had left the cave, the mother and sister were killed by flying stones. The cave people pitied them and buried them in a pit, erecting a tomb which they called "The Tomb of Regretful Women." The cave people worshiped them as the goddesses of matrimony, and whoever asked them a favor regarding marriage was sure to have her prayer granted.

The king returned to his island and made Yeh Hsien his first wife. During the first year of their marriage, he asked the fishbones for so many jades and precious things that they refused any longer to grant his wishes. He then took the bones and buried them close by the sea, with a hundred bushels of pearls, lined with a border of gold. When his soldiers rebelled against him, he went to the spot, but the tide had washed them away and they have never been found to this day.

This story was told me by an old servant of the family, Li Shih-yuan. He comes from the cave people (aboriginal tribesmen) of Yungchow, and remembers many strange stories of the South.

12. THE CRICKET BOY

~~~~~~

From Liaotsai, by P'u Sungling. (See note for Jojo, No. 10.)

WHEN Kiti, a boy of eleven, came home with his father after a day's fruitless search for crickets, he had a most wonderful feeling — the discovery of his father as a play companion. Kiti was an extremely impressionable child. Once, when he was five, his father held a stick to punish him for something, and Kiti's face turned so pale with fright that his father let the stick drop out of his hand. He had always had a great fear of his father, a taciturn man of forty-five.

He was small for his age, about the size of other children of nine or ten, and the jacket which his mother had made for him a year ago, thinking he would grow up quickly, still seemed ample and long. His slim, childish figure was accentuated by a disproportionately large head and a pair of big, black, playful eyes and plump round cheeks. He jumped and skipped, rather than walked normally, and he was still very much a child in his emotions. When his brother was Kiti's age, he was already a great help to his mother, but not Kiti. Now the brother was dead and his only sister was married into a family in another town. Kiti was perhaps pampered by his mother, a sad but strongly built woman, who could be made to smile only by Kiti's unusual pranks and wiles. He still retained many childish ways in his looks and smiles, and in the intense joys and sorrows of childhood.

215

Kiti loved crickets as only boys can love, and, with a child's keen enthusiasm and poetic imagination, he found in the beauty and delicacy of the insect something utterly perfect, noble, and strong. He admired the cricket's complicated mandibles and thought that no animal of a larger size in this world had such a lacquered, armored body and legs. He thought that if an animal the size of a dog or pig had such a beautiful outfit — no, there was no comparable animal. Crickets had been his passion since his early childhood. Like all village children, he had played with them and had come to know the worth of a cricket by the sound of its creak, the size and angle of its legs, and the proportion and shape of its head and body. There was a northern window in his room, adjoining a back garden, and as he lay in bed listening to the song of the crickets, it seemed to him the most pleasing music in the world. It represented to him all that was good and strong and beautiful in this world. Confucius and Mencius he learned quickly from his teacher, who was now his own father, and forgot just as quickly; but this song of the crickets he understood and remembered. He had heaped a pile of bricks and stones under the window for the purpose of attracting them. No grown-up seemed to understand this — certainly not his cold and severe father — but today for the first time, he had come out with Kiti and run over the mountainside to look for a champion fighter.

There had been a memorable incident when Kiti was six. He had brought a cricket to the classroom, and the teachers discovered it and crushed it. Kiti was so furious that when the teacher turned his back, Kiti leaped from his chair, saddled on his back and pummeled the teacher with all the strength of his small fists, to the amusement of the students, until the teacher had to shake him down.

That afternoon, he had watched his father silently making a hand net with a bamboo handle for catching crickets. When the net was made, his father had said to him, "Kiti, bring that bamboo box. We will go to the southern hills." It was beneath the scholar's dignity to announce that he was going to catch crickets.

But Kiti understood. He went out with his father and felt as if he were on a New Year holiday. It was like an answer to a child's prayer. He had gone out to catch crickets, but had never had the luxury of a proper net. Furthermore, he had never been allowed to go to the southern hills, about a mile and a half away, where he knew there were plenty of crickets.

It was July and the day was hot. The father and child, net in hand, ran all over the foothill slopes, making their way through thickets, jumping over ditches, turning over and peeping under stones, listening for that most important sound, the clear, metallic chirp of a good champion. They had found no worthy champion, but they had found each other as companions. That was a wonderful new sensation for Kiti. He had seen his father's eyes shine when they heard a clear, sharp note, and heard him curse under his breath when they lost one in the underbrush. On their way back, his father was still uttering sighs of regret over missing the beautiful one. For the first time, his father had become human, and he loved his father then.

His father had not bothered to explain why he suddenly took an interest in crickets, and Kiti, though secretly delighted, saw no reason to ask. But when they got home he saw his mother standing at the door, waiting for them to return for supper.

"Did you catch any?" asked his mother anxiously.

"No!" The father's reply was solemn and heavy with disappointment.

Kiti wondered greatly about it. That night he asked his mother, when they were alone, "Tell me, Mother, does Father love crickets, too? I thought I was the only one."

"No, he does not. He has to do it."

"Why? For whom?"

"For the emperor. Your father is the head of the village.

He received an order from the magistrate to catch a good fighter. Who dares disobey the emperor?"

"I do not understand." Kiti was still more puzzled.

"Nor do I. But your father has to catch a good one within the next ten days, or he will lose his job and be fined. We are too poor to pay, and he may have to go to jail if he fails."

Kiti gave up trying to understand and asked no more questions. He only knew that it was something of terrible importance.

At this time, there was a great craze for cricket fights among the ladies of the court, with heavy betting going on, and culminating in the annual mid-autumn championship contests. It was perhaps an old tradition at the court, for the last premier of Sung Dynasty was known to have been watching his cricket fights when the armies of Genghis Khan marched into the capital. The district of Hwayin where Mr. Cheng lived was not known for producing the best fighters, but a year ago, an alert magistrate of the province had obtained a good champion and sent it to the court. A prince had written a letter to the governor of the province asking him to send more champions for the annual mid-autumn contest, and the governor had issued an order to all his magistrates to send their choicest selections from the districts to him. What had been a private request from a prince had become an edict of the emperor, as far as the common people were concerned. The price of good crickets skyrocketed and one magistrate was known to have offered as much as a hundred dollars for a good champion. Cricket fights had also become a popular pastime among the local people, and those who had champions were reluctant to part with them for any price.

Some heads of villages had taken the occasion to extort money from the people to buy crickets for the emperor, calling it the "crickets' levy." Mr. Cheng could have collected one or two hundred dollars from the villagers, pocketed half of it, and with the other half bought a cricket from the town. He, however would do nothing of the kind. If it was his duty to submit a champion, he would go and catch it himself.

Kiti shared his father's anxiety and felt important because his child's pastime had now become a dignified, grown-up affair. He watched his father's expression, as they were taking a rest in the cool shade. His father took out his pipe, lighted it, and his eyebrows danced a little as he puffed. He seemed to want to say something but paused and puffed away at his pipe, opened his mouth and then stopped to puff again. Finally, he said with an almost guilty expression on his face, "Kiti, you can catch a good champion for me. It is worth a lot of money."

"How, Father?"

"You see, son, there is a national championship at the imperial palace on mid-autumn festival. The winner will be awarded a big prize by the emperor."

"Really — by the emperor himself?" exclaimed Kiti. "Does the emperor love crickets, too?"

"Yes," replied the father reluctantly, as if a shameful confession had been forced from his lips.

"Hey, Father, we might catch a good fighter and win the national championship!" Kiti was greatly excited. "Will you be able to see the emperor?"

"No, I will send the cricket through the magistrate, and then through the governor, if it is good enough. It has got to be good. There is a big award in silver for the champion owner."

"Father, we will catch one, and we will be rich!"

It was difficult to repress the child's enthusiasm. But the father, having told him an important secret, looked serious once more. They got up and continued the search. Kiti now felt it was his responsibility to catch a champion fighter for his father, and for his mother as well because he had often heard her complain about being poor.

"I will catch one and fight and fight till we win," said the child.

The father was now glad that Kiti knew so much about

crickets and was able to help him. For three days, they could
not find a champion, but on the fourth day, they had a streak
of good luck. They had gone over the top of the hill and
descended on the farther side where there was a deep thicket
and heavy underbrush. Far down the slope was an ancient
tomb site. The outline of the tomb, some fifty feet across,
was clearly visible. Kiti suggested going down to the tomb
where they might catch some good crickets, especially because
the sand there was reddish yellow. They followed a small brook
and reached the site where a great many stone slabs lay about,
showing the outlines of the ancient tomb. Their hope was
justified The crickets were singing on that July afternoon,
not a few, but dozens of them in concert. Kiti's senses were
sharpened. A frog suddenly leaped from the grass under
his feet and disappeared into a hole, from which sprang out
a big, beautiful insect, hopping away in long, powerful
strides. The big cricket disappeared into an underground
hole protected by stone slabs. The father and son crouched
down and listened with bated breath to the rich, resonant
chirp. Kiti took a long blade of grass and tried to stir the
insect out of the hole, but it stopped its singing. They were
sure now that the prize champion was in that hole, but the
crack was too small even for the child's small hands to reach
down through it. The father tried to smoke it out without
success. Then Kiti went to fetch some water to pour down
the hole, while the father held the net in readiness outside
the entrance.

In a few seconds, the cricket sprang neatly into their net.
He was a beauty, of the kind called "blackneck," with wide
jaws, slender body, and powerful legs bent at a high angle.
His whole body was of a fine and deep reddish-brown lacquer
finish. Their labor was rewarded.

They returned home happily and placed their prize in an
earthen jar on a table in the father's room, carefully covered
with a sheet of copper wire netting. Mr. Cheng would take
it to town the next day to present it to the magistrate. He

instructed his wife to guard it carefully against neighbors' cats, and he went out to get some chestnut meat to feed it. Nobody was to touch it while he was away.

Kiti was excited beyond measure. He could not help coming into the room to listen to the insect's chirp and stare at it in sheer joy.

Then a tragedy happened. There was for a time no noise whatever in the jar. Kiti tapped it and still there was no sign of a movement. The cricket was apparently gone. He could not see into the dark jar, so he took it near the window and removed the wire net slowly to look when out hopped the cricket and landed on a book shelf. Kiti was desperate. He closed the window quickly and started to chase the insect around the room. In his excitement he neglected to use the net, and by the time he had caught the cricket under his palm, he had crushed its neck and broken one of its legs.

Kiti was pale with terror. His mouth was dry and he was without tears. He had destroyed what had promised to be a national champion.

"You accumulated debt of ten generations!" scolded his mother. "You are going to die! When your father returns, I do not know what he will do to you!"

Kiti's face was deathly white. He finally broke into sobs and ran away from the house.

At supper time Kiti still had not returned. His father was enraged and mortified, and threatened to give him a sound thrashing when he returned. The parents thought that he was hiding away, afraid to return, but believed that he would come home when he was hungry.

Toward ten o'clock, there was still no sign of Kiti, and the anger of the parents had turned into anxiety for him. They went out with a lantern into the night to search for him; and toward midnight they found Kiti's body at the bottom of a well.

When the child was brought out, he was apparently lifeless. There was a big wound on his head, but a trickle of fresh blood was still oozing from a cut on his forehead. It was a shallow well, but his whole body was drenched. They dried him and bandaged him, laying him on the bed, and were glad to find that his heart was still beating. Only a feeble breath indicated that the child was still alive. The shock was apparently so great that Kiti remained unconscious for a whole day, hovering between life and death. That evening they heard him mumbling in his sleep, "I have killed the champion — the blackneck, the blackneck!"

The next morning, Kiti could take some soup, but he was a changed child. All life seemed to have gone out of of him. He could not recognize his father and mother. His sister, hearing of the incident, came to visit him, and he made no sign of recognition. An old doctor told them that he had been badly frightened and that his illness was too deep to be cured by medicines. The only coherent words Kiti said were, "I have killed him!"

Happy that Kiti was at least alive, and hopeful of an eventual recovery, Mr. Cheng remembered that he had still four more days in which to catch another fighter. He had a faint hope that if he could catch a good one and show it to Kiti, it might help to cure him. After all, there were plenty of crickets in the ancient tomb site. He slept lightly and at dawn he heard a chirp in his house. He got up and traced the sound to the kitchen, where he saw a small cricket resting high up on the wall.

A strange thing now happened. As the father stood looking at it, he thought how small and probably useless it was for such a loud chirp. But with three loud chirps the little one hopped down onto his sleeve, as if asking to be caught.

The father captured it and examined it slowly. It had a long neck and a plum-flower design on its wings. It might be a good fighter, but it was so small. He would not dare to offer it to the magistrate.

A neighboring young man had a local champion which had won every bout in the village. He had put a high price on it, but he had found no buyer, so he brought it to Mr. Cheng's house, intending to sell it to him.

When Mr. Cheng suggested a match, the young man took a look at the little cricket and covered his mouth in laughter. The two insects were placed inside a cage, and Cheng felt ashamed of his cricket and wanted to withdraw. The young man insisted on a fight to show his insect's prowess, and Cheng, thinking it would be no great sacrifice if the little one should be killed or maimed, yielded. The two insects now stood facing each other inside a basin. The little one stood still while the big one opened its fangs and glowered as if eager for combat. The young man teased the little one with a pig's bristle to provoke it, but it remained unmoved. Again he prodded it, repeatedly, and suddenly the little fellow sprang into action, and the two insects fell at each other. In an instant, they saw the small cricket tilt its tail, raise its feelers, and with a powerful leap, sink its jaws into the opponent's neck. The young man quickly lifted the cage and called the fight off in the hope of saving his pet. The little cricket raised its head and chirped triumphantly.

Cheng was greatly pleased and amazed, but while he was admiring his new find, along with his family, a cock came along unnoticed by them, and pecked at the prize. The little cricket hopped away, chased by the cock, and in immediate reach of its claws. Cheng thought all was lost. Then he saw the cock shaking its head repeatedly, and observed that the little cricket had perched safely on the cock's neck and was harassing it from that position. They were all astounded and delighted.

Now confident of the little cricket's fighting power, Cheng decided to present it to the magistrate, telling him the story. The magistrate was far from impressed and was very skeptical, but he gave the insect a trial. The cricket won every fight over others collected in his office. He tried it again on a cock, and the little "plum-flower-wing" repeated his tactic of landing on the cock's neck, to everybody's astonishment. Satisfied with the district champion, the magistrate put it in a copper-wire cage and sent it to the governor. It was already the last day of July, and he dispatched it on horseback.

The father waited and hoped; one cricket had brought on his son's illness, another one might cure him. Then he heard that the little cricket had become the provincial champion, and his hopes went higher. It would take probably a month before he heard the results of the national championship match.

"Huh!" said Kiti's mother to her husband when she was told of the little cricket's fighting tactics. "Is it not just like Kiti riding on the teacher's back and pommeling him from behind?"

Kiti did not recover from his shock. Most of the time he was asleep and his mother had to force food down his mouth with a spoon. The first few days, his muscles twitched and he perspired heavily. The doctor came again and after hearing the symptoms announced that Kiti had burst his gall bladder in fright, and said that his *yang-yin* system of internal secretions had turned backwards. His three spiritual and seven animal spirits had been frightened away. It would take a long and slow cure to restore his vitality.

After three days, Kiti suffered another fit of paroxysms. Then his head seemed clearer for a day — it was the last day of July, his mother remembered clearly — and he could even smile when he said to his mother, "I have won!" His eyes stared vacantly.

"You have what?"

"I have won."

"Won what?"

"I do not know. I must win." He seemed to be still in a delirium.

Then his spirit left him again, and he fell into a profound coma for half a month.

At dawn, on the morning of August the eighteenth, Kiti's mother heard him calling, "Mother, I am hungry!"

It was the first time Kiti had called his mother since the incident. She jumped out of bed, called her husband, and they went in together to see their boy.

"Mother, I am hungry."

"My darling child, you are well again!" The mother wiped her eyes with the hem of her jacket.

"How are you feeling?" asked the father.

"I am feeling fine, Father."

"You have slept a long time."

"Have I? How long?"

"About three weeks. You scared us."

"Was it that long? I did not know anything. Father, I did not mean to hurt that champion. I was trying to capture him for you." Kiti's voice was perfectly normal, and he spoke as if the incident had happened only a day ago.

"Do not worry, Kiti," said the father. "While you were ill, I caught a better champion. He was small, but a terribly good fighter. The magistrate accepted it and sent it to the governor. I hear that he has won every fight."

"Then you have forgiven me?"

"Of course I have. Do not worry, son. That plucky little fighter may be a national champion yet. Now put your mind at rest, and soon you will be able to get up."

The family was happy once more. Kiti had a good appetite and only complained that his thighs were sore.

"That is very strange," said his mother.

"I feel, Mother, as if I had run and jumped hundreds of miles."

His mother massaged his legs, while Kiti kept on saying that his thighs were stiff.

In a day, Kiti was able to get up and walk a few steps. On the third day after his recovery, father, mother, and the boy were sitting by the lamp after supper, eating chestnuts.

"This is like the chestnut meat I had at the palace," Kiti remarked casually.

"Where?"

"At the imperial palace," Kiti replied, not knowing how strange his words must have sounded in his parents' ears.

"You must have been dreaming."

"No, Mother, I was there. Now I remember. All the ladies were dressed in red and blue and gold, when I came out of my golden cage."

"Did you dream that when you were ill?"

"No, it was true. Believe me, Mother, I was there."

"What did you see?"

"There were men with long beards and there was one I thought must be the emperor. They had come to see me. I only thought of father and said to myself that I must win. When I was let out of the cage, I saw a big fellow. He had very long feelers and I got frightened, until the fight started. Night after night, I fought with only one idea that I must win for Father. On the last night, I met a redhead. He was fearful to look at. I was not afraid any more. I went at him, but when he came at me, I leaped away. I was in perfect form and felt very light and alert. I tore at his tail and bit off one of his front legs. He got mad and came at me with open fangs. I thought I was done for, but I bit him somewhere. Then he became confused. I saw his eye was bleeding. I sprang on his neck and finished him."

Kiti told all this so realistically that his parents listened in silence, knowing that he was perfectly sincere in describing what he had seen in his dreams.

"And you have won the national championship?" asked the father.

"I think I did. I wanted to so much. I only thought of you, Father."

The parents did not know whether to believe his story or not. The child was not lying, they knew. They would wait and see.

The little cricket, sent in a golden cage by the imperial system, had reached the capital just one day before the contests began. The governor was risking a great deal in submitting such a small cricket to the prince. If the insect gave a good account of itself, well and good, but if it failed, he stood a chance of being ridiculed for being in his dotage. He trembled at the thought. The official document of three thousand words accompanying the cricket was something unusual, both apologetic and bombastic at the same time.

"My friend is mad," said the prince, after reading his letter.

"Why not give it a trial?" remarked his wife, the emperor's daughter.

The plucky little fighter fought with supercricket powers. As far as they could see, he had shown no fear when put in a basin opposite the other provincial champions.

After the first night in which he felled a champion almost twice his size, the little plum-flower-wing was regarded as a marvel and became the talk of the court.

Night after night, the little one won. It was true that he had the advantage of lightness and agility. While no champion could get at him, he always harassed the big fellows by his lightning attacks and bit the opponent here and there before he came in with deadly accuracy for a crushing bite. His accomplishments seemed incredible.

The contests lasted five nights from August fourteenth to August eighteenth. On the last night he became the champion. The next morning, the little champion had completely disappeared from his cage.

When the news reached Kiti's family, the father wept, and they were all overjoyed. The father put on his best gown and took Kiti along to the magistrate. He was told that he would be made an honorary member of the district college with monthly stipends for his support.

The family fortunes turned, and Kiti eventually was able

to go to college. Kiti not only felt embarrassed to have his story told, but he stopped watching cricket fights altogether. He could not stand it.

Later he became a *hanlin* and was able to support his parents in ease and comfort in their old age. Mr. Cheng, now a proud grandfather, never tired of telling the story of his son, which grew better and better every time, and he always ended with the words, "There are many ways of showing filial piety. When one's heart is good, the spirits of heaven and earth will show mercy to them that love their parents."

Satire

13. THE POETS' CLUB

~~~~~~

From T'aip'ing Kwangchi, No. 490. The story was written by Wang Chu (997-1057). Wang was a many-sided scholar who lived in the beginning of the Sung Dynasty, and the decline of Tang poetry in his time may be the reason for this whimsical satire upon the latter-day poets. I have necessarily rewritten the story, for the verses written by the animals would have little meaning in translation I have been compelled to translate the names of the poets into English, for the names in the original contain hints as to the true character of the poets.

FOUR YEARS AGO, I was stopping at Yungyang when I ran into an old friend of mine, Mr. Cheng. He was on his way back from the capital to his home in Pengcheng, and we spent a few days together. He was a very witty fellow, besides being a poet, and in the course of our conversations, he told me one of the funniest and strangest experiences he had ever had. Just how much of it was true and how much he added to it to make it more interesting, I do not know, but he swore to me that it had happened to him just a month before. Mr. Cheng told me the story in these words, as near as I can remember.

It was November the eighth. I had been far up to the northwest, and had not been there a day before I heard of my mother's illness and had to break off the journey and start home at once. On the second day, I arrived at Weinan in the afternoon. The weather had turned suddenly very cold, as if it was going to snow. The magistrate, Mr. Li, whom I know, asked me to stop for a few drinks. It must have been about midafternoon, and I told my servant to go ahead with the luggage and wait for me in the next town. It was not such a great distance, and I had a good horse and expected to get there by myself probably before midnight.

It began to snow and my friend asked me to stop overnight. I did not particularly care for the place, so I told him I was in a hurry to get home and insisted on leaving. When I got outside the city, there was a whirling mist of snowflakes which filled the sky and blinded my eyes. My horse's black mane was peppered with white flakes. I had to go slowly and met few passengers on that road leading toward Chihshui. It was getting dark by the time I got to Tungyang where I had a light supper at the relay station, and proceeded on my way.

With the countryside blanketed in white, and the diffused light of the moon hidden behind soft cloud masses, the world lay before me in all the beauty of a wintry landscape, like a realm of eternal twilight. I had had a drink at the station and felt warm and comfortable, but the animal seemed to feel the eerie effect of the strange light and pawed and whinnied, as if he had been ghosts. The snow thickened and confused my vision. I turned the ear flaps of my hat down and kept my eye on the road, for fear of getting lost. I could not have gone much farther than a mile from the relay station when the land began to slope toward a valley. A little distance away I saw an old temple. I gave up the idea of reaching the next town and headed toward the temple to seek shelter for the night. Horses, as you know, are timid animals, and they have a sixth sense that we humans lack. When I tied my horse to a tree in the front yard of the temple, he began to buck. His eyes were distended and his nostrils quivered, and it was with some difficulty that I was able to calm him.

"Is there anyone in?" I called aloud, as I went into the temple. It was dark inside and apparently deserted.

No one answered. I went around the altar to peer into the inner court, and saw a dim oil lamp shining inside.

"Is anyone in?" I called out loud again.

An old monk with a hunched back, which stuck up beneath his light-brown cloak came to the door. "Come in," he said. I walked across the yard. The poor monk was very old. His lower eyelids hung loosely. The hump on his back forced him to stretch his neck to keep his head level. This, and the way he tilted his chin up to survey me gave him a queer, almost comical effect, like an old person peering down at a child over his spectacles. He had evidently been expecting some guests, for when I went in, he took me for an old friend and remarked, "Mr. Chu (Hogg) is already here."

I quickly explained that I was a traveler caught in the snowstorm and would appreciate if he would give me shelter for the night.

"Where are you going in this storm?"

"To my home in Pengcheng."

"You evidently are a scholar," said the monk, surveying me over his upturned nose. "We are having a meeting of a few friends tonight, and if you wish, you may sit in with us. Are you a poet, too?"

"I write verse," I answered politely.

"That is excellent. We shall be honored to have you with us."

I was surprised that there should be a gathering of poets in such an out-of-the-way place and on such a night, too. I did not know till later that it was a small, exclusive group, known only to themselves, and making up a special cult with the avowed purpose of pushing out frontiers for a new kind of poetry. Each of them had given earnest, through his poetical compositions, of being launched, in his opinion at least, on the road to immortality.

In one corner of the room sat a big-bellied gentleman, too comfortable or too careless of convention to get up when I entered. His name has already been mentioned as Mr. Hogg.

"This is Mr. Cheng, Mr. Hogg," said the monk in the brown cloak. "He is traveling home and he is a poet, too. I have asked him to join us."

Mr. Hogg looked up from his spectacles and made a gesture to rise.

"Please do not get up. Glad to meet you."

I liked him. He was a short, stout man, with lumps of fat under his chin and shiny white, stubby fingers were locked across his chest.

"I have not the honor of knowing *your* name," I said, turning to the host.

My name is Frederick Dromedary Humphrey," he replied in an extremely heavy, low voice, somewhat sententiously.

I could see that his brown robe was much too ample for his shrunken frame. He must have been quite tall in his youth, for when he sat — crouched would be a better word — on his seat, I could see his long, gangling legs.

"We call him Humphs," interposed Hogg and laughed throatily.

"What is your grand age?" I asked him.

"I am eighty now. I have traveled a great deal in my time, as you are doing. I could go for days, hundreds of miles at a stretch, without food and without fatigue. Now these joints of mine are getting stiff." He showed me that he had a rheumatic knee which troubled him a great deal on cold, wet nights. His words were disjointed and he seemed to be ruminating over the past. Then he said abruptly, "I wonder why Professor Pine is not here yet. He is usually the first to arrive."

"Who is this Professor Pine?" I asked, as I was interested to know the gentlemen I was going to meet.

"Professor Porter Q. Pine, his name is," said the monk. "He

will be here in a minute. He is our great critic. Perhaps the
storm is delaying him. Come and sit near the fire."

The host, old as he was, was quite an amiable fellow. He
turned his long neck slowly and constantly toward the yard
to watch for the expected guests. I admired the old man's
spirit, for his eyes shone when the subject of poetry was mentioned. He told me that he was a great admirer of Chia Tao,
perhaps because the latter, too, was a monk.

I sat beside Hogg, and I learned that he lived on a farm
with his progeny. From the way he talked about his children,
I gathered that he was very much of a family man.

Soon we heard the sound of wooden clogs across the
front yard, and a lively energetic voice called, "Bahoo! Bahoo!
Here I am!" A jolly young man, with a rather thin, bony face
and an old gray blanket thrown around his shoulders, almost
danced into the room.

"I trudged and trudged the tortured miles," he repeated.
"What do you say of that?" He threw his blanket on a bench
and danced to the edge of the fire. "Phew, what a night!"
he said, blowing out a long breath.

"Let me introduce you," said Humphrey. "This is Mr.
Donald Key — Don for short. He is our most original and most
promising poet."

"Pleased to meet you." As he greeted me, he grinned and
showed his white teeth. His face and grin were almost face-
tious. His stiff black hair and stiff neck gave him the appearance of great vitality, but his long narrow face could hardly
be called handsome. He turned to Hogg immediately, calling
the latter by his first name, "Swiney, what do you say to this
line of mine:

> I trudged and trudged the tortured miles,
> Lonely, sad and depressed."

"Tolerable, tolerable," grunted Hogg good-humoredly. "I
grant you a certain smooth rhythm, that is all."

"Don, I am not impressed either by your sadness or your state of depression, to judge from your present appearance," said a thin squeaky voice from a dark corner.

"Why, Professor! When did you come in? I did not know you had arrived," said the monk. Both Hogg and I turned our eyes toward the dark corner where a short, small man sat huddled in his seat, two little bright eyes shining against the light.

"There is an apparent discrepancy between your professed state of loneliness and dejection — no, depression is the word you use — and your present exhibition of exuberant jollity, don't you think?" continued the professor.

"Why, Porter," said the monk. "You always creep in so noiselessly."

"It is not my habit to dance on clogs and make my entree with a lot of noise, like our dear Don."

I looked carefully at the small, cranky professor. He was carelessly dressed, but his eyes shone with great intellectual fervor, an impression heightened by his shaggy, bristly hair which fell over his shoulders. His whole appearance suggested tremendous learning and scholarship.

"Come and sit down by the fire, Professor," said Humphrey the monk. "We love to listen to your brilliant comments, but it is difficult to hear you."

"I was comfortable here," protested the professor as he yielded to the invitation and rose. He shifted his short legs awkwardly and slowly and sat almost silently in an armchair which seemed to be the seat of honor. When he was near us, I became aware of a curious, sharp smell. His beauty, I assure you, was entirely spiritual.

Soon three other persons arrived. There was a young, athletic young man who was introduced to me as Wolfson Hunter Barkeley, and another handsome young man who came in, head high, walking in very stately steps. His face was unusually red, which, Hogg informed me, came from his being constantly and eagerly in love. Hogg whispered to me that he was a bachelor, quite a coxcomb, and a devil with women. They called him Henry, but his full name was Henry Wattles Combes. He wrote nothing but love lyrics, a little off color, but he was distinctly popular with the younger generation.

But the most singular and unforgettable person was Anambuli Katz, who spoke in a high-pitched girlish voice and had an almost effeminate appearance. He moved about gracefully — rather too gracefully for a man — and sometimes he clasped his two hands, which had very long fingernails, and laid his inclined cheek on them as he spoke. Hogg, who was not jealous of any of them, being a contented, good-natured man, said that Anambuli Katz was a great passionate poet, distinguished for the ambient grace of his lines and the dark passion of his sentiments. Barkeley had confessed to Hogg that he could not stand Katz's lachrymose sentimentality. Katz and Barkeley hated each other, though both of them were too polite to let their feelings toward each other come to the surface.

I was intrigued to have walked into such a group of eccentric individuals, whose enthusiasm for their Muse made them brave the snowstorm to come and discuss poetry. As a matter of fact, I had never heard of them. But their devotion to the Muse was admirable, and they regarded themselves as the vanguard of a new school of poetry, priding themselves on the uniqueness and unintelligibility of their versifications. Tu Fu, Li Po, and a host of very distinguished poets had sung before them, and the late-comers were struggling for new paths and novel effects. This uniqueness of expression, its novelty and unintelligibility, united them together into a secret coterie, but I had no doubt that the human sentiments meant to be expressed by them and underlying them — the excuses for their tortured obscurity — were common to mankind. Many of their poems, I learned in the course of the evening, could not be understood by others, and some even not by all of them. I remember coming across a particular expression which at first confused and later amused me: *"By the horned glistening rosebuds roundish square."* This was a line composed by Don Key and much admired by Professor Porter Q. Pine. Embarrassed by my inability to make head or tail of it, I asked to be enlightened on the allusion, for I had in all my reading never come across a "roundish-square rosebud." The professor kindly explained to me that this referred to the poet's wife's toe, "horned" being a refined expression for the toenail, and "roundish-square" referring, of course, to its shape.

"But why 'glistening'?" I asked timidly.

"Ah," replied the professor. "You have not read the context carefully. Don has privately communicated to us an intriguing bit of information on the source of his inspiration. Last month he had gone out walking with Mrs. Key and on returning rather late that evening, he found that his wife's cloth shoes were wet through and her toes, as he expressed it so graphically and poetically, were bedewed with the pearly moisture of the meadows. You see, compressed in that little poem is a rich store of hidden associations, which, coupled with the sonorous rhythm of the language, is pregnant with suggestive power. Of course, to enjoy it fully and esthetically, you have to know of the poet's private walk with his wife."

I swallowed hard. I know that, for centuries, poets have employed allusions as refinements of language. Allusions flatter the reader's pride. Everybody knows, of course, that Confucius said of himself that he "reached thirty and stood (firm)." Therefore to say that a man has reached "the age of and stood," as we commonly do, is a form of subtle flattery, assuming he has read Confucius. And of course the more obscure the passage referred to, the rarer is the delight in understanding its covert reference.

"Do you not think this has gone too far?" I asked the professor.

"Too far for whom? For the ignoramuses, yes. But not for those who appreciate the personal emotions, the delicate nuances, the fine shades, and delightful novelty made possible by such allusions."

As a guest and a stranger to the group, I did not wish to be dragged into an argument, but the professor had merely asked a rhetorical question to hear himself answer it.

"It is like this," said Professor Porter Q. Pine. "It is the poet's duty to create a mood by the use of his words, and moods are evoked by words and phrases associated with them. That is why poets for ages have used classical allusions. A phrase evokes an entire episode or story. However, these allusions have, as it were, become public property and, through overuse, have lost much of their value of suggestion. The better poets today have searched further and further for less well-known references. Some have gone to Sanskrit, and thereby display a greater learning, and therefore give to the reader who understands the source of the reference the rare pleasure of recognition. You see how inevitable it all is. As for unintelligibility, it is up to the learned scholar to search for that obscure allusion. I have spent a lifetime hunting up the sources of Tu Fu's simple words. The more full of allusions a poem is, the richer is its suggestive power. Hence today poetry has become a pastime worthy of a scholar's effort. The true appreciation of poetry becomes the reward of hard, painstaking discovery. If a poem is readily understood by everybody, there can evidently be not much to it."

Soon the different poets began to read to one another their individual compositions of the past month and offer them for mutual appreciation and criticism, with the result, of course, that there was more appreciation than criticism. Their desire to understand and enjoy fully each other's verse was quite sincere, and the elucidations of particularly obdurate passages or phrases offered by authors provided much fun and comment. It is not necessary to offer more examples of their verse. Mr. Donald Key appeared to be the acknowledged leader of the New School, while Anambuli Katz had an inimitable charm of his own when he read his own compositions himself with a soft purring voice. Mr. Henry Wattles Combes, the lyricist, was the only one who had not written anything in the past month, being too busy, as he explained with a cackle, with his "harem." He stuttered a great deal and on hearing another's verse often exclaimed, "Co-co-could not believe it!" Hogg grunted smugly with his hands across his chest, while Barkeley, being a forthright person and loyal to his group, howled with delight when one of Don Key's verses was explained to him by the poet himself. As I listened to them, I had the delightful sensation of being initiated into the innermost sanctum of a literary Pleiad. The host, Drome-dary Humphrey, refrained from exuberant demonstrations, and sat ruminating over the past, playing with a stalk of hay in his mouth.

The discussions went on deep into the night. Anambuli Katz was the first to leave. He had silently stolen outside without anybody's notice when it came Barkeley's turn to read his lines. What with drinking and munching of nuts and discussing the delightful practice of the New Poetry, the hours passed very rapidly. The professor, who was the cham-pion critic and who had made himself exponent of the new theory, fell asleep in his seat, his head buried in his chest so that I could see only his bristly, shaggy hair. At about three o'clock, Henry Wattle Combes suddenly jumped up and said he had to go home; he reminded the company that he had to get up at dawn and he had been out all night. Mr. Hogg was comfortably asleep in his seat, his big belly moving rhythmically with his snore. Only the two young men, Key and Barkeley, were fully awake and never seemed to need sleep at all.

I do not know when I fell asleep myself. Now do not ask me to explain these things. I am only telling you what hap-pened. When I heard the temple bells and woke up, I found myself sleeping on the floor in a corner of the temple. A strange sharp smell assailed my nostrils.

The sky had cleared and I felt hungry. I quickly got up

and looked around. Everything had disappeared. There was no fire and no furniture; the temple was deserted and absolutely bare. I went inside in the hope of finding someone, and the smell became sharper as I stepped into the inside room. There I found a sick and old camel crouching on the ground, proudly ignoring my presence. Surprised by what I saw now and what I had seen in the night, I explored the grounds. On the north, I found a scrawny donkey, whose skin was bruised in several places. He was covered by a gray blanket and almost too weak from hunger to bray for food. Greatly touched by the condition of these animals, I went to look for some hay. On my way I saw something moving under a plank against the temple wall, and discovered a cock standing in his sleep. I found some hay in a broken-down outhouse, with old delicate paintings on its gray wall. Reaching out for the hay, I saw a black cat suddenly spring out and disappear into the yard.

Hugging a bunch of hay, I returned to feed the donkey, which looked up at me gratefully, and then went in to feed the old camel. I saw he had a swollen knee. My recollection of the night meeting was so vivd that I said to the animal, "I appreciate your hospitality of last night." But he merely sniffed at the hay, licked his tongue and stared at me.

Coming out through the yard, I stepped over an abandoned broad-brimmed farmer's hat and discovered something moving under it. It was a porcupine. I recognized the bright little eyes of the professor, and would have liked to greet him with some phrase like, "It was a great pleasure — " But his bristles stood up in angry self-defense, and I hurriedly left. I must have been crazy, for I heard a thin, squeaky voice behind me, "There is an apparent discrepancy — " Unceremoniously I left without stopping to hear him finish his sentence.

I found my horse still tied to the tree. It was now broad daylight, and when I passed through the village, the villagers were up. I stopped at a rustic inn to have a light breakfast

and order some fodder for my horse. A dog came and
sniffed at me, wagging his tail affectionately, as if he knew
me.

"Hullo, Barkley," I said, patting him gently.

"Why do you call him that?" asked the owner.

"I do not know," I replied.

"He is quite a hunter," remarked the innkeeper. "The
villagers' chickens are not safe from him unless I keep him
leashed."

Without telling the innkeeper of the strange things I had
seen during the night, I went on my way. I found my servant at an inn in the next town waiting for me.

14. THE BOOKWORM

wwwwwwwwwwwwwwwwwwwwwwwwwwwwwwwwwwwwwwwwwwwwwwwwwwwww

From Liaotsai, by P'u Sungling (see note on story No. 10). P'u was an original and extremely gifted scholar, but he failed in the imperial examinations. This in no way reflected upon his literary talent, for gifted scholars often had contempt for official success. In P'u's case, his contempt found expression in this humorous and very lively satire upon politicians.

MR. LANG of Pengcheng came from a scholar's family. Since his childhood, he had heard his father talk of rare editions and the "only extant copy," and regale company with chats about manuscripts and ancient poets and their lives. Being an honest official, his father had not acquired much property; whatever money he earned, he invested in books for his library, which had been started by his grandfather. Consequently, the family library was almost the only inheritance Lang had when his father died. Then something like an exaggeration of inbred family traits occurred, for in the case of the son who had been brought up in the world of books, and knew almost nothing else, the love of books assumed abnormal proportions. He had no idea of money or how to make it, and often had to sell bits of his personal property to get cash. In no circumstances, however, would he part with a single volume of the library, and it was therefore kept intact.

One of the objects in his study, which he personally valued

very much, was a copy of Emperor Sung Chentsung's "Invitation to Learning," in his father's own handwriting. The father had written it especially for his son, intending it to be his dying advice, and the young man had it framed and hung over his desk, so that he could look at it daily as the guiding motto for his life. He covered it with a piece of gauze to protect it from dust. It was to him a sacred text:

> Let not the rich people invest in farms and lands, for in books is to be found a rich harvest of corn;
> Or the wealthy build themselves spacious mansions, for the volumes of learning contain houses of treasure;
> Or the young people search for romance, for within book covers are women whose countenances are like jade;
> Or any man be too much concerned over carriages and a long retinue of servants, for liveried horses and carriages will come to studious scholars.
> Let those young men of ambition who wish to rise to fame and wealth apply themselves to earnest study of ancient tomes.

The meaning of this injunction to learning was clear enough: From learning and scholarship one could win distinction and honor and become a member of the ruling class of scholars, enjoying all the comforts of worldly success, including gold and corn and women. Mr. Lang, however, took the words literally, and pathetically believed that bushels of corn and pretty women were literally to be found in books, if he persisted long enough at his studies.

At eighteen, nineteen, and then twenty — the age when young men are more interested in the opposite sex than in musty volumes of ancient lore — he still kept a commendable devotion to his books. He would not go out to meet people or seek other forms of relaxation, his greatest pleasure being to sit in his chair and recite aloud his favorite passages. He had all the symptoms of a bibliomaniac. Through winter and summer, he wore the same gown, and being a bachelor living alone, he had no one to remind him to change his underwear. Sometimes his friends came to visit him, but after a few words of greeting and perfunctory remarks about the weather, his mind turned once again to his books. He would close his eyes, throw his head back, and recite certain poems or prose selections, intoning the lines with great satisfaction. His friends soon left, seeing he was such an incorrigible book lover that he had no use for them.

He failed in the imperial examinations and was not able to obtain a degree, but he showed an unflagging devotion to learning because he believed so completely in Emperor Sung Chentsung's words. He did want gold and carriages, and perhaps a woman of wondrous beauty whose countenance was like jade, but the emperor had said that he could win all these things and success in life just by being a learned scholar — the emperor could not lie.

One day a sudden gust of wind blew away the light volume he was holding in his hand and sent it twirling to the garden. He chased after it and put his foot down on it to retrieve it. In doing so, his foot slipped into a hole covered by weeds. He examined the hole which his book had led him to discover, and found at the bottom decaying roots, mud, and some grains of millet. He picked up the millet piece by piece. It was soiled and must have lain there for years, and there was not enough even to make a bowl of congee for breakfast. To him, however, it was like a phophecy come true, and it confirmed in him his faith in the words of the emperor.

Some days later, mounting a ladder in search of some old volumes, he found hidden behind the volumes on a top shelf a miniature carriage about a foot long. Wiping off the dust, he saw the bright shining color of gold. Happily he took it down and showed it to his friends. They found it was gilt only, not solid gold, and this was not what he had expected. Soon afterward, however, a friend of his father, an inspector who was passing through the district, came to see the carriage. He was a devout Buddhist and wanted to obtain the ancient object of art for one of the temples, to be placed before a niche, and he gave Lang three hundred taels of silver and two horses in exchange for it.

Lang was now absolutely convinced that the words of the "Invitation to Learning" were true, for the promises of gold and carriages and corn were already fulfilled. Everybody had read the emperor's famous essay, but only Lang showed unlimited faith in the literal truth of its words.

When he was thirty and still unmarried, his friends urged him to find a good girl for a wife.

"Why should I?" asked Lang confidently. "I am sure I will find in these volumes of wisdom and learning a lady whose countenance is like jade."

The story of this bookworm's faith in books, and his pathetic hope of having a beauty leap forth from their pages got around and provoked a great deal of mirthful comment. One day a friend said to him, "Dear Lang, the Spinning Maid is in love with you. Some night she will fly down from her abode in heaven and come to you."

The bookworm knew that his friend was teasing him, and did not argue with him, but only replied, "You will see."

One evening, he was reading the *History of Han Dynasty*, Volume VIII. About the middle of the volume, he found a bookmark, a broad silk ribbon, with the picture of a beautiful woman cut out in thin gauze and pasted over it. On the back were written two tiny words: "Spinning Maid."

His heart warmed as he looked at the picture. He turned it over and examined it, whispering and fondling it before he laid it back in its place. This was it, he thought to himself. He would get up in the middle of the dinner to have a look at it, and at night just before retiring to bed, he would go to that volume, take out the bookmark and hold it fondly in his hand. He was very happy.

He was thus contemplating the beauty in his volume one evening when the girl suddenly sat up on the page and smiled graciously at him. Surprised and not a little shocked, he stood up and made a courteous bow, and the girl grew to be a foot tall. Again he bowed, clasping his hands tightly before his chest, and he saw the girl step forth from the page, revealing a pair of beautiful legs. As her foot touched the ground, she became a full-grown figure, rolling her eyes at him provocatively. She was a feast to behold.

"Here I am! You have waited long enough," said the girl in an ingratiating voice.

"Who are you?" asked Lang tremulously.

"My name is Yen [countenance], and my personal name is Juyu [like jade]. You did not know it, but I have known you for a long time, even hidden up there. Your faith in the words of the ancient sages touched me, and I said to myself, if I do not come and show myself to him, nobody will believe in the ancient sages any more."

Now the young scholar's dream was fulfilled and his faith justified. Miss Yen was not only beautiful, she was friendly and familiar to him from the first moment she appeared. She bestowed on him affectionate kisses and showed in every way that she loved him dearly. Mr. Lang, as was to be expected of such a bookworm, did not take advantage of the situation. Alone with her, he discussed literature and history and the arts deep into the night. Soon the girl began to look drowsy, and she said, "It is late. Let us go to bed."

"Yes, we should."

Out of modesty, the girl blew out the light before she would undress, but the precaution was not really necessary. When they were in bed, she kissed him and said, "Good night."

"Good night," Lang replied.

After a while the girl turned over and again said, "Good night."

"Good night," replied the young scholar.

So it was, night after night. Happy with such a charming companion by his side, Lang worked still harder and read deep into the night. Miss Yen was always obliged to sit up with him.

"Why are you studying so hard?" the girl said to him, quite annoyed. "I have come to help you. I know what you want — to be a success and become a high official. Then for heaven's sake, do not study so hard. Go out and meet people and become sociable and win friends. See for yourself how many books the so-called successful candidates for degrees have read! You can count them on the fingers of your hands — the *Four Books* with Chu Hsi's *Commentary* and perhaps three of the *Five Classics*. Not all who passed the examinations are scholars. Do not be an idiot. You listen to me and forget about your books."

Mr. Lang was both surprised at the girl's words and depressed by what she asked him to do. This was the hardest kind of advice for him to accept.

"You must listen to me if you want to be a success," she insisted. "Forget your books and your scholarly studies, or I shall leave you."

Reluctantly he obeyed her, for he appreciated her company and loved her. But the moment his eyes fell on his books, his mind was lost in them and he started to recite aloud. One day when he turned around, the girl was gone. Silently he prayed to her to come back to him, but there was no sign of her. Then he remembered that she had come out of Volume VIII of the *History of Han Dynasty*, and he went to open the volume and found the bookmark lying there on exactly the same page. He called her name, but the girl in the picture did not move. He was very miserable. Again and again he begged and entreated her to come out, and promised to obey her.

Finally, the girl rose again from the book and stepped down, her face still angry.

"If you do not listen to me this time, I shall leave you. I really mean it."

Mr. Lang gave her his solemn promise. Miss Yen drew a chessboard on a piece of paper and taught him to play chess and instructed him in card games. Afraid of losing her, Mr. Lang tried to enjoy these games, but his heart was not in them. Whenever he found himself alone, he would surreptitiously open his books again, and afraid that she might go back to her hiding place, he placed Volume VIII on a different shelf, hidden among other books.

One day he was occupied in his reading, and so absorbed in it that he was not aware of the girl's presence in the room. Seeing that he was discovered, he closed the book quickly, but the girl was gone in a second. He searched all the volumes for her frantically but in vain. Could she have known where Volume VIII was? He looked for the bookmark in it, and found her picture on the same page in the same volume.

This time, it took her longer to yield, and only on his promise never to open a book again; and when she consented to step out, she pointed a finger of warning at him and said in a tone of great exasperation, "I wanted to help you to become an official and be a success, but you were too stupid to listen to my advice. This is absolutely the last time I shall be patient with you. If you do not make any progress in chess within three days, I will leave you forever, and you will die an unrecognized scholar."

On the third day, Lang happened to win two games of chess, which delighted Miss Yen. She then taught him to play on a seven-stringed instrument, and required him to master a song in five days. Bound now by his pledge, he concentrated on his music lessons and gradually his fingers became more nimble and more responsive. The girl did not demand perfection, but she wanted him to learn to enjoy music.

Lang found himself acquiring a very liberal education. He was taught to drink and gamble, and to be witty and sociable at parties.

She saw the emperor's text and remarked, "That is only half the story," and gave him a secret, esoteric book, entitled *True Path to Success*. From this small volume, the girl taught him many things: not to say what was on his mind, and to say what was not on his mind; and, most important of all, to say what was on the mind of the person to whom he was talking. After he acquired this polish, the last stage was learning to say half of what was on his mind, so that he would never be caught affirming or denying anything, and when things turned out not to be what he had thought at first, he could always conveniently deny what he had affirmed, and affirm what he had denied. Lang was not an apt student, but the girl was very patient with him. She assured him that to say what was not on his mind would gain him a position of at least fourth or fifth rank, whereas not to say what was on his mind would gain him only a post of sixth rank, like a district magistrate. She avowed that in all history, officials of the first and second ranks, such as governors and ministers and prime ministers, had all perfected the art of saying half of what was on their minds so as not to be caught affirming or denying anything. This last stage required a great deal of practice and refinement of language, but Miss Yen assured Lang that he could at least master the art of saying what was on the other person's mind, which was basic and would get him a post of the seventh rank, such as a *hsien* magistrate. Actually, it was very simple, consisting only of always remembering to say, "You are right," and this Mr. Lang learned easily.

Miss Yen sent him out to meet his friends and spend nights in drinking and revelry. His friends noticed that a great change had come over him, and he soon acquired a little reputation as a drinker, gambler, and "good fellow."

"Now you are fit to become an official," said Miss Yen.

Perhaps it was an accident, or perhaps the girl had skillfully guided him toward the last lesson needed to complete his education in manhood, but one night he said to her, "I notice that when a man and woman sleep together, they produce a baby. Yet I have slept with you for a long time and we have produced no baby. How is that?"

"I told you it was foolish of you to study books all the time," she said. "And now at thirty-two, you do not know even the first chapter of human life. And you boast of your *knowledge*. Shame on you!"

"What I will not stand for is having anyone chide me with ignorance," replied Lang. "Let anyone call me a thief or a liar, but I will not let anyone say that I am deficient in knowledge. You speak of the first chapter of human life. Will you please enlighten me?"

Miss Yen then initiated him into the mysteries of man and woman, and to his great surprise Lang discovered them to be extremely enjoyable. "I did not realize that there was such exquisite happiness in the relationship between man and wife!" he exclaimed.

And he went about telling his friends about his new discovery and his friends covered their mouths in laughter. When Miss Yen learned about it, she blushed and scolded him. "How can you be so stupid? One does not speak of the intimacies of the bedroom to one's friends."

"What is there to be ashamed about?" he asked. "I can understand that one should think it a disgrace to have an illicit affair, but there is no need to be ashamed of a relationship which is the foundation of the home."

A baby was born to them and a maid was hired to take care of it. When the baby was over a year old, his wife said to him one day, "I have lived now for two years with you and have begotten a child by you. It is time that I leave. I am afraid that something will happen if I remain much longer, for I have come only to reward you for your faith. It is best to say good-by now, and not regret it afterward."

"No, you must not leave me. You cannot leave me. And think of our child!"

The woman looked at the pretty child, and her heart

was moved with pity. "Very well," she said, "I will stay.
But on the condition that you dispose of the books in your
library."

"Darling," Lang replied, "I beg you, I implore you, to
stay, but please do not ask me to do the impossible. This
library is your home, and it is all that I have of value in
this world. I beg of you! I will do anything else you tell
me to do."

The woman yielded, unable to part from the child, and
consented to stay without extracting from him the promise
to give away his books. "I know I should not do this. However, everything is destined by Fate. I only gave you a
warning."

Now the story that Mr. Lang was living with a strange
woman and had had a child by her had been spread about.
His neighbors never knew where the woman had come from,
or whether she and Lang were married at all. Some questioned Lang, but he evaded the question, for he had already
learned not to say what was on his mind. It was rumored that
he had begotten a child by an evil spirit, or at least a woman
of mysterious and questionable origin.

The story reached the ears of the magistrate, a man by
the name of Shih. He was from Foochow, and was a dashing
young man who had obtained a degree early in his youth and
made quite a name for himself. He sent for Lang and the
woman he was living with, curious to have a look at her.

Miss Yen disappeared without a trace. Shih had Lang
brought to court and questioned. Even under torture, he
refused to divulge his secret, in order to protect the mother
of his child. Finally, the magistrate extracted the information from the maidservant, who told him what she knew.
The magistrate did not believe in evil spirits. He came to
Lang's house and made a thorough search, but found nothing.
To prove that he did not believe in superstitions, he ordered
all the volumes of the library to be taken out to the yard and
burned. It was observed that the smoke from the fire hung

like a mist over the place for days. Lang was released, but now he saw his library of books burned and the woman he loved irretrievably lost. In great anger he swore revenge.

He determined that he would rise to official power, by whatever means. Following the woman's advice, he soon made remarkable progress in acquiring friends who liked him and were willing to help him. He left visiting cards at every important home, and was attentive to the ladies of high families. He was promised an appointment.

He had not forgotten Miss Yen or the man who destroyed his library. He made a spirit tablet for Miss Yen and burned incense to it, and prayed daily to her, "Listen to my prayer, and grant that I be appointed to a post in Foochow."

His prayer seemed to have been answered, for soon afterward he was made inspector of the Foochow district. His duty was to examine the records of the officials. He took special pains to look into the records of Shih, and found evidences of corruption and abuse of official power. He impeached Shih and had his property confiscated. Thus satisfied, he sent in his resignation and, taking a Foochow girl to look after his child, returned home.

15. THE WOLF OF CHUNGSHAN

wwwwwwwwwwwwwwwwwwwwwwwwwwwwwwwwwwwwwwwwwwwwwwwwwwwwwwwwwwww

This remarkable tale was written by Hsieh Liang of Sung Dynasty, but some texts give the author as Ma Chungshi of Ming Dynasty. It is possible that Ma revised and improved upon Hsieh's text. The style is highly classical, making the wolf talk in the language of cultured gentlemen of Tsochuan (which I have, of course, not followed), but this fault may be forgiven in consideration of the author's very original comment on human ingratitude toward animals, who are our friends and faithful servants.

ONE DAY, with a great hullaballoo, the Baron of Chao set out for a chase in the Chungshan Mountains, accompanied by a pack of hounds and professional hunters armed with spears and arrows, some bringing trained falcons. On the way the baron saw a wolf standing a little distance away right across the road. Strangely enough, the animal was standing on its hind legs and howling as if to attract attention, thus presenting a perfect target. The baron shot an arrow and wounded the animal, but it got away. Then the hunters gave chase, and the cries of men and hounds resounded through the forest, and a cloud of dust was raised which must have helped the animal to escape.

At this moment, one Mr. Tungkuo was traveling to Chungshan, riding on a thin donkey and carrying only a bag containing his books and a few articles of clothing. He was

one of the Motseans, or followers of Motse, which were then
a flourishing religious sect characterized by their austere
life of self-sacrifice and devotion to the service of their fellow
men. They went about preaching the gospel of universal love,
trying to convert kings, the aristocracy, and the common
people with fanatic zeal. They consecrated themselves to a
life of poverty, often risking their own lives to help others
and make them happy.

Tungkuo heard the noise and commotion and then saw
the wounded wolf rushing in his direction with the hunters
in hot pursuit. When the animal saw the Motsean, he growled
pitifully for help, and Tungkuo's heart was touched with pity,
for he saw an arrow stuck in the poor animal's back.

"Do not be afraid," said Tungkuo. "I will take the arrow out
for you."

"Oh, you are a Motsean," said the wolf. "You are a good
man. The hunters are coming after me. Let me hide in your
bag until the chase is over. I shall be eternally grateful to
you, if you save my life."

"Poor wolf, why did you get yourself into this trouble? You
need wisdom, that is what you lack. However, get into the
bag quickly. Do not talk of gratitude. I am glad to do what
I can for you."

The Motsean then took the things out of his bag, and
began to squeeze the wolf into it. But the wolf was full-
grown and the bag was too small. When he went in head first,
his hind legs and bushy tail stuck out, and when he put his
tail in first, he could not jam his front paws and head in
without breaking his neck. He tried and tried again, in every
possible position, but without success.

"Hurry! The chase is coming near!" cried the wolf. "Come
on, tie me up!"

The wolf huddled on the ground and let the Motsean tie
his body and legs together into a bundle. Finally, with much
pressing and squeezing, Tungkuo succeeded in tying up the
wolf in the bag, and put him on the donkey's back. To his

dismay, he saw drops of blood oozing out of the bag. Moreover, the wolf had left a bloody track, and Tungkuo's own
hands were smeared. As quickly as he could, the Motsean
covered up the traces and turned the donkey around so that
the bag was less noticeable.

When the party arrived, the baron asked him if he had
seen a wolf.

"No," replied Tungkuo calmly, as he stood on the side
of the road. "The wolf is a cunning animal. He would not
come down the road. He must be somewhere hidden in the
big forest."

The baron glowered at him. Whacking the sword in his
hand, he said, "If anyone tries to help the animal escape,
he will have to pay for it."

Tungkuo calmly mounted his donkey and waved good-by
to the baron. "If I see him anywhere, I will let you know.
Good luck!"

When the wolf heard the hoofbeats of the hunting party
dying out in the distance, he cried out from the bag, "Let
me out, quickly! I am being suffocated!"

The Motsean quickly dismounted and helped the wolf
out of the bag. He untied him and touched the wound
gently, saying, "Does it still hurt? My, I had such a scare
for you!"

"No, the wound is only a slight scratch. Now that you
have saved my life, will you do another favor for me?"

"I will be glad to — anything within my power. We are
Motseans, you know. Only the gospel of love can save the
world. What is it you want me to do for you? I am at
your service."

"Well, I am famished," said the wolf, looking at him
sideways.

"Yes?"

"You might really save me. I have had nothing to eat
for three days, and if I die tonight, you will have saved

my life in vain. Why do you not let me eat you? Just a bit of self-sacrifice, you know. I am not asking much, am I?"

Tungkuo was now terrified, as the wolf opened his fangs and pounced at him. Quickly the man dashed to the other side of the donkey, trembling for his life.

"You cannot, you cannot do this to me!" he remonstrated.

"Why not?"

"You cannot. I have just saved your life!"

They began to chase each other around the donkey, who was very much puzzled by all this action.

"Now be reasonable," the Motsean addressed the wolf across the donkey's shoulders. "There is no use our arguing and trying to settle it by force. I shall not be convinced that you are right, even if you do succeed in tearing me apart, and your conscience will hurt you, will it not? I presume you are interested in knowing that when you eat me, you are doing the right thing."

"Of course," growled the wolf. "But I am hungry and I am tired of this argument."

"Then let us settle this dispute reasonably. I propose that we submit to arbitration. According to custom, we will ask three elders to decide whether you have the right to eat me, considering the fact that I have saved your life."

"All right, all right, but do not be so long-winded," replied the wolf. "I am convinced that God has created men to be eaten by wolves. We are so immeasurably superior to your race. You cannot defend yourself, you are degenerate, that is what you are."

They went together on the road but met nobody, for the day was getting dark.

"I am really famished. I cannot wait much longer," said the wolf. Pointing to an old stump on the roadside, he said, "Let us ask him."

"But he is only a tree. What does he know?"

"You ask him. He will tell you."

The Motsean bowed to the old tree and told him how

he had saved the wolf's life at great risk to himself. "Tell us, is it fair, in your opinion, and does it show common gratitude that I should be eaten by him now?"

A big, booming voice came out of the tree and said, "Good sir, I see what you mean. You speak of gratitude. Let me tell you my story. I am an apricot. When the gardener planted me, I was only a seed. In a year I flowered, and in three years I bore fruit. In five years my trunk was the size of an arm, and in ten years, the size of a child's belly. Now I am twenty years old. All my life I have fed the gardener and his family with my fruit. I fed him and his friends, and he even sold some of my fruit at the market and made a profit on it. Now the gardener sees that I am old and can no longer bear fruit. He tore off my leaves, broke off my branches, and sawed off my limbs for fuel. Not satisfied with that, I hear he is going to sell what is left of me for timber, to be chopped up and chiseled. Well, that is life. Why should the wolf not eat you?"

"Here speaks a wise spirit," said the wolf with great delight and he started to pounce on Tungkuo.

"Wait a minute. We have to hear two elders yet."

"All right, as you say," replied the wolf. "But I must say, you smell sweeter to me than ever."

They had gone a little distance when they saw an old water buffalo standing against a fence, looking as if he was very much tired of life.

"Ask this fellow," said the wolf. "I am sure he has seen a great deal of life."

The Motsean again told his story and asked for a fair judgment. The buffalo stared at him coolly and, Tungkuo thought, a little cynically. The animal thought a while, licked his tongue, and replied, "Well, what old Apricot told you is right Look at me, old and thin and slowly starving to death. You should have seen me when I was young. A farmer bought me at market and made me work on his farm. The other cows were getting old and I was doing most of the

work. The farmer said I was his favorite. When he went
on a journey, he harnessed me, and when he wanted to open
up barren land, I plowed it for him and made it into culti-
vable land. At planting time, I waded and splashed in the
mud, and at harvest, I worked his mill. I did not spare
myself and did the work of two or three farm hands. As a
result of my labor, the farmer got along quite well. His
food, his clothing, and the money with which he paid his
taxes, all came from me. Now he has been able to add a
wing to his granary and get his son married, and he lives
like a comfortable squire with children and grandchildren
around him. You should have seen him when I came to his
house. Talk about table service — why, he used to eat out
of clay spoons and bowls and basins. Now he has jars of
wine in his cellar. What did you do for the wolf that I have
not done for the farmer's family? But his wife thinks I am
useless — I am old, that is all — and she lets me wander about
and sleep in the open, exposed to the wind and the cold.
You see me standing here, trying to get a bit of the sun's
warmth, but when night comes, I am alone. I do not mind,
everybody must get old. But I heard his wife say that she was
going to send me to the butcher. She said, 'His meat can be
preserved, his hide can be made into leather, and his horns
and hoofs can be carved into useful utensils.' Ah, such is life!
Do not talk about human gratitude. I do not see a single
reason why you should not be eaten by the wolf."

The wolf again made ready to dig his teeth into the
Motsean's arm, but Tungkuo said, "Not yet. You have been
so patient. Let us hear what the third elder will say, according to our agreement."

They soon saw an old man, walking with a stick, coming
toward them. He had a long, white beard and looked like
a saint. Tungkuo was happy to find a human being and
ran to him, begging him to solve the dispute between him
and the wolf. "A word from you will save my life, old
uncle," he implored him.

The old man listened to the story. "What ingratitude!" said the saint, looking at the wolf with angry eyes. "Do you realize that an ungrateful man will be rewarded in his old age with an ungrateful son? You will one day have a son who will be brutal and unkind to you, in spite of all that you may have done for him. Get away, or I will kill you!"

"But you have not heard my story," pleaded the wolf. "Please listen to me. The Motsean tied me up and squeezed me into a bag so tightly that I could hardly breathe. I thought I was going to die. You have no idea how uncomfortable it was in the bag."

"In that case, the Motsean is to blame also," said the saint, and the argument started all over again.

"I do not know whom to listen to and whom to believe. You said you saved the wolf's life and the wolf said you injured him. The only way to prove who is right is to have an actual demonstration. I will see for myself how uncomfortable he made you in the bag."

"You will see," said the wolf, and allowed himself to be tied up and shoved into the bag.

"Have you got a pointed knife?" whispered the saint.

"Yes," said Tungkuo, puzzled.

"Well?"

"You are not asking me to kill the wolf, are you?"

"Whatever you like. You kill him or be killed by him. What an impractical moralist you are!"

So saying, the saint laughed and helped the Motsean run a knife through the wolf in the bag, which settled the argument.

Tales of Fancy and Humor

16. A LODGING FOR THE NIGHT

〜〜〜〜〜〜〜〜〜〜〜〜〜〜〜〜〜〜〜〜〜〜〜〜〜〜〜〜〜〜〜〜〜

*A Lodging for the Night, The Man Who Became a Fish,
The Tiger,* and *Matrimony Inn*
*Four stories by Li Fu-yen (see Introduction). They are
preserved in* T'aip'ing Kwangchi *as Numbers 418, 471,
429 and 159 respectively. Another story by the same
author may be found in my* Vigil of a Nation (John Day),
*pages 155-58; it is told against the same weird back-
ground of magic and answers the question: When is it
hardest for a person to keep his mouth shut? Among the
four here, "Matrimony Inn" is the best known, and the
phrases "the old man under the moon" and "tying red
threads" have passed into current Chinese vocabulary.*

WHEN Li Tsing, the great general,° was an unknown
young man, he used to hunt in the Huo Mountains. He
became a familiar sight among the villagers in that moun-
tainous region, and because he was tall and handsome and
friendly to everybody, they liked him. He often stopped at
a certain village for supper or lunch on his hunting trips.
There was an elder of that village who always provided
him with food and shelter whenever he was out late and
could not get back to the city. The elder was well-to-do
and would not accept pay for the lodging. He always provided a hot supper and a warm bed for Li Tsing, and
thus they became great friends.

*See also Li Tsing's story in "Curly-Beard."

One day Li sighted a herd of deer and started to follow their track. He was a good horseman and went rapidly over hill and dale, sometimes following goat tracks to the crest of a hill where he hoped to sight the herd again; but the deer had completely eluded him. He knew he could see anything moving five hundred yards away, and he was too good a hunter to give up halfway to his goal. He crossed crest after crest, and by the time it was pitch dark, he did not know where he was. Mortified and tired, he tried to find his way back, but the land was unfamiliar to him. Soon he was delighted to see a light shining from the top of a mountain opposite him, which he could reach a half an hour, and he struck out in that direction, hoping to find a lodging for the night.

Arriving at the place, he found a mansion enclosed by a high white wall with a red gate. He knocked and waited. After a long while, a servant came to open the side door and ask what he wanted. Li told him that he had been out hunting and had lost his way and begged their hospitality.

"I am afraid it is impossible," said the servant. "The men are away and only the mistress of the house is at home."

"Will you please speak to the lady for me anyway?"

The servant went inside and soon returned, saying, "Come in. Madam was at first unwilling, but on hearing that you had lost your way, she reconsidered and said she would give you a room for the night."

Li was ushered into the hall, which was elegantly furnished with many crystal lamps and plates and other fine objects. Soon a maid came to announce, "Madam is coming."

The mistress appeared, a dignified-looking lady of over fifty, simply dressed in black. Li noticed that everything she wore was of the finest material. He made his bow and apologized for the intrusion.

"My sons are away tonight, and ordinarily I would not receive guests. However, you are lost on such a dark night and I have not the heart to send you away." She spoke with great poise and refinement, and her tone was that of the kindly mother of a happy, well-ordered family. Even her graying hair was beautiful.

Li was served a simple, excellent supper, consisting mainly of fish. He ate with ivory chopsticks from bowls of crystal.

After supper, the lady excused herself, saying to him, "You must be tired and will want to retire at once. My maids shall see that you have everything."

Li rose to thank her and said good night.

The lady said good night sweetly and added, "It may be noisy at night. I hope it will not disturb you."

Li's eyes registered surprise, and she noticed it.

"My boys often come back in the middle of the night and make a lot of noise," explained the lady. "I just wanted to let you know so that you would not be frightened."

"I shall not," replied Li. He wanted to ask how old her boys were and what they were doing, but he thought it best not to be too inquisitive.

Two maidservants soon brought out a roll of fine clean bedding to make his bed and, having seen that he had everything, went out and closed the door.

It was a comfortable, warm bed, and he was tired after the day's chase. But he wondered what kind of people he was stopping with, who lived so far away from everything and had business at night. His limbs were fatigued and ready for a good sleep, but his head was fully awake. Like a hunter stalking his prey, he lay perfectly still in bed, waiting to hear what might happen.

Toward midnight, he heard a loud and urgent knock at the gate. Soon he heard the creak of the side door, and the servant talking to someone in whispers. Then he heard the servant's steps coming to the parlor, and heard the lady come out and ask, "What is it?"

"The messenger brought this scroll, and said it is urgent," reported the servant. "The elder young master is ordered to make rain in this region for seven miles around the mountain, and the rain is to stop before dawn. He said not to make too much rain, for fear of hurting the crops."

"What can I do?" said the lady in a quick, excited voice. "Both of them are away and it is too late to send for them. I cannot send anybody else."

"Can you ask our guest to do it?" suggested a maid. "He is a strong fellow and a hunter. He rides a good horse."

The mistress was delighted with the suggestion and came to knock at Li's door. "Are you awake?"

Li answered, "What can I do for you?"

"Please come out. I have something to talk over with you."

Li got out of bed at once and came out into the parlor. The mistress explained, "This is not an ordinary house. You are stopping at the Dragon's residence. I have received an order from Heaven to make rain at once, between now and dawn, and I have nobody to send. My eldest son is away attending a wedding in the Eastern Sea, and my second boy has accompanied his younger sister on a distant journey. They are thousands of miles away, and it is too late to send them a message. Will you be so kind as to take the job? Making rains is our duty, and my sons will be punished if they do not obey this order."

Li was delightfully astonished by such a novel request. "I would be glad to oblige, madam, but it is beyond my power and experience. I suppose you have to fly up above the clouds to make rain."

"You can ride a good horse, I presume?"

"Certainly."

"That is enough. All you need do is mount a horse I shall give you — not your own, of course — and follow my instructions. It is quite simple."

She ordered a black-maned horse to be brought and saddled, and handed Li a small bottle containing rain water, which was to be hung in front of the saddle.

"This is a celestial steed," she said. "You must hold the reins lightly and let him trot where he likes. Do not hurry him. He knows where to go. When you see him paw with his hoofs, you just take this bottle and sprinkle one drop over his mane. But be careful not to sprinkle too much. Do not forget."

Li mounted the celestial steed and set off. He was surprised at its steadiness and speed. Soon it trotted a little faster but still maintained an even pace, and Li had a feeling that he was climbing. As he looked about, he saw that he was already on top of the clouds. A swift, moist wind blew fiercely against his face, and below him thunder rolled and lightning flashed. Following the instructions, he sprinkled a drop of the divine water, whenever the horse stopped and pawed. After a while, with the help of flashes of lightning, he saw through an opening in the clouds the village where he used to stop for the night. "I have bothered the old man and the village people a great deal," he thought to himself. "I have been wanting to repay them for their hospitality, and now I have the power of making rain. Yesterday I saw their crops parched on the field, the blades wilted and yellowing. I will sprinkle a little more for those nice people."

He sprinkled twenty drops on the village and felt happy watching the rain pour down. When it was over, he returned to the Dragon's residence.

The hostess was weeping in a chair in the parlor.

"What a terrible blunder you have made!" cried the lady when she saw him return. "I told you to sprinkle one drop of water, and you must have poured down half a bottle. You did not know that one drop of that liquid means one foot of rainfall on earth. How many drops did you sprinkle?"

"Only twenty," Li replied, feeling very silly.

"*Only* twenty! Can you imagine a village suddenly flooded with twenty feet of rain in one night? All the people and cattle will be drowned. Of course a report will be made to Heaven, and my sons will be held responsible for this disaster."

Li was ashamed of himself and did not know what to say except that he was very sorry. But of course it was too late.

"I do not blame you. You could not have known. But I am afraid that when the Dragon comes home, it will not be pleasant for you. I should advise you to leave immediately."

Li was touched by the lady's kindness, and prepared to leave at once. It was already daybreak. He was glad to get away so easily, but to his surprise the hostess said to him when he was all ready, "I must repay you for the trouble you took. I should not have asked a guest to get up in the middle of the night. It was my fault. Out here I have no costly gifts to give you, but I can furnish you with two servants. You can take either of them or both, as you wish."

Li looked at the two servants standing beside her. The one on the east looked gentle and kind. The one on the west was tough and muscular and looked a bit ferocious.

Li thought he could use a servant, and he would like to have a souvenir of the strange night's visit.

"I will take one," he said.

"As you like. Make your choice," replied the hostess.

Li paused and considered. The gentle one looked intelligent and amiable, but he might not be such a useful companion on a hunting trip. Li said he would take the strong fellow with the rather savage-looking appearance.

He thanked his hostess and left. He turned around to look at the house once more and saw that it had disappeared. When he turned back to question the servant, he, too, was gone.

He found his way back alone. On reaching the spot where the village had stood, he saw a huge flood covering everything except the tree tops. All inhabitants had been drowned during the night.

Later, Li became a great general, leading victorious campaigns which ended in the founding of the Tang Dynasty. But through the long years of his service to the emperor who was his friend, he never became a premier or civilian head of the government, because he had not chosen the good and gentle servant. It is a proverb that good generals come from the west of the Tungkwan Pass (northwest), and good premiers come from the east (the central plains). Perhaps the position of the two servants was symbolic. Had Li chosen both and taken them with him, he would have become the civilian, as well as the military, head of the government.

17. THE MAN WHO BECAME A FISH

~~~~~~

SHAY, a man over thirty, was serving as a section chief in the magistrate's office of Chincheng in Szechuen. The chief magistrate was a man by the name of Tsou, and his colleagues were the two vice-magistrates, Lei and Pei. In the autumn of the year 758, Shay became severely ill. He ran a high fever and his family consulted many doctors in vain. On the seventh day he lost consciousness, and lay in that state for days. His friends and family almost gave him up for dead. At first he was thirsty and was able to ask for water, which he drank in great quantity, but toward the end he was in a comatose state and could not take anything. He slept on and on until the twentieth day, when he suddenly yawned and sat up.

"How long have I been asleep?" he asked his wife.

"About three weeks."

"Yes, I suppose it must have been that long. Go and see my colleagues and tell them that I have recovered. Find out if they are eating minced carp at this minute. If so, they must leave the dinner at once. I have something to talk to them about. And bring the servant Chang at the office. I want him, too."

A servant was sent to the magistrate's office. He found that the staff was indeed having the midday dinner, and it was a dish of steaming hot, minced carp. The servant gave them the message, and the men came over to Shay's house accordingly, happy to learn that their friend had recovered.

273

"Did you people send the servant Chang to buy fish?" Shay asked.

"Yes, we did."

He turned to Chang and said to him, "Did you not go to buy fish from the fisherman, Chao Kao, and did he not refuse to sell you the big fish? Do not interrupt me. You found the big carp hidden away in a small pool, covered by reeds. Then you bought the fish, but you were angry at the fisherman for deceiving you and took him with you. When you entered the office building, the clerk of the tax bureau was sitting on the east of the door, and the sub-altern was sitting on the west, playing chess. Correct? Then you went up the hall, and you saw Magistrate Tsou and Vice-Magistrate Lei playing cards, and Pei was watching them, munching on a pear. You told Pei about the fisherman and Pei gave him a kick which sent him rolling out into the yard. Then you took the fish to the kitchen and the cook, Wang Shihliang, killed it for dinner. Is not this exactly what happened?"

They questioned Chang and checked with one another and found that every detail was correct. Greatly puzzled, they asked Shay how he knew all this, and this is the story that he told his friends:

When I fell ill, I had a burning fever, as you all know. Overcome by the unbearable heat, I fell unconscious, but the feeling of hot fever remained inside, and I wondered to myself how I could find relief. I thought of taking a walk along the delightful river bank, and took a cane and went out. The air was perceptibly cooler as soon as I got outside the city, and I immediately felt better. I saw the hot air rising from the roofs of the houses and was glad that I had left them behind me. Besides, I was thirsty and only wanted to get near the water. I struck out toward the foot-hills, where the East Lake joins the river.

I arrived at the lake, pausing on the bank under a willow tree. The blue water looked extremely inviting. A gentle breeze blew over its surface and creased the water like fish scales, so that I could visibly follow the movement and direction of the breeze over the lake. All was quiet and peaceful. Suddenly I thought I would like to have a bath. I used to swim as a boy, but for a long time I had not had a swim in the lake. I took off my clothing and plunged in, and felt a delightful sensation as the water closed around me and caressed my body and limbs. I dived below the water several times, feeling an immense relief. All I can remember was saying to myself, "I pity Pei and Lei and Tsou and all my friends, sweltering in their offices all day. I wish I could become a fish for a while and have no more to do with stamps and seals, signatures and documents. How happy I would be if I could turn into a fish and swim for days and nights, with water, and nothing but water, around me!"

"That is easy to arrange, I believe," said a fish coming up at my feet. "You can become a fish for life like me, if you want to. Shall I arrange it for you?"

"I shall very much appreciate it, if you will be so kind. By the way, my name is Shay Wei, section chief at the city. Tell your people that I would be glad to exchange places with any one of them. Just allow me to swim and swim and swim!"

The fish left and soon came back with a man whose head was like a fish, and who came riding on a *wawa* — you know, the kind that has four legs and lives in the water, but can climb up trees, and when you catch it or kill it, it makes a noise like a baby's cry. This fish-headed man came with a retinue of a dozen assorted fish and read an order from the River God. Believe me, it was written in excellent prose style, and it went as follows:

Man, a creature born on land, has different habits from the denizens of the sea. So long as he retains his form and shape, he makes execrable progress in the water. Section Chief Shay Wei has great depth of mind and is seeking relief and solace in a life of freedom. Dissatisfied and weary of the round of official duties, he yearns for the cool depths of blue lakes and rivers, for the freedom and unlimited time for sports of our watery kingdom. His wish to become a member of the scaly tribe is hereby granted. He shall be made a brown carp and assigned to the East Lake as his regular abode. Alas! Many are the temptations and pitfalls in the way of inhabitants of the sea and rivers. Some have ruthlessly attacked boats, and some, with insufficient experience and self-control, have been caught and trapped by the various devices of man. It is never truer than in the water that caution is the best insurance for a long life. May you conduct yourself wisely and honorably, in a manner worthy of the tribe of which you have the privilege to become a new member. Be a good fish!

As I listened to the order, I found I had been transformed into a fish, and my body was covered with beautiful, shining scales. Delighted with the transformation, I swam gracefully and with perfect ease, rising to the surface and diving to the bottom at will with the slightest movement of my fins. I sailed down to the river, and explored every nook and cranny on the shore and all the streams and tributaries, but I always returned to the lake at night.

However, one day I was terribly hungry and unable to find food. I saw Chao Kao dropping his line and waiting to catch me. The worm looked very tempting and my gills literally watered. I knew perfectly well that it was a horrible thing which I used to dread even to touch, but I felt it was just what I needed, and could not imagine anything more delightful to my palate. Then I remembered the words of caution and turned away from it, and with great self-control swam away.

But a terrific hunger was gnawing inside my stomach, and I could not stand it any longer. I said to myself, "I know Chao Kao and he knows me. He would not dare to kill me. If I am caught, I will ask him to bring me back to the office."

I went back to gobble up the worm and was caught, of course. I struggled and fought, but Chao Kao pulled at me and my lower lip was bleeding, so I gave up. When he was about to haul me up, I cried, "Chao Kao, Chao Kao, hear me! I am Shay Wei, the Section Chief. You will be punished for this."

Chao Kao did not hear me, and put a string through my jaw and put me away in a pool covered with reeds.

I lay there, waiting. Soon, as if in answer to my prayer, Chang from our office came. I heard the conversation during which Chao Kao refused to sell Chang the big fish. However, he found me and took me out of the pool, and I was dangling by the string, quite helpless.

"Chang, how dare you? I am your employer. I am Section Chief Shay, only temporarily disguised as a fish. Come, kowtow to me!"

But Chang did not hear me, either, or chose to ignore me. I shouted at the top of my voice, and cursed and flapped back and forth, but all to no avail.

When I entered the gate, I saw the clerks playing chess near the door, and I shouted to them, telling them who I was. Again I was ignored. One of the clerks exclaimed, "My, what a beauty! He must weigh three and a half pounds." Imagine my mortification!

In the hall, I saw you people, as I told you a minute ago. Chang told you how Chao Kao had concealed the big fish and wanted to sell only the small fish, and Pei was so angry that he aimed a powerful kick at him. You were all delighted with the big fish.

"Take him to the cook" — I think it was Pei who said

that—"and ask the cook to make a nice dish of minced carp, with onions and mushrooms and a dash of wine."

"Wait a minute, my dear colleagues," I said to you all. "Listen to me. It is all a mistake. I am Shay. You ought to know me. You cannot kill me. How can you be so cruel?" I protested and protested.

I saw it was useless, for you were all deaf. I looked at you with my imploring eyes and opened my mouth and begged for mercy.

"Onions and mushrooms and a dash of wine! How these heartless rascals could turn against their friend just like that!" I thought to myself. But there was nothing I could do.

Chang then took me to the kitchen. The cook opened his eyes wide when he saw me. His face gleamed as he sharpened his knife and laid me on the kitchen table.

"Wang Shihliang! You are my cook. Do not kill me! I beg you!"

Wang Shihliang took me firmly by the waist. I saw the white flash of the knife about to descend over my head. Whack, it came down, and in that instant, I woke up.

Shay's friends listened to the story, greatly touched by it, and all the more astonished at what he told them because every detail was true and exact. Some said that they had seen the fish's mouth move, but no one had heard a single sound. Thereafter, Shay recovered completely, and his friends abjured the eating of carp for the rest of their lives.

18. THE TIGER

CHANG FENG was traveling in Fukien in the beginning of the reign of Yuanho (806-820). He was a northerner, and the luxuriant subtropical vegetation was new and interesting to him. Among other things, he had heard of tigers in the south. One day he was stopping with his servant at an inn in Hengshan, a small town near Foochow, lying on the watershed of the high mountain ranges which divide Fukien from Chekiang. Having deposited his luggage, he went out to take in his first impressions of the land, its people and the women's costumes. Walking alone with a cane in his hand, he went on and on, attracted by the refreshing green of the country after rain, and the bracing winds which came over the mountain. He felt strangely excited. Before him lay a landscape which was a riotous display of colors. It was autumn and the hillsides literally glowed with the gold and red of maple forests. A beautiful white temple stood halfway up the mountain above a thickly wooded slope. The golden sunset transformed the mountainside and the fields into a landscape of brilliant pastels, blue and purple and green, changing in hue every moment, mingling with the dazzling red and gold. It was like a magic land.

Suddenly he felt a fainting sensation: stars danced before his eyes and his head reeled. He thought it was due to the altitude, the overexertion, and the sudden change of climate, or perhaps he was affected by the strange light. Just a few steps before him he saw a pasture land covered with velvety lawn, lying just where the wooded slope began. He took off his gown and put it with his walking stick against a tree, and lay down to take a rest. He felt a little better. As he looked up at the blue sky, he thought how beautiful and peaceful nature was. Men fought for money and position and fame; they lied and cheated and killed for gain; but here was peace—in nature. As he rolled in the grass, he felt happy and relaxed. The smell of the sod and a gentle breeze soon caressed him into sleep.

When he woke up, he felt hungry and remembered it was evening. As he rolled his hands over his stomach, he touched a coating of soft fur. Quickly he sat up, and he saw his body covered with beautiful black stripes, and as he stretched his arms, he felt a delightful new strength in them, sinewy and full of power. He yawned and was surprised at his own powerful roar. Looking down his own face, he saw the tips of long white whiskers. Lo, he had been transformed into a tiger!

Now, that is delightful, he thought to himself. I am no longer a man, but a tiger. It is not bad for a change.

Wanting to try his new strength, he ran into the woods and bounced from rock to rock, delighting in his new strength. He went up to the monastery, and pawed at the gate, seeking admittance.

"It is a tiger!" he heard a monk inside shouting. "I smell it. Do not open!"

Now that is uncomfortable, he thought to himself. I only intended to have a simple supper and discuss Buddhist philosophy with him. But of course I am a tiger now, and perhaps I do smell.

He had an instinct that he should go down the hill to the village and seek for food. As he hid behind a hedge on a country path, he saw a beautiful girl passing by, and he thought to himself, I have been told that Foochow girls are famous for their white complexion and small stature. Indeed it is true.

As he made a move to go up to the girl, she screamed and ran for her life.

What kind of a life is this, when everybody takes you for an enemy? he wondered. I will not eat her, she is so beautiful. I will take a pig, if I can find one.

At the thought of a nice, fat pig, or a small juicy lamb, his mouth watered, and he felt ashamed of himself. But there was this infernal hunger gnawing at his stomach, and he knew he had to eat something or die. He searched the village for a pig or calf, or even a chicken, but they were all under good shelters. All doors were shut against him, and as he crouched in a dark alley, waiting for a stray animal, he heard people talking inside their houses about a tiger in the village.

Unable to satisfy his hunger, he went back to the mountain, and lay in wait for some wayfarer in the night. All night he waited, but nothing came his way. For a while, he must have fallen asleep.

Toward dawn, he woke up. Soon travelers began to pass along the mountain road. He saw a man coming up from the city who stopped several passengers to ask whether they had seen Cheng Chiu, a bureau chief of Foochow, who was expected to return to his office today. He was evidently a clerk from the bureau who had been sent to welcome the chief.

Something told the tiger that he must eat Cheng Chiu. Just why he must eat that person he could not tell, but the feeling was very definite that Cheng Chiu was destined to be his first victim.

"He was getting up from the inn when I left. I think he is coming behind us," he heard a man reply to the clerk's question.

"Is he traveling alone, or is he accompanied by others? Tell me his dress so that I can recognize him, for I do not want to make a mistake when I go up to greet him."

"There are three of them traveling together. The one dressed in a dark green is Cheng."

As the tiger listened to the conversation from his hiding place, it seemed as if it were taking place expressly for his benefit. He had never seen or heard of Cheng Chiu in his life. He crouched in a thicket and waited for his victim.

Soon he saw Cheng Chiu coming up the road with his secretaries, along with a group of other travelers. Cheng looked fat and juicy and delicious. When Cheng Chiu came within pouncing distance, the tiger, Chang, rushed out, felled him to the ground, and carried him up the mountain. The travelers were so frightened they all ran away. Chang's hunger was satisfied, and he only felt as if he had had a bigger breakfast than usual. He finished up the gentleman and left only the hair and bones.

Satisfied with his meal, he lay down to take a nap. When he woke up, he thought he must have been mad to eat a human being who had done him no harm. His head cleared and he decided it was not such a pleasant life, prowling night ofter night for food. He remembered the night before, when the instinct of hunger drove him to the village and up the mountain, and he could do nothing to stop himself.

"Why do I not go back to that lawn and see if I can become a human being again?"

He found the spot where his clothing and walking stick were still lying by the tree. He lay down again, with the wish that he might wake up to be a man once more. He rolled over on the grass, and in a few seconds found that he had been restored to his human shape.

Greatly delighted, but puzzled by the strange experience, he put on his gown, took up his cane, and started back to the town. When he reached the inn, he found he had been away exactly twenty-four hours.

"Where have you been, Master?" asked his servant, "I have been out looking for you all day." The innkeeper also came up to speak to him, evidently relieved to see him return.

"We have been worried about you," said the innkeeper. "There was a tiger abroad. He was seen by a girl in the village last night, and this morning Cheng Chiu, a bureau chief who was returning to his office, was eaten by him."

Chang Feng made up a story that he had spent the night discussing Buddhist philosophy up in the temple.

"You are lucky!" cried the innkeeper, shaking his head. "It was in that neighborhood that Cheng Chiu was killed by the tiger."

"No, the tiger will not eat me," Chang Feng replied.

"Why not?"

"He cannot," said Chang Feng enigmatically.

Chang Feng kept the secret to himself, for he could not afford to tell anybody that he had eaten a man. It would be embarrassing, to say the least.

He went back to his home in Honan, and a few years went by. One day he was stopping at Huaiyang, a city on the Huai River. His friends gave him a dinner and much wine was consumed, as was usual on such occasions. Between the courses and the sipping of wine, the guests were each asked to tell a strange experience, and if in the opinion of the company the story was not strange enough, the teller of the story was to be fined a cup of wine.

Chang Feng began to tell his own story, and it happened that one of the guests was the son of Cheng Chiu, the man he had eaten. As he proceeded with his story, the young man's face grew angrier and angrier.

"So it was you who killed my father!" the young man shouted at him, his eyes distended and the veins standing up on his temples.

Chang Feng hastily stood up and apologized. He knew he had got into a very serious situation. "I am sorry. I did not know it was your father."

The young man suddenly whipped out a knife and threw

it at him. Luckily it missed and fell with a clang on the
floor. The young man made a rush at him, and would have
fallen on him, but the guests, greatly disturbed by the sudden
turn of events, held him back.

"I will kill you to avenge my father's death. I will follow
you to the ends of the earth!" the young man shouted.

The friends persuaded Chang Feng to leave the house
at once and hide himself for a while, while they tried to calm
Cheng Chiu's son. It was conceded by everybody that to
avenge one's father's death was a noble and laudable undertaking, but after all, Chang Feng had eaten Cheng Chiu
when he was a tiger, and no one wanted to see more blood
shed. It was a novel situation and posed a complicated moral
problem as to whether revenge under such circumstances
was justified. The youth still swore murder to appease his
father's spirit.

In the end, the friends spoke to the commander of the
region who ordered the young man to cross the Huai River
and never return to the northern bank, while Chang Feng
changed his name and went to the northwest to keep as far
away from his sworn enemy as possible.

When the young man returned to his home, his friends
said to him, "We entirely sympathize with your determina-
tion to avenge your father. That is a son's duty, of course.
However, Chang Feng ate your father when he was a tiger
and not responsible for his action. He did not know your
father and had no purpose in killing him. That was a strange
and special case, but it was not intentional murder, and if
you kill him, you will be tried for murder yourself."

The son respected this advice and did not pursue Chang
Feng any more.

19. MATRIMONY INN

W EI KU wanted to find a good girl to be his wife, but so far he had been unsuccessful, because he was particular about the girl he was going to marry. In the year 807, he was traveling to Tsingho and stopped at an inn outside the South Gate of Sungcheng. Someone had suggested a match with a daughter of the Pan family which was socially his equal, and the matchmaker made an appointment to meet him at Lungshing Temple in the morning. Excited by the proposed union with a girl of wealth and reputed beauty, Wei was unable to sleep and got up at dawn. He dressed and washed and went to keep his appointment. A crescent moon was shining in the pale sky, for it was still before daybreak. When he arrived at the place, Wei found an old man sitting on the steps of the temple, reading a book by the light of the pale moon. A small bag lay on the floor by his side.

Curious about what this old man was reading at that unearthly hour, Wei looked over his shoulders and found it was nothing he could understand. He had studied all the known ancient and archaic scripts, even Sanskrit, but he could not make out what this writing was.

"May I ask what that volume is you are reading, old uncle? I thought I knew every kind of writing on earth, but I have never seen this kind of script."

"Of course you have not," answered the old man with a smile. "It is not written in any language that you would know."

"Then what is it?"

"You are a mortal and this is a book of the spirit world."

"So you are a spirit! What are you doing here?"

"Why should I not be here? You came out too early. You see at this time, between night and daybreak, half of the wayfarers abroad are human beings and half are spirits. Of course you would not be able to distinguish between them. I am in charge of human affairs and I have to go around during the night to check up on the persons and addresses whose affairs are my concern."

"What affairs?" asked Wei.

"Matrimony."

Wei Ku was greatly interested. "You are the man — excuse me, the person I want to consult. I have never been successful in finding a girl from a suitable family for my wife. In fact, I have come here for an appointment about a union with a girl of the Pan family who is said to be very beautiful, refined, and of excellent character. Tell me, will I succeed?"

"What is your name and address?" asked the old man.

Wei Ku told him. After thumbing the pages of the volume in his hand, the old man looked up and said, "I am afraid not. You see all marriages are arranged in Heaven. They are all written down in this book. I see your wife is only three years old now. When she is seventeen, you will marry her. Do not worry."

"Do not worry! You mean I shall have to remain a bachelor for another fourteen years?"

"That is the situation."

"And I shall not be able to arrange this match with the Pan girl?"

"You are right."

Wei did not know whether to believe him or not, but he asked, "What have you got in that bag?"

"Red silk strings." The old man's face melted into a generous smile. "You see this is my job. I note the different pairs to be matched off in the book, and when a baby girl and a baby boy are born and destined to become man and wife, I go around in the night and tie their feet together. Once the knot is tied — and I tie it very securely — nothing can separate them. One may be born in a poor family, and the other wealthy, or they may be separated by thousands of miles, or there may even be a feud between the two families, but they will end up as man and wife. There is nothing they can do about it."

"You have tied mine, I presume."

"Yes, I have."

"And where is the three-year-old baby who is destined to be my wife?"

"Oh, she lives with a woman who sells vegetables at the market. They are not far from here, and the woman comes to the market every morning. If you are interested, follow me to the market after daybreak and I will point her out to you."

Dawn was already breaking, but the man who had made the appointment with Wei failed to arrive. "You see there is no use waiting for him," remarked the old man.

They chatted together for a while, and Wei found the old man very pleasant to talk with. The old man told him that he liked his job immensely. "It is passing strange," he said, "what a little piece of silk string does. I see the boy and girl grow up, each in his or her home, sometimes unconscious of the other's existence, but when the time comes, they meet and fall head over heels in love with each other. All they know is that they cannot help it. And if some other boy or girl comes in between, he stumbles over the string and gets so tangled up he commits suicide. I have seen it happen again and again."

The market which was only a short distance away, was now filling up with people.

"Come, follow me." The old man made a signal with his head, took up his bag, and arose.

When they came to the market, the old man pointed to a stall where a dirty old woman with floppy hair was selling vegetables, holding a child to her breast. There was a film over the woman's eyes, and she could hardly see.

"There she is. That child will be your wife."

Wei cursed audibly. "What do you mean? You are joking with me." He turned to the old man angrily.

"No, I assure you that child is born under lucky stars. She will marry you, live in comfort, and later become a lady of high rank on account of her son."

Wei looked at the skinny waif and was disheartened. He would have liked to dispute the old man's words, but when he turned around again the old man had vanished.

He went home alone, disappointed because the man who was to meet him had not come and because he could not make up his mind whether to believe the old man or not. I am a scholar, he thought to himself, and even if I should fail to marry a girl from a good family, at least I shall take a pretty mistress from the theatrical world. The more he thought about it, the more he found the idea of marrying that dirty child distasteful and downright ridiculous. He worried about it so that he could not sleep that night.

The next morning he went to the market with his servant. He promised the servant a big reward if he would kill the child with a knife. They found the woman in the stall holding the baby. When an opportunity presented itself, the servant flashed out his knife, stabbed the baby and ran away. The child cried, the woman shouted "Murder!" and there was great confusion in the market, during which Wei and his servant made their escape.

"Did you get her?" Wei asked.

"No," replied the servant. "As I aimed the knife at her, the child turned abruptly. I think I scraped her face near the eyebrow."

Wei hurriedly left town, and the incident was soon forgotten.

He then went west to the capital, and disappointed with the last proposal which had failed to come off, he turned his thoughts away from marriage. Three years later, he succeeded in making an excellent match with a girl of the Tan family, quite well known in society. The girl was well educated and known for her beauty. Everybody congratulated him, and preparations were being made for the wedding when one morning he heard the awful news that his fiancée had committed suicide. She had loved another man.

For two years, Wei stopped thinking of marriage. He was twenty-eight already, and he had changed his mind about marrying a girl from society. One day when he was stopping at a temple in the countryside, he found a farmer's daughter and fell in love with her. Moreover, the girl was madly in love with him. They became engaged and he went to the capital to buy her silks and jewels. On his return he found that his fiancée had been struck with a severe disease. He was willing to wait, but the illness dragged on and after a year, the girl had lost all her hair and become blind. She refused to marry him and asked him to leave her and find someone who would be a worthy wife for him.

Several years passed before the perfect match was made. The girl was not only pretty and young, she was a great lover of books and art and music. There were no rivals and they became engaged. Three days before her wedding, when she was walking on a pavement, she tripped over a loose boulder and fell down and died. It seemed as though Fate was mocking him.

Wei Ku now became a fatalist. He did not want to be bothered with women any more. He worked at a post in Shiangchow, fulfilling his duties, and thought no more about marrying. But he did his work so well that the magistrate, Wang Tai, proposed to marry his niece to him.

The subject was painful to Wei. "Why do you want to marry your niece to me? I am too old to marry."

Under pressure, he consented, but without enthusiasm. He did not see his bride until the wedding took place, but she

was young and he was satisfied. In every way she was a
good wife to him.

She always arranged her hair in a peculiar way to cover
her right temple, and he thought it beautiful but wondered
about it. After a few months he loved her dearly, and he
asked her, "Why do you not change the style of your hair
sometimes? I mean, why do you always let it fall on one
side?"

The wife lifted her hair and said, "See?" she pointed to
a scar.

"How did you get it?"

"I got it when I was a child of three. My father had
died in his office, and my mother and brother died also in
the same year. I was taken care of by my wet nurse. We had
a house near the South Gate, at Sungcheng where my father's
office was, and she grew vegetables and sold them at the
market. One day a thief, for no reason whatsoever, tried to
kill me. We could not understand it, for we had no enemies.
He did not succeed, but it left a permanent scar on my forehead. That is why I have to cover it up."

"Was that nurse almost blind?"

"Yes. How do you know?"

"I was that thief. It is most strange. Everything has happened according to Fate."

He told her the whole story of the meeting with the old
man exactly fourteen years ago. The wife told him that when
she was six or seven, her uncle found her at Sungcheng and
took her to live with his family in Shiangchow where Wei
found her. Then they knew that their marriage was destined
in Heaven and loved each other all the more for it.

Later, a boy was born to them, by the name of Kun, who
eventually became the magistrate of Taiyuan, and the mother
received an honorary rank on account of her son.

When the magistrate of Sungcheng learned what had happened in his town, he named the inn where Wei Ku had
stopped "The Matrimony Inn."

20. THE DRUNKARD'S DREAM

‸‸

This is one of the best known of the Tang tales, written by Li Kung-tso, who also wrote several other popular stories. Like Li Fu-yen, he lived in the first half of the ninth century. "The Dream of Southbough" has now become a standard Chinese expression signifying that all life is but a dream.

CHUNYU FEN was a man much given to drink. The name "Fen" (meaning "Fine Confusion"), which he had adopted, was evidently indicative of his ideal of life and of the actual state of his finances. He had already squandered half of his fortune. It can never be definitely established whether he had dissipated his wealth in drinking with his friends and orgies with women, or because his life was already a mess or, to put it more generously, in a state of beautiful confusion. He had once received a commission as lieutenant colonel in an army, but had been discharged for intoxication and insubordination. Now he was unemployed and carefree, spending his days with his convivial friends, while his financial capacity dwindled as his drinking capacity doubled. Sometimes when he was sober, he thought of his youthful ambition for a great official career and shed a few tears over his lost hopes, but when he was filled with the "divine fluid," he was his happy natural self again.

He lived in his ancestral home near Kwangling, about three miles from the big city. There was a vacant plot to the south of his house, in which stood a very large, old locust tree, under whose green shade he and his friends held great drinking parties.

Such trees often live to a great old age. Sometimes, after being apparently dead for thirty or forty years, green shoots sprout up from an old stump and the tree has a second lease of life. This tree in front of Fen's house had reached great age, as one could see from its long branches reaching out in all directions. The ground under it had eroded, and the roots lay exposed in gnarled twists and knobs, providing a home for a great many insects.

One day Fen was so drunk that he began to weep. (It was in September of the year 792, according to his friends.) He declared that he was profoundly touched by the grand, old tree. He had played under it as a child, and so had his father and his grandfather. Now he was growing old (as a matter of fact, he was only approaching thirty). He cried so hard that his friends, Chou and Tien, carried him back to the house and laid him on a couch by the wall of the eastern corridor.

"You go to sleep for a while, and you will be all right. We will stay for a while to give the horses their feed and wash our feet, and wait till you feel better."

Fen fell into a profound sleep. No sooner had he closed his eyes than he saw two messengers in purple uniform come up to him, make a profound bow, and say, "The king of Locustania sends his greetings. He has sent a carriage for you and invites you for a visit."

At once Fen got up and put on his best cap and gown, and when he reached the gate, he saw a beautiful green carriage, pulled by four horses with gilt accouterments and red tassels, and a retinue of seven or eight royal attendants waiting for him.

As soon as he got into the carriage, it headed toward a depression in the ground where a big cavity was formed by the roots of the tree. To his surprise, the carriage drove

right through it. On the other side of the entrance, he saw
a new and wonderful landscape with hills and rivers which
were all strange to him. Three or four miles ahead, he saw
a high city wall with battlements and towers. The road leading toward the gate was jammed with traffic, and the pedes-
trians stood by the roadside to let the royal carriage pass
and watch the royal guest. When they reached the gate, Fen
saw large, gilt characters across the tower proclaiming, THE
KINGDOM OF LOCUSTANIA.

The walls stretched for miles around and the streets were
jammed with people. They seemed to be industrious and
active and, somewhat to his surprise, they were neat and
courteous. They greeted each other and stopped for hardly a
second's exchange of good wishes before proceeding each
on his way, as if the day was too short for all the work. He
could not understand what they were so busy doing. Laborers
carried huge sacks on the top of their heads. There were
soldiers, too, standing at their stations, tall and handsome,
and dressed in clean uniforms.

A royal delegation had met him at the gate, and he was
escorted to a stately mansion with many yards and a special
garden, reserved for state guests. He had been there hardly
five minutes when the attendant announced that the premier
had come to call on him. They bowed to each other and the
premier informed Fen that he had come to take him to see
the king.

"His royal majesty would like to marry his second daughter
to you," the premier informed him.

"Your humble servant is entirely unworthy of the honor,"
the drunkard replied, but inwardly he was greatly pleased
with his good luck.

"My luck has turned at last," he thought to himself. "I
will show the people what I, Chunyu Fen, can do. I will
be an honest and dutiful servant of His Majesty and a good
official to the people. My life will no longer be a mess.
I will show them what I can do."

A hundred yards from the house Fen and the premier entered a big red gate with golden knobs. Guards and soldiers with spears and tridents stood at attention, while officials in full court dress lined up on both sides of the causeway to see the distinguished guest. Fen had never felt so important. He saw his friends, Chou and Tien, among the bystanders and passed them by with a gesture, thinking to himself how they must envy him on this day.

Accompanied by the premier, he went up the steps into a great hall, which he knew must be the king's audience room. Fen hardly dared to raise his head. The officer of ceremonies asked him to kneel down and he did so.

"We have received a request from your venerable father," said the king. "He has condescended to honor us with a proposal to marry you to our second daughter, Yaofang. We have decided that the princess, our dear second daughter, shall be your wife."

The drunkard was so overwhelmed that he could barely stammer his thanks.

"Well, you may retire now and have a good rest for a few days. See the city at your leisure. My premier will accompany you and show you all the sights. I shall have the preparations for the wedding in a few days."

No sooner was it said than it was done. A few days later, the whole city turned out to see the wedding of the princess, who was dressed in the finest and flimsiest gauze, bedecked with jewels, and surrounded by beautiful girl attendants. The princess, too, was good and wise and kind. Fen fell madly in love with her at first sight.

On the wedding night, the princess said to him, "I can ask my father to give you an office — almost any one you want."

"To tell you the truth," replied the drunkard-bridegroom, "I have led a lazy life all these years. I am not acquainted with administrative procedures and do not know the rudiments of governing a country."

"Do not worry. I will help you," said the princess sweetly.

Now this was too much, the drunkard thought to himself, to be husband of a princess and have a high office, besides. He wanted to weep, but he was afraid of being misunderstood and restrained his tears.

The next day, the princess spoke to her father, and the king said, "I think I will make him ruler of the Southbough District. The governor there has just been discharged for neglect of his duty. It is a beautiful town, situated in a foothill district, with a big forest and waterfalls and grottoes outside the city. The population is industrious and lawabiding. Their skins are darker than ours, but they are brave fighters. They will be pleased to have my son-in-law and my princess ruling over them. They will adore you. I am sure you will like it."

Fen was delighted with the appointment. He did not care where he lived so long as he had the princess by his side.

"So I am to be Governor of Southborough!" he said.

"Dear, the district is called Southbough," corrected the princess.

"It does not matter what name you call it, does it?"

Fen's only request was that his friends, Chou and Tien, be allowed to go with him as aides. A royal farewell dinner was given for the couple and the king himself saw them off at the palace gate. Big crowds came out to see the princess riding in her own carriage with the royal bridegroom, and the women shed tears, for the inhabitants of Locustania were a sentimental people. The royal carriage was preceded by horse guards and bugles and trumpets, and followed by a great escort of soldiers who were to accompany them to Southbough. The journey took three days, and when they arrived, they were received with a rousing welcome.

They spent a wonderful year in Southbough. The residents were dutiful and well-disciplined, and each one had a trade. There were no loafers nor beggars in the town.

Fen heard that in case of war, all men and women turned out to defend their homes, and fought without regard for their lives. But they rarely got into a fight among themselves. The princess was gracious and kind, and the people adored her. Fen was lazy by nature, but his wife urged him to get up early in the morning and attend to his duties, to set an example for his people, and this was the only thing he did not like. He kept a bottle hidden in his office, but in all conscience he did his best to make himself worthy of the princess' love. He knew that he had to live an exemplary life; that was the price for being connected with royalty. In the afternoons, however, his time was his own, and he often drove with his beloved wife to the forest, and there walked hand in hand with her on the bank, or sat down with Chou and Tien to have a drink in one of the grottoes. It was there that he found the penalty of greatness almost too much.

"Not a drop more, darling," said the kind princess.

Well, he thought, one cannot have everything in this life. He was grateful to her, for she had helped him with official reports to the king and other important documents. With Chou and Tien as his secretaries — they now regarded him with awe and respect — he thought, in all fairness, he should not demand more of life.

After a year had passed, his dearly beloved princess caught a cold and died. His grief was so great and inconsolable that he began to drink again. He requested that he be relieved of his post and asked permission to return to the capital. He followed the princess' coffin and gave her a royal funeral. Out of his own savings, he built her a beautiful white mausoleum on the crest of a rocky hillock, and wept bitterly, refusing to leave the place for three months.

With the death of the princess, everything went wrong. In his bereavement, he went about the city, frequenting the wine shops and getting drunk day and night. The king, having lost his daughter, was now cool toward Fen. Reports of his disorderly behavior in the capital had reached the king's ears, but in memory of the princess he did not wish to disgrace him publicly. This was known to the people, and his friends began to desert him. He was reduced to the state of having to borrow money from Chou and Tien for a drink. Once he was found lying on the floor of a public house for a whole night.

"Turn the rascal out!" demanded the populace. "He is a disgrace to the nation."

The king was ashamed to have such a son-in-law, and the queen said to Fen one day, "You are so unhappy because your princess died. Why do you not go home for a change?"

"This is my home. Where else can I go?"

"Your home is in Kwangling, do you not remember?"

Fen hazily remembered that he had a big house at Kwangling and that he had arrived here about a year ago as a stranger. Dejectedly he said he would return to his home.

"Very well, then, I shall send two servants to take you there."

He saw again the two messengers who had brought him to the kingdom, but this time when he reached the gate, he saw an old, rickety carriage. There were no foot soldiers, no retinue, and no friends to see him off. Even the livery of the servants was old and torn and discolored, and when he passed through the city gate, nobody paid any attention to him. He thought of the days of his pomp and glory and realized how vain and fleeting all such worldly honors were.

He recognized the road by which he had come a year ago. Soon the carriage passed through a rock entrance, and as soon as he saw his old village, he shed tears. The attendants took him to his house. They pushed him down on a couch by the wall of the eastern corridor and shouted gruffly, "You are home now!"

Fen woke up with a jerk. He saw his friends still washing their feet in the middle of the yard. The evening sun was still casting shadows on the eastern wall.

"What a life!" he exclaimed.

"What! Have you waked up so soon?" asked Chou and Tien.

"So soon? I have lived a lifetime since I fell asleep."

He told his friends of the extraordinary dream and his visit to the kingdom of Locustania, and they marveled greatly.

Taking his friends to the old locust tree, and pointing to a big cavity under the winding roots, he said, "Here is where my carriage went through, I remember distinctly."

"You must have been bewitched by the tree-spirit. It is a very old tree."

"You come tomorrow," Fen said to his friends. "I am going to examine the hole and see."

The next day he asked his servants to take axes and shovels and dig up the hole. They chopped off some of the big roots and discovered a big cave underground about ten feet square, crossed by zigzag offshoots. On one side of the cave, situated on a raised level, there was a miniature city with roads and compartments and connecting corridors. Thousands of ants swarmed around the place. A raised terrace stood in the center, on which sat two giant ants, with white wings and red heads, and dozens of big ants stood guard around them.

"So this is the kingdom of Locustania, and there sits the king in his palace!" Fen was amazed.

A long passage led from the central cave in the direction of the southern branch, where they found another nest in a big hollow, also built up with mud structures and passageways. The ants were darker in color than those in the central cave. He recognized the gate tower of the district of Southbough and the little town where he had spent such a happy year. It touched him to see his subjects dashing madly about when their nest was disturbed. The bottom of the decayed branch was cut up in grooves, and on one side there was a patch of green moss. Unquestionably this was the forest where he and his princess had spent so many happy hours together, and nearby were the little grottoes where his wife had said to him, "Darling, not a drop more."

Excited by this curious discovery, he explored the passage leading toward the central cave, which had taken him three days to travel through in the princess' carriage. Finally, he discovered another small hole about ten feet to the east. This was more rocky, and only a few ants wandered about here aimlessly. A small mound about three inches high rose in the middle, capped by a jagged pebble whose shape reminded him of the princess' mausoleum. He knew it was a dream, but the affection he felt for her still lingered in his heart and gave him a sense of the futility and transitoriness of life.

With a profound sigh, he remarked to his friends, "I thought I was dreaming, but now I know that the kingdom of Locustania is real — as real as you and me. Perhaps, we are all dreamers."

Fen was never quite the same man again. He became a monk, took to drink again, and drank harder than ever, and in three years he was dead.

Washington Square Press

A new and growing series presenting distinguished
literary works in an inexpensive, well-designed format

• • • • • • • • • • • • • •

NOVELS

HAWTHORNE, NATHANIEL, *The House of the Seven Gables*. W 215 (45¢)

HAWTHORNE, NATHANIEL, *The Scarlet Letter*. Afterword by Maxwell Geismar. W 226 (45¢)

READE, CHARLES, *The Cloister and the Hearth*. Introduction by Morris Gall. W 1003 (90¢)

SCOTT, SIR WALTER, *Ivanhoe*. W 219 (45¢)

STEVENSON, ROBERT LOUIS, *Kidnapped*. Introduction and Glossary by Hardy R. Finch. Illustrated. W 234 (45¢)

STEVENSON, ROBERT LOUIS, *Treasure Island*. Introduction by Max J. Herzberg. Illustrated. W 249 (45¢)

TWAIN, MARK, *The Adventures of Huckleberry Finn*. Illustrated. W 242 (45¢)

TWAIN, MARK, *The Adventures of Tom Sawyer*. Illustrated. W 239 (45¢)

TWAIN, MARK, *A Connecticut Yankee in King Arthur's Court*. W 150 (45¢)

WILDER, THORNTON, *The Bridge of San Luis Rey*. W 236 (45¢)

OTHER TITLES NOW IN
WASHINGTON SQUARE PRESS EDITIONS

CRANE, STEPHEN, *Maggie and Other Stories*. Selected and with an Introduction by Austin McC. Fox. W 133 (45¢)

FRANKLIN, BENJAMIN, *Autobiography*. Postscript by Richard B. Morris. W 218 (45¢)

SAINT AUGUSTINE, *Confessions*. Translated by Edward B. Pusey, D.D., Introduction by Harold C. Gardiner, S.J. W 245 (45¢)

SOPHOCLES, *Oedipus the King*. Translated and with an Introduction by Bernard M. W. Knox. W 99 (35¢)*

*Price will be changed to 45¢ at the time of the next printing.

• • • • • • • • • • • • •

If your bookseller does not have the titles you want, you may order them by sending retail price, plus 5¢ per book for postage and handling, to: Mail Service Department, Washington Square Press, Inc., 1 West 39th Street, New York 18, N.Y. Please enclose check or money order—do not send cash. WSP-2 (B)